MW01135388

THE REBEL KIND

by C.R. Anderson

CR Anderson

ISBN-10: 1985306131
ISBN-13: 978-1985306134

You were better than the best, stayed a notch above the rest. It was raining in Heaven when you went down. Your mama cried, said she told you so, but you touched the devil and couldn't let go.
No one controls The Outlaw.

You wrote the story with the movie in mind. An angel face with a criminal side. Celebrated as the rebel kind.
The Outlaw.

I wonder if they knew you would turn your bad deeds into good. Paint you as a modern Robin Hood. It's high noon everywhere you go, and the guilt you feel is the weary soul.
Of The Outlaw

Holly Knight/Simone Climie

CHAPTER ONE

If I smile and don't believe
Soon I know I'll wake from this dream
Don't try to fix me I'm not broken
I'm the lie living for you so you can hide

Hello by Evanescence

I woke up feeling groggy, my head pounding. My body felt stiff as I slowly sat up and took in the unfamiliar scene around me. The room was bare. Other than a window on one side and a heavy looking door on the other, the small twelve by twelve space was empty. A bed sat dead center in the room, its feet bolted to the cold, tiled floor. I glanced toward the door and noticed a small window near the top, just the right height for someone to look in and observe.

Where was I?

Afraid to move, I sat still for several minutes just trying to get my breathing under control. Maybe Corie was in another room. But how we had gotten here I didn't know. And where were Jesse and Kelly?

Slowly, I crept off the bed and realized I was wearing a flimsy, thin hospital robe over my underwear. I grabbed at the material, holding it tight around me, and tiptoed over to the door to peer out the window. The room on the other side was large with several stuffed chairs and couches scattered around on one end, and a large table with smaller, cushioned chairs around it at the other. There were people sitting around, writing, reading, talking to each other in low voices. Luckily no one seemed to be paying attention to my door. I made my way back to the bed and curled up on it, feeling lost and afraid. I didn't recognize a single person out there. I didn't even know where *there* was. If my friends were anywhere in this building with me, I couldn't see them. I could only hope that someone came for me soon and answered my questions.

The bed was hard. Narrow and stiff. I noticed on the head and footboards there were thick, leather straps with buckles attached to them. Then I noticed my sore wrists and knew that they'd been strapped in at some point. I shook my head in confusion, but I just couldn't remember a single thing about how I'd gotten there. Vague memories flashed behind my eyes of an ambulance ride, but it didn't make any sense. I found that it was too difficult to recall and ended up crying into the pillow in frustration.

Sometime later a person peered through the window and the door opened to admit a stoutly woman with a sour face. She reminded me of Nurse Hatchet and I found myself shrinking into the bed involuntarily. She announced herself as Brenda, the head psychiatric technician, which I soon learned was little more than a babysitter. A tech's jobs was to watch us, herd us around, tell us what to do, and to make sure we didn't try to off ourselves in the bathroom with our environmentally safe shampoo. I soon found out that I couldn't have a hairdryer or makeup. Even the pull strings from my sweatpants and hoodies had been taken. My shoestrings. How the hell was I supposed to hurt myself with a shoestring?

She motioned for me to follow her and led me through the ward, past the common area and the long hallway where I could see door after door on either side of me leading into what looked like regular rooms, each with two beds. We continued past the nurses' station and through a heavy, locked door into a hallway with elevators. She pressed a button and waited silently. I wasn't sure if it was strange or not that she hadn't said another word to me, but I didn't care. Stepping inside the elevator, she pressed the button for the first floor and I noticed we were on the fourth of the five-story building. Then she led me through two more sets of locked doors and into a small waiting room.

I stepped inside, and the door was promptly shut and locked behind me. The air conditioning was on full blast as I waited. There was no phone, no TV, no radio, not even a magazine. There was nothing to do. I beat on the door, yelled for someone, for anyone to come. When that didn't yield any results, I started to kick methodically, pouring out every profanity there was. No one came. There was an electric pad on the wall beside the door. It was the same kind that was on either side of every heavy, locked door I'd walked through. I didn't know the code of course but I figured if I pushed a few buttons someone might come running, but nothing happened. An error code popped up on the tiny screen, the little red bulb flashed, then was gone. Someone was probably watching it all on a monitor and laughing their ass off at me right now.

When the door finally buzzed opened I was asleep, stretched out over several crappy chairs with about enough cushion I'd require a back alignment afterwards. Slowly I opened my eyes and looked with dread at the man standing on the other side. I knew him, a psychologist colleague of my father's where he worked as a professor at the University of Chicago. I had always thought Phillip was a nice enough person, but I doubted it would be helpful now that I realized where I was. He looked at me grimly.

"Wake up, Jade," he said.

I sat up wearily.

"How are you?" he asked. Stupid question.

"Cold."

He only nodded at that, then said, "I'm sure you've been wondering about what's going on. It's been several days now, and you weren't coherent enough to talk to."

I didn't really have a reply to that. "Still cold," I reminded him.

He frowned but pulled off his suit coat and placed it around my shoulders. Then he sat down across from me and leaned his elbows on his knees, his hands clasped together.

"You're in trouble," he informed me.

Obviously, considering the last place I remember being was somewhere in Texas. But I didn't say it. Instead I asked, "Where are the others?" He only looked at me blankly.

"You came alone," he said simply, his voice low. I knew what he was doing. Like talking to a wild animal in a steady voice to keep them calm, Phillip was treating me as if I were some volatile feral.

I shook my head. "I wasn't alone."

"You were by the time you got here." Then he sighed. "I'm willing to tell you how you got here, but you've got some talking to do yourself. So, let's help each other, okay?"

I stared blankly back at him. I had no idea what he wanted me to say, where he expected me to start.

He stood up, punched a code into the pad on the wall and spoke through the intercom to have a tech come get me. When another woman appeared, he introduced her to me as Lori and told me she'd be taking me back up to my ward. He said he'd see me soon and gave me a reassuring smile before leaving the room and disappearing down the hallway in the opposite direction Lori was leading me.

She led me back the way I had come with Brenda earlier, only this time the large common room was dark and full of patients watching a movie. I could feel every pair of eyes on me as I kept my head straight and trooped into my cell. When Lori left, shutting the door behind her, I sat down on the floor in a corner of the room and cried. This was real. It was really happening. I hadn't been dreaming those other times I'd woken up feeling disoriented and out of place. I really was out of place. And even worse, I was alone.

The bright ceiling lights burnt into my head as I squeezed my eyes to shut it out. It was either that or sit in total darkness. With the lights on I felt as if I were under a microscope, but with them off I'd feel completely vulnerable in the darkness.

Someone knocked on my door and before I could push myself off the floor, a young girl popped her head in and smiled. I could see that the lights had come on in the common room. The movie had ended, and everyone was making their way out into the long hallway, toward their rooms.

"Hi," she said, coming further into the room. She pushed the door shut behind her before perching on my bed. "I'm Kari."

Slowly, I stood up and waited, uncertain of what to do. I fiddled with my robe and then quickly swept a hand over my wet eyes.

"What's your name?" she finally asked.

"Jade."

"Oh, that's nice," she smiled again. "So anyway, they told me to check on you and make sure you're okay. I guess I'll be taking you under my wing, you know, in case you have any questions. It's not hard to learn the ropes around here."

I wondered how she could be all smiley and happy in this place as I watched her bounce gently on the bed while she talked. "You been here long?" I asked her.

"Oh, no, not too long," she said, and put a finger to her chin. She looked at her shoe with a hard, concentrated expression on her face, then perked up and said, "About six weeks."

Six weeks? I couldn't stay in here for six whole weeks! What would Jesse do without me? I had to get out of here.

I didn't realize I'd said it out loud until I heard Kari say, "Oh, you can't get out. There's no way. It's all locked up tight!"

I looked to see her throw her hands up in an animated gesture and thought, *she's brainwashed.*

I sat there looking at her stupidly, not having a single reply for the nitwit bouncing happily on my bed, when a knock sounded on my door a second time. Kari bounded up and opened the door to a skinny guy with very long and straight brown hair. His bangs almost covered his eyes and he stood holding a plastic bin full of jello cups and containers of juice.

"Snacks," he said in a dull, bored voice. Kari said thank you and selected a jello. The boy looked at me expectantly and I shook my head.

"Mark, this is Jade," Kari told him. He nodded his head at me and I continued to stare back expressionless.

"You sure you don't want anything?" he finally asked me. "It's all you get until breakfast."

"Who says I'll be eating breakfast?"

"You will," was his reply as he laughed and turned from the door.

"He's been in here forever," Kari informed me as she closed the door behind him. I sighed as I watched her settle back on my bed, wondering if she was ever going to leave. She pulled back the foil top of her jello and started to eat it with her fingers. "So, what are you in here for?"

I shrugged. I wasn't sure. I mean, yeah, I could make a list of probabilities, but I honestly didn't know exactly what I was in for since I couldn't remember anything specific. She only looked back at me and nodded. Like she knew I knew but it was obvious I wasn't going to say anything.

"How long have I been here?" I asked her instead.

She glanced at the door before replying, as if talking about it was some big secret. "You've been here for five days as far as I know. You really don't remember anything?" I shook my head, sure my face was registering some level of shock. "Wow."

"Did I come alone?" I whispered, fearful of the answer. She only looked confused, so I said louder, "Was anyone with me?" She only shrugged, still clearly confused by what I meant. "No other people have come in since?" I asked roughly. She shook her head at me and I slumped down dejectedly. I really was alone in here.

"You've been in a lot of trouble, huh?"

"I suppose," I said, getting irritated. "What about you? Why are you here?"

She sighed heavily. "I had an abortion, but mostly I think my parents are giving me a kick in the pants, you know?"

An abortion? I looked at her stupidly. "How old are you?"

"Fourteen," she smiled. I didn't see what she was so proud of. "You?"

"Sixteen."

She looked at her watch and jumped off the bed. "I'd better go. Lights out at ten. See you in the morning."

I grunted something in reply as I shut the door behind her. Turning off the light switch, I crawled between the sheets. I could feel the panic starting to set in. Five days and I didn't remember any of it. It's been five days since I was in Texas with the others. Where were they now?

CHAPTER TWO

It's a damn cold night
Trying to figure out this life
Won't you take me by the hand
Take me somewhere new
I don't know who you are
But I'm with you

I'm With You by Avril Lavigne

The first time I met Jesse he was standing at my backdoor as snow filtered down around him and his breath came out in small wintery puffs. I won't stretch the truth and say he looked like an angel, even though he did have a sort of brooding Adonis thing going for him, but he sure looked like a gift to me.

He'd come with my best friend Kelly, who although I'd seen him only a week before, I hadn't in nearly eight months before that. This was Kelly's way, to disappear for weeks or even months at a time, never letting me know where he is or if he's alive and well until I get some random phone call, which is what I got over two weeks ago on Christmas Eve. The following conversation was predictable between us.

"Merry Christmas!" he said. "How are you?"

"Well, I'm here, so…." I let my reply end there.

"Always a ray of sunshine."

"Where are you?" I demanded into the phone.

"I'm fine," he assured me. "I've been living out in Elgin with some friends. It's kind of cool out here." He was never very good at answering questions, still I was relived I'd gotten a direct answer out of him without having to pull some teeth.

"Elgin?" I squawked. I'd have been less angry had he told me he'd been in California. But Elgin was barely an hour drive from Deerfield. "I've been worried sick! And people keep asking me where you are and when you're coming back."

"You wouldn't tell anyone, would you?"

"Why, who's looking for you now?"

He paused. He probably wasn't sure who he had pissed off, but pretty sure he had. "I dunno." I could hear the shrug as he said it.

"Stay out of trouble," I begged him. "I'm too broke to bail you out of jail. And stay in touch more, dammit!"

"Jade," he sighed. "I'm tired of this. Just come on the road with me already, alright?"

"No," I said, shaking my head. "Stop asking me that." I was going to hate it when the day came that he stopped asking me that.

"Why not?" He didn't sound convinced at all. "I know you want out of there so bad you can taste it." His voice was low, almost hypnotizing the way he said *taste*. He was mocking me. "Besides, your whole family hates each other just as much as mine does. Yours just hates with more money and nicer cars."

Man, he really knew how to cut to the quick. And he was right. Well, to a point anyway. I didn't hate my brother and sister. My older brother, Johnathon, was several years older than me and already gone, finished with college and everything. My sister, Anne, was twenty-one but still living at home, planning for her wedding next August. We got along alright. It was our parents; career-driven and emotionally constipated people who barely knew us because we'd been raised primarily by a nanny until I "came of age" four years ago. When I said they were out of town a lot on business trips, I wasn't lying except half of those trips were vacations (that didn't include us kids), and if they were home they were drinking. They didn't want much to do with us, we could tell.

Kelly didn't say he was coming home. He didn't really say anything at all, which was very Kelly-like. More than anything I figured his arbitrary phone calls to "touch base" were more about checking in to see if I had heard anyone talking about him. The thing was people did talk about him, but when they asked me about where he was or what he was up to it was because as his best friend everyone expected me to know. And I rarely did. And when I say "checking in" I'm guessing it's because he's pissed someone off and wants to see if the coast is clear. But people know better than to be too honest with me about their dealings with Kelly. I'm his best friend and fiercely loyal. It's not that I don't know all about him; it's not that I don't hear the stories or believe that anything they say could be true. I don't put much past him. But they don't know how hard his life has been. They don't know how his step father resented him from the time he was little and pushed him around and threatened him, and how his mother didn't care. Growing up on the North Shore of Chicago in a moderately wealthy suburb, none of them could understand what it was to be homeless and unwanted at seventeen. If anyone had anything to say about Kelly to me, whether it was warranted or not, they understood where my loyalties lie.

He called again about a week later in the middle of the night, waking up my sister. It was a good thing she and I shared our own landline. I couldn't imagine why he was calling so late. My friend Lynn was sleeping over and we'd crashed on the couch in the family room watching movies. I woke up to Anne hitting me on the shoulder, still half asleep herself, at four-thirty in the morning.

"What!" I demanded, peering out from under my arm. "Why are you hitting me?"

"Kelly has called five times in the last hour," she told me. "You better come upstairs and talk to him the next time he calls."

"What the hell is he calling for?"

"Go listen to the voicemail," she told me and headed back upstairs. "I'm not getting any sleep with that damn phone ringing all night!"

"Turn your ringer off," I called to her. She grunted in reply and I pulled myself off the couch as Lynn stirred, and asked, "What's going on?"

"Something's wrong with Kelly," I said. "I'm going upstairs. You want to sleep in my bed?" She followed me up to my room groggily. I closed my bedroom door and checked my cell phone as well. Blown up with missed calls. Maybe he intended to call the landline, knowing it would wake someone up. I pushed play on the receiver and could almost hear Kelly's teeth clattering from the cold.

"We're stranded," he said. "The car died in Long Grove at some gas station."

"What is he doing there?" Lynn muttered sleepily as she curled up with my pillow. "I thought you said he's living in Elgin now?" I shrugged at her and listened to the four more messages, all pretty much the same.

"Where are you, Jade? It's freezing out here!"

As if on cue the phone rang again, and I snatched it up halfway through the first ring. Kelly immediately started to babble in my ear, begging me to come get him. I couldn't understand half of what he was saying through his clacking teeth, but I couldn't risk waking up my parents by opening the garage door. He'd just have to wait until they left for work.

"That's three more hours!" he squawked in my ear.

"What the hell are you doing in Long Grove anyway!" I hissed at him as quietly as I could. But what I was really asking him was why did he come back to the North Shore without calling me or telling me or stopping by. "Stop calling. Anne is getting pissed. I'll be there soon."

I turned off the ringer on both phones and fell asleep. By the time I woke up there were four more messages from him on the machine. "Hurry up! We're freezing!" When we finally picked them up, Kelly and two other people squeezed into the backseat of Anne's little Ford Escort, and Kelly glared at me.

"What?" I asked him innocently.

"It's nine o'clock!" was all he said. Lynn and I looked at each other and giggled.

I took them back to my house because I didn't know what else to do with them. The girl, Corie, was Kelly's girlfriend. The other one, some 40-year-old guy named Mike, finessed my last fifty bucks out of me to tow his car, which I never got back. I doubted it was enough to get his piece of junk towed all the way to Elgin, but since I never saw him again it didn't seem to matter. It seemed like they were there all day. Finally, I called Anne's fiancé and asked him to help me. I piled them back into the Escort, met up with Tom, and handed them over with relief. I still don't know where Tom took them, but eventually they got back to Elgin.

A week later Kelly turned up on my doorstep again.

"Well," I said as I let him enter past me. "I might start to feel special or something if you keep coming back."

He gave me his charming, lazy grin, and said, "You'll always be special, baby."

Corie was with him again. I said hi and was surprised to see that they were still together. I never minded his girlfriends, even if most of them were a little on the dippy side. In fact, most of them resented me more than anything. Kelly had a nasty habit of coming whenever I snapped my fingers, even if it meant blowing off a girlfriend. You can see why they never liked me much. Corie didn't seem to have that jealousy problem. I liked that.

Kelly said, "This is Jesse."

I looked at the tall, dark-haired guy standing behind Corie. I took it all in within seconds. Broad shoulders, dark and stormy eyes that pierced right through mine, and a beautiful bow-lipped smile. He was the most beautiful and dangerous person I'd ever seen.

You ever experienced that love at first sight feeling when your mouth goes dry and your heart stops and falls into your stomach all at the same time? That wasn't what I felt. It was something more than that. Something I couldn't identify.

My parents hated Corie and Jesse immediately. Of course, they never liked anyone, but they had an intense distaste for what they summed up in two seconds as trouble-makers. They weren't real fond of Kelly either, but he had been around so much over the years that they learned to tolerate him. Kelly wasn't the type to care what other people thought of him. He didn't come to my house or stay away because of how my parents felt.

Anne came flying through the kitchen to grab a Coke from the fridge, barely acknowledging us. Kelly said hi to her. She looked back at him on her way out of the room, and said, "Don't be calling here at four-thirty in the morning anymore or I'll have to beat the shit out of you, little man."

"You're a foxy mama!" Kelly called after her and laughed.

We decided to leave the house. My parents had been sitting in the next room, bourbons in hand, making more nasty comments about the "riff raff" in the kitchen. I don't know how they got to the point where they felt like they were so much better than everyone else in the whole world. Maybe success and money do that. Then again, I didn't know them very well.

Kelly and I decided to take Corie and Jesse to the Nike Base. It was dark and cold and there must have been at least three feet of snow on the ground. The woods were black, and the trail was covered and frozen over, but Kelly and I knew the turns and distance by heart. It was the only place I could honestly say I wasn't afraid of. When I say that I mean it's because I could walk the trails through the woods and every long runway at two in the morning by myself without a care. No matter if there was snow everywhere, not a lick of moonlight that never made it through the thick treetops anyway, or sometimes it rained so hard the trails would change completely. I didn't need a flashlight either. I had walked that trail so many times, day and night, stoned, drunk, and sober. Back and forth, back and forth.

Kelly led us through the woods, and as he held the fence where it had been cut between the woods and the sewage field, we crawled through and headed toward the first runway. The field wasn't as bad as it sounds. It didn't even smell bad, and in some spots was actually quite warm, which was good when you were passing through on a cold January night.

The runway to the abandoned naval base lay straight ahead of us, stretching a good quarter mile.

We had walked it so much in the past that it seemed little more than a short walk. At the end of the runway was a long, half-moon-shaped hill that surrounded a smaller, internal one. We used to party on the hills a lot. And whenever people were approaching from a dark distance, they would whistle back and forth, hoping for a reply. No one wanted to walk all the way out to the base only to find there was no party going on.

Beyond the hills was a smaller runway, maybe a hundred and fifty feet or so before it ended in the overgrown brush of the surrounding fields. But this small path led to an old missile bunker. The openings had been sealed shut, packed with dirt, and over time a large group of us had dug our way through one of the shafts, creating a slide-like tunnel. The shoot made your jeans real dirty, and climbing back up was a bitch, especially when you'd had too much to drink or smoke. But the bunker was an interesting place to see. It was completely dark inside but if you had a flashlight you could see all the graffiti that had been spray painted and written in magic markers on the walls over the years. Most of the time we'd sit down on the ground, crack open a few glowsticks on the walls, and tell stupid stories by the light of our Zippos.

The main runway made a big L-shape, as it also jutted to the left from the entrance at the sewage fields. The left runway was about half the distance as the first and not as interesting. It led to nowhere in fact, but if you veered to the right you'd end up in a small clearing just past a thicket of bushes where we'd build bonfires. There was a lot of land in between those two runways, and during the years I don't think I explored it all; mostly because I wasn't the exploring type. There were other, smaller runways but years of growth had covered them with weeds and bushes.

The Base had always been a reliable place to party on days and nights when there wasn't much to do. During the summer there were always people up there, so I rarely ever arrived to find myself alone or amongst strangers. Even though it closed in 1972, the government still owned the land and occasionally the cops would raid it. I never found out exactly how they got in, but every occasionally you'd see headlights from security cars and then everyone would be running frantically over the hills and hiding in the bushes.

Corie and Jesse liked the Base and listened to me and Kelly told stupid stories of the past. We were in hysterics as I recalled a night from the winter before in which Kelly had been staying at my house and we'd gotten a little too wasted. By the time I was done, Kelly was laughing so hard that no sounds were coming out of him, but he was holding his stomach as if he were in pain.

I lived in a big two-story house and we were in my bedroom lying on our backs on the floor trying to play Sega while looking at the TV upside down. We had an eight-pack of Little Kings in the refrigerator and two doses of acid between us. We soon tired of going downstairs every time we wanted a beer though, so I had the brilliant idea of tying it to a rope and hanging it out of the bathroom window. So, I tied the pack of beer to one end, and the other end to my bathroom doorknob. The rope, however, was so long that the beer reached all the way down to the redwood deck on the first floor below. We thought this was genius. The beer would stay cold and all we had to do was pull them up whenever we wanted one.

At one point we were lying on the bed staring at all the ceramic masks I had on the walls. The faces were melting and contorting into ugly expressions. Little things were flying all around the room in different shapes and colors. I wanted to swat them away but couldn't lift my arms.

"Kel," I finally managed to say. "Kel." I forced my arm onto his leg.

"What?" he groaned, and then started to laugh.

It took me a while to stop laughing as well.

"Go get a beer," I told him as soon as I could catch my breath. He started to laugh harder, which had *me* laughing harder. I didn't even know why.

"I don't think I can move," he finally said. But within a few minutes he dragged himself off the bed and crawled into the bathroom.

I don't know how long he was in there. It could have been seconds; it could have been an hour. He was so quiet that I had completely forgotten about him. It was him erupting into laughter from the bathroom that brought me back to reality. I finally remembered I asked him to get me a beer, and I couldn't figure out what was so damned funny to be laughing about in the bathroom. I lay on the bed laughing along like an idiot until I was able to roll off and shuffle over to see what was going on. I found Kelly bent over and hanging out of the window, laughing uncontrollably.

"What are you doing?" I asked him, unable to stop laughing. My back literally hurt, and he looked so stupid just hanging out the window, laughing like a hyena.

"I can't reach it!" Kelly yelled between gulps of air. "The beer, it's too far away!"

After I picked myself up from rolling on the floor laughing, I told him he needed to *pull* the rope up to get to the beer. I pushed him aside and started to grab for the rope myself but couldn't get a hold of it. I was still laughing stupidly, and my eyes were blind from tears. Kelly started to laugh harder, if that was possible, and fell over me, almost pushing me out of the window. I screamed through my laughter as he grabbed me by the waist and hauled me back in.

I don't even remember really wanting that beer.

We stayed down in the bunker until the cold crept in and we couldn't stand it any longer. Seeing as they were all pretty much living out of Jesse's car, we headed back to my house where I slipped them into the basement for the night, throwing blankets at them and telling them to be quiet.

CHAPTER THREE

A monster press machine in on her body
While she is stepping on the quicksand
A beautiful rose, stay at the corner
She is living in and out of tune

Vitamin C by Can

I don't know how I slept that night, thinking about the beautiful, quiet boy I'd hidden in the basement two floors beneath me, but I did.

I got up for school the next morning, went through the motions of taking a shower, drying my hair, putting on makeup. Kelly silently led the others out while my parents were still upstairs getting ready for work, and they waited for me down the street in Jesse's car. We stopped at a gas station so the guys could put their last few bucks in, while Corie called me out sick at school.

We drove for forty minutes and reached Elgin. Jesse stopped first to check in with his probation officer before driving to a trailer I soon learned was his mother's, where he expertly broke in. We all followed him inside and Corie went straight for the shower, while Kelly began throwing their clothes into the washer. It was apparent this was their routine.

As days went on and I stayed with them, I found that they had other places to go as well. Sometimes it was Kelly's house, sometimes even mine. If there was no place to go then we'd all suffer without showers for a day. We usually managed pretty well. It was the same routine for maybe a month after that first day in Elgin. I was trying to play it safe by going home, or at least making it look like I still lived there. At first, I was still going to school occasionally, especially when it seemed like my parents were looking at me more curiously, as if to say, "I don't believe I've seen you in a week." Then I'd pretend that I'd been there all along and they were the ones who weren't paying attention. It worked, because for the most part, they didn't pay attention.

Lynn and some of my other friends kept me up to date on my classes and I found it was quite easy to slip in and out for a test when needed. I have no idea why I even bothered. But somewhere inside of me I was afraid of getting busted. Busted for what, I didn't know exactly. Only that I was afraid to lose Kelly again and the thought of never seeing Jesse tore a hole in my gut. He was like a drug to me. I needed to be with him. Kelly couldn't understand why I was even making the effort to keep up the pretense, but Jesse just smiled and looked amused.

It was fun at first, running around with them. I was having a blast and doing exactly what I wanted to do. But as time went on it got more serious. It was becoming a life style. After a while I was no longer just someone to party with or someone to loan money or food or a dry place to sleep. I was expected to be there with them, to travel with them, and to become part of their private world. No words were spoken, it just happened. I didn't mind because it was exactly what I had wanted all along.

I was accepted into this elite little club for the rebel kind only.

Kelly used to depend on me for so much that at times I felt like his mother. But now things were so different. Before when he was in and out of my life, I was used to the way things were. Now I saw him in a much more independent light, and I found myself depending on him just as much. My decision to run away wasn't made by me alone. My mother helped, though that's not the way she'd look at it. It was near the end of that first month with Kelly and Jesse, and the tension in my house had gotten really bad between all of us.

It was a Monday afternoon, President's Day in fact, because we'd had no school that day, when my mother had us all arrested around three o'clock. We'd come up to the house thinking it'd be safe to go in because I wanted to get my hairdryer and a few more things. Neither of my parents ever got home from work before six. I'd long ago lost my key to the house and the spare was no longer in its hiding spot. I had no doubts that it was missing on purpose. Jesse said he could get in through the basement window and let me in the backdoor.

After showing him where the window was, I walked back to where Kelly and Lynn were waiting. We had picked her up earlier that day and were getting ready to take her home as soon as we were done. We watched the back door, waiting for Jesse to go through the house and open it for us, but he didn't. I gave Kelly a confused look and he shrugged back at me. I took a step toward the door and saw it slowly open. Jesse stood in the doorway, staring at me with an odd expression and I stopped.

All of this occurred in a matter of seconds, but to me it was very much in slow motion. Jesse continued to stand in the doorway, looking at me with some kind of warning on his face. I started toward him again and he suddenly moved aside as my mother appeared behind him. My heart started to skip. I could almost feel the blood drain out of my face, and I prayed for a faint spell or something to take the vision away from my eyes. That image of my mother in the doorway, holding a phone in her hand, and looking more pissed off than I could ever remember seeing her.

I don't remember anything being said, just that slow motion feeling of standing still and staring at each other as the rest of the world whizzed by. Jesse came down the steps and started toward his car, and within that one minute of silence I turned to see at least three policemen approaching us from different sides of the house. There were no sirens, no footsteps, no sounds.

The police packed us into two cars; Lynn and I in one and the guys in the other. An officer took me by the arm and pushed me into the backseat as I fumbled and stared, shocked and speechless. Surely this wasn't happening. What could this all be about? I watched in horror as Lynn was placed next to me and the door slammed shut. I glanced at her and saw that she had turned a pale shade of green. Her mother was going to kill her.

I twisted around to see the guys in the other cruiser. All I could see were their silhouettes, the sunlight playing over the windows, reflecting the trees. I looked at Lynn again to see the expression on her face. Shock. I was glad that Corie wasn't with us, that we had left her in Elgin that morning, or surely she'd be in a lot more trouble. She'd been labeled a runaway for months. If the police found her there'd be no getting her back, and no telling what her abusive father would do to her, either.

The police officers got into the cruiser and started the engine, slowly driving in reverse down the driveway, followed by the other car. I looked back at my mother to see her still standing in the doorway. I saw nothing in her eyes and I felt nothing.

"I live here!" I pounded on the grate divider. He ignored me.

When we reached the police station, Lynn and I were put into the Youth Officer's office, where we sat and watched the cops fill out their reports. Kelly and Jesse had been taken into another room, and though no one would tell me anything, I had a feeling it was a holding cell. Kelly was seventeen, an adult by Illinois law. Jesse was nineteen with a record. They weren't getting out of there.

Lynn and I were, of course, let go after sweating it out at the station for two hours. They wouldn't let us leave without a parent, and I could feel the anxiety permeating off Lynn as she waited for her mom to come collect her. I had no idea what was going to happen to me. While we waited, the youth officer asked us what we were doing at my house earlier.

"It's my house," I told him, disgusted with the whole thing. "I forgot my key and was locked out."

"Then explain why your mother called in a burglary." The words *B and E* filtered through my brain and I wondered what would happen to Jesse if he were charged.

I shook my head. "I don't know what happened," I pleaded. "I didn't even know she was there. I thought she was at work."

"She said you were trespassing."

"She didn't know it was me!" I insisted, though I knew even if it were the truth it wouldn't matter.

My parents came for me before Lynn's mother arrived and they made me leave her there, just waiting in fear. I knew she didn't have any answers or a plausible explanation to give to her mother as to why we were arrested.

I walked out of the police station with my parents leading me toward the car. It was obvious my mother had me sit in the police station while she waited for my father to get home from work so she wouldn't have to face me alone. I slid into the backseat and took a last look at the building before the tears started to spill. I didn't even see Jesse's old beat up station wagon anywhere. I wondered if it had been impounded, and I wondered what the guys were going to do now or if they were going to remain in jail. I wondered if this was going to split us up, and I wondered what Corie would think when she realized that no one was coming back for her tonight. Where would she go; what would she do?

It was a weird thing being in that car with my parents, like I had never been before.

"Why the hell are you crying?" my mother started yelling as soon as the engine started. "Don't you dare waste your tears on those people."

"My tears are not wasted!"

"Well, I don't agree," she argued. "Just look at what you're doing with your life."

"I've done exactly what I've wanted to," I seethed.

"What's that? Start your career toward being a bum? Because that's exactly what you're going to be, a bum and a tramp."

"I am not a tramp!"

"Well, you sure as hell are in a hurry to start working on your vices."

"You're a fine one to go pointing fingers. Neither of you spend much time talking to your children in case you forgot. You don't know the first thing about me, so I wouldn't go around accusing people about their lack of ethics when the best example you and dad can show me where to find them is at the bottom of a Tanqueray bottle."

She had been screaming at me to shut up. Finally, at the end of my tirade, she hollered, "Enough! I don't want to hear a lecture from you. I don't even want to hear your voice right now." She paused. "You know, Jade, I-"

"I don't care!"

"Shut up, Jade!" my father yelled suddenly.

I seethed in the back seat as we crawled toward home at a snail's pace. Was this some new form of torture, turning a five-minute ride into twenty minutes?

"You arrested *me*, for trying to get into my own house!" I accused them.

"Oh please," my mother said dramatically. "I don't want to hear it. Do you know I even asked the police if there was any way I didn't have to take you home?"

"Isn't that a coincidence?" I blurted. "I asked him the same thing!" But the only thing that was running through my head was what were those police thinking of us right now? They must think we're crazy.

"If that's what you want, then fine. Gregg, stop the car," my mother yelled. My father stopped the car in the middle of the road without a word, and my mom said, "You want out, get the hell out! See how you like it without having the luxuries of a home."

I didn't even look back. I darted out of the car and ran back the way we'd come as fast as I could.

I didn't know where I was going. Most of my friends lived too far away. Lynn would have been my first choice, but I knew that was impossible now. It didn't bother me that it was freezing outside, or that I had no jacket or money. All that mattered was that I was free and I had to know what was happening to Kelly and Jesse. I thought about Corie, but I didn't know where she was or how to get in touch with her.

I only had two friends who lived close enough to walk to their houses, and even then it was a couple of miles. I hated living in this residential part of town, so far away from everyone and everything.

There weren't any public phones or anything around me, just miles of houses.

By the time I made it to my friend Lisa's house I was hyperventilating through my sobs. She lay on her stomach on her bed, reading a magazine and listening to The Grateful Dead. She looked up surprised as I burst into her room, but her expression changed quickly into worry.

"Hey, what's wrong?" she asked me, sitting up.

"I just got kicked out of my house," I told her as I panted and paced the room.

She didn't look surprised, but rather curious, as if that shouldn't have bothered me too much considering I had barely been living there for the past month.

"Why?"

"Trespassing!" I said, flinging my arms up in the air. "My mom caught Jesse trying to break into the basement window because she'd locked me out, and then had us and Kelly and Lynn arrested."

"Whoa, that really sucks," she agreed.

"And now I can't find the guys. I don't even know if they're in jail or what's happened to them."

"This is so heavy," she exclaimed lamely. "Dude, I'm sorry but you can't stay here. I'm grounded."

"Again?"

She nodded. "Yeah. Ever since my parents caught us up here getting high with Carrie."

Lynn had been with us, too. I bet her mother was never going to let her see me again.

"That was months ago."

"Yeah," she said again. "Seems they got mad about it all over again when report cards came out. This is the third time I've been grounded for the same thing. It's pretty comical, man. Just a stupid, repetitive cycle."

Comical when you're stoned, maybe, which she was. I guess she figured there wasn't much more they could do to her since she was grounded for smoking pot in the first place.

"By the way, how *did* you get in here?" she asked me.

I shrugged and looked at her stupidly. I was still trying to catch my breath. "I just walked in. I didn't even think about it. I didn't see anyone," I assured her. Neither of us were surprised. Her house was bigger than mine and with less people in it.

She just laughed and said, "Classic."

"I don't know what to do," I complained. "If I knew where Jesse's car was I'd go get it. It doesn't need a key to start because he rigged it somehow, but it's probably impounded anyway, and I don't have any money or a place to stay."

"Why don't you go to Carrie's house? It's only two blocks away and I know she's home. There are so many kids in that house they probably won't even notice you're there."

That was true. Carrie had two brothers and three sisters. They were all between the ages of fourteen and eighteen. Her mother had been having problems conceiving for a long time and they had started adopting, when all of a sudden she started getting pregnant. Hence the herd.

Lisa gave me two cigarettes and sent me on my way.

When I got to Carrie's house I called Lynn. She was still wired from the whole ordeal and couldn't talk long because her mom was still pissed off and listening close by. She told me the police had called her hoping she knew where to get in touch with me, saying they wanted me to call them back.

"Your mom called the police station and told them what happened," she explained in a whisper. "They didn't know where else to look for you, so they called here. They only want to talk to you."

"I don't think so," I murmured into the phone. "Did you find out anything about Kelly and Jesse?"

"They were let go."

"Really? Why?"

"I don't know," Lynn signed into the phone. "Maybe they got off with a warning, or maybe your mom just didn't press any charges. Anyway, there's a peace bond out on them now, so they aren't allowed back in Deerfield at all, especially your neighborhood."

"Did the police tell you all this?" I sounded doubtful.

"No, the guys were here about an hour ago."

"They were? Where are they now?" I started to get excited. Maybe I could find them!

"I don't know, Jade," Lynn said in a tired voice. "My mom was still mad and she made them leave. They wanted me to call you, but I couldn't. I don't know where they went."

I still couldn't believe it after I hung up with Lynn. They had been let go. They were free, I was free, and yet we couldn't find each other. How was it possible that none of us had a stinking cell phone?

I picked up the phone again in a trance and dialed the police station, asking for the youth officer. After I identified myself he said that he'd only wanted to assure me that he was aware of the situation and to make sure I'd found a safe place to go.

"What situation?"

"Your mother explained what happened. Based on the circumstances we can't list you as a runaway, but we will pick you up as one if you don't go back to school."

"Is this a joke?" I asked. "Are you forgetting that I am sixteen and old enough to drop out of school if I want?"

"You are still a minor and dropping out would definitely put you at risk." His voice was calm, but the threat was audible.

"Fine," I grumbled.

I hung up and thought about my options. I didn't have any intention of going back to school, but if I couldn't find the guys then that might be the best place for them to find me. I picked up the phone one last time to call my friend Paul and asked him to come get me.

By this time it was dark, maybe six o'clock, and the possibilities of where Kelly could be found in our town were limited. We drove all over, looking in every possible place. The only place we didn't look was at the Base. Jesse's car wasn't in front of the entrance to the woods, even though there was a slight chance they parked on the other side. Very slight. Next to nil. No one ever went in that way. Plus, I didn't think it was fair to Paul to drag his butt all the way out to the bunker in the freezing cold after I had ordered him to drive me all over town.

Paul mentioned that there was a big party planned for Friday night as the Base. I figured if I didn't find the guys before then I'd most likely run into them there. It was wishful thinking more than anything. We finally gave up and he drove me back to Carrie's house. As I slipped into the bed next to Carrie I kept thinking, only five more days and I'll find them. Then I'll be able to start my life.

"No luck, huh?" she whispered into the darkness.

"No," I whispered back, close to tears. "We looked everywhere. Paul is such a good sport."

I remember overhearing Carrie tell her mom why I was there and asking if I could stay the night, and her mom saying, "That poor girl." I felt like some charity case and was almost embarrassed. I hated the fact that I was supposedly free, yet I was now bound by different chains. Against my will I found myself boarding the school bus the next morning with Carrie and Lisa, with a bag of Carrie's clothes on my shoulder and five bucks her mother gave me for lunch in my pocket.

CHAPTER FOUR

You better start running
When you hear the man coming
Won't do you no good
It won't do you no good

No Good by Kaleo

When I got to school, the principal called me out of my first class, and I went to his office wondering what sort of trouble I was in for missing nearly a month. It was one of the reasons I hadn't wanted to return, feeling trapped and unable to avoid punishment. I could see all the hours of detention and in-school suspension adding up in front of me, and then I figured he could bestow all the punishments he wanted to when I remembered that this was only temporary.

I sat across from him at his desk and listened as he informed me that my mother had called him earlier that morning to tell him what was going on. I was livid. This woman wanted nothing to do with me, and now all of a sudden, she's calling everybody and telling them our private business. If her goal was to humiliate me and make me even more miserable then she was doing a bang job of it.

"I realize you are having a hard time at home," Leighton started. He was leaning back in his large, leather, swivel chair, with his hands templed beneath his chin in a condescending way. "It may be against my better judgment but I'm not going to administer a suspension for you just yet." His voice sounded like some tyrannical dictator who was deciding which form of torture would be the most amusing. He was such a masochist.

I didn't know if he expected me to be grateful or what, but I only sat there looking at him, wishing I were anywhere but there. He pushed the phone at me and I looked at him confused.

"Your mother wishes to speak to you and has asked that I have you call her."

"I don't wish to speak to her," I said evenly.

"Jade, I'm not letting you out of this office until you at least let her know that you are here and okay. It's the least you can do."

I didn't think it was the *least* I could do.

"You can tell her that, can't you?' I said to him, not really asking. He only looked at me. "She knows I'm here because that's what the police told me to do or else I'd be arrested. She doesn't care. She's just being a bitch."

He didn't look moved.

In the end I called. Not because I wanted to or because I was curious about what she'd have to say, but because if I was going to be stuck at school I sure as hell wasn't going to be locked away in ISS all day without even a chance for a cigarette, let alone the possibility of Kelly coming for me.

It was strange talking to her. I didn't know what to say at first. It seemed foreign to me since we rarely spoke much to each other. It felt as if we were strangers, and I realized that she didn't know what to say any more than I did. In my mind I was never going back, but I didn't know what else I was doing. I was waiting in limbo for Kelly and Jesse to come along and tell me what I was doing with my life. In my mother's mind I was coming home. I didn't even know why she would think that way except because anything else where your sixteen-year-old daughter is concerned is socially unacceptable.

Before we hung up I told her I would come by after school to get some of my stuff. Since most of it was in Jesse's car I didn't really know what there was to get, except I did still want my hairdryer and I knew I couldn't wear the few clothes Carrie had lent me for very long. She said that was fine as long as I stayed away from Kelly and Jesse. I told her not to worry because I didn't know where they were anyway.

"You didn't need to call the school and involve them," I told her. "It's none of their business what's going on here. You did that just to piss me off."

"That's not true," she said angrily. "I wanted to make sure you were okay."

No, she didn't.

"You were checking up on me."

"I wanted to talk to you."

"You haven't said anything significant yet!" I snapped.

"You're a very difficult person to love, Jade," my mother finally said.

There were a million things I wanted to say in reply. Like how about the fact that parents were supposed to love their children unconditionally and show that love. She was a walking contradiction and actions spoke louder than words. I hung up then, no longer interested in hearing about my failures as a daughter.

My friend Ona told me I could stay with her and I had Tom swing us by my house on the way. They waited outside while I went inside to pack a bag. Once again, my mother was home early, standing in the doorway of my bedroom, watching me pack a bag. Neither of us said a word. In my defiance I kept my back to her as I stuffed clothes and makeup into the bag, walking in and out of my bathroom until I had everything I could carry. I closed the bag and slung it over my shoulder, then breezed past her and down the winding staircase. She followed me down through the hallway and to the backdoor where Tom's truck waited, idling in the driveway. I knew she stood watching as I jumped up onto the high seat as Ona slid in between me and Tom and the truck backed out.

I never gave her a second glance, but the whole time I wanted to shout, *What do you want from me?* In the past twenty-four hours I had gotten more attention from her than I'd normally get in six months.

I hung out at Ona's that night, waiting until the last minute for her to tell her mother that I was sleeping over. She made up some story about why I was there, but I knew the next day I would have to find another place to go. I had stopped looking over my shoulder for Kelly and Jesse. I knew they weren't around. I figured they had gone back to Elgin and when things cooled down, hopefully they'd come back for me. I had to hope.

The next day was Wednesday and I couldn't wait until the bash on Friday night at the Base. I just knew I'd find them if I gave it enough time. I could only hope that Kelly had heard about the party somehow, because I was sure he'd know I would be there, looking for him, too.

My friend Drea said I could stay at her place that night, but when Paul dropped me off after school her mother slammed the door in my face. I walked to the convenience store and sat down on my bag, completely at a loss as to what to do. I had spent all day looking for a place to crash; there was nowhere else to go. Four cigarettes, no money, and it was snowing again. I felt more alone than ever.

I called Lynn. More to talk than anything because I knew I couldn't stay with her. It was only four-thirty and already the sky was getting dark. I had a lot of cold, dark hours ahead of me and nowhere to spend them. I couldn't just sit in front of the 7-Eleven all night. I had to think. Lynn talked to me for a while then said she had to get to work. About twenty minutes later she came walking down the street, huddled into her winter coat, and handed me the keys to her apartment.

"My mom will be home around seven," she said. "I told her your parents had a business meeting in the city and you didn't want to stay by yourself."

"Oh my God, are you serious?" The relief I felt was physical. "Thank you so much, Lynn. I didn't know what I was going to do."

"Well, I wasn't going to let you sleep in the snow. I hope you like lasagna." I laughed and said I did. "I have to get to work. I'll be home just after ten."

Spending the evening with Lynn's mom wasn't an easy thing to do. I had met her many times before and thought she was a nice enough woman, but this past incident put an obvious strain between us. Even though Lynn explained it away as an innocent misunderstanding, there was still the pot-smoking offense we had all been busted for several months prior. I didn't know her any better than she knew me, really, and she tried to make the time pass as comfortably as possible by asking questions about my family. It was hard for me to pretend like we were a normal, loving family, but the conversation became much smoother when I spoke of neutral things like what my parents did for a living.

Thursday night I stayed with my friend Jenni, who said I could stay with her all weekend if I wanted to. She told her mom that my parents were going through a nasty divorce and didn't want me around to see all the fighting. Her mom asked for my phone number so she could talk to my mom herself, but Jenni kept putting it off. I asked her if she wanted to go to the Nike Base party with me on Friday night and she said she would.

Jenni's mom was great. She was the kind of mom that I thought moms should be. She said, "You just stay here as long as you need to, honey." She made me feel so welcome that I felt a twinge of guilt. I never asked any of my friends to lie for me, though Carrie's mom did make me feel like an outcast. Maybe my friends thought their parents couldn't accept the truth, like when Ona told her mother my house was being fumigated. I guess they were more willing to accept a lie than me and the truth.

Friday afternoon came and I was waiting with baited breath for the time to go to the Base. Jenni still had one more class but I was done for the say so I decided to wait for her in the Pit. When I walked outside I saw a crowd had gathered and there was Jesse's car in the middle of it. I was so glad to see them that I actually started laughing. I ran as fast as I could toward them and punched Kelly in the shoulder.

"Hey!" he said, rubbing his arm. "What's that for?"

"That's for leaving me behind, you dillhole," I ragged at him. "I didn't know what happened to you. Why didn't you come for me four days ago?" As soon as the words were out of my mouth I wanted to bite them back in. How presumptuous of me to assume they *were* coming back for me. Kelly was an out-of-sight-out-of-mind kind of guy. The fact that I had been looking for them was an entirely different thing.

"We had to go back to Elgin, Jade," he explained in a whiney voice that satisfied me. "They followed us back, but look, we're here now, okay?"

"Did you really come back for me?" He looked at me like I had just sprouted a second head, and then smiled. I stood with my arms crossed, looking back at him stubbornly, and he broke into laughter.

"So, I heard you got kicked out of your house," he said smugly.

"Yeah, it's been a hell of a week."

"Can we go now?"

I looked through the mess of bodies to see Jesse standing by the car talking to a boy I had never seen before. He caught my eye and winked. There were so many things I wanted to do right then, so many things I wanted to say. But I wasn't much for public affection and I wasn't completely sure where we stood. Our relationship this past month had teetered between codependency and lust, with no real answers as to what we were to each other yet.

I looked back at Kelly and sighed. "I have to find Jenni before we leave. I've been staying at her house and she needs to know what's going on. You'll take me over there later to get my stuff, right?"

"Sure, whatever," he said noncommittally. So Kelly-like.

"I'll be right back. Don't you dare leave without me!"

I ran back into the building and found Jenni's class just as the second bell rang. The teacher hadn't shown up yet and the students were all laughing and throwing spitballs at each other.

"What's up?" she hurried to the door where I waved at her.

"Kelly is here," I told her. "I'm gonna go with him but we'll be over at your place later to get my stuff."

"Where are you going?" she asked me, alarmed.

"Thank you for letting me stay with you, Jen. Don't say anything to your mom until I get there, okay?"

"Wait a minute!" she yelled after me. "What are you talking about?"

I hadn't realized that she didn't know what had been going on for the past month. She wasn't in my normal crowd. She probably didn't even really know who Kelly was. All she knew was that I was bailing on her and it made no sense. She had no idea what this was about; that for me it had been about finding Kelly and Jesse. That it was all about Jesse.

"For heaven's sake," I faked a laugh that didn't sound very convincing. "You're going to see me later. I'll be fine, Jen. Kelly is going to take care of me."

That was a mistake. I didn't realize at the time what I should have said. I just didn't know how it was all going to play out, and the next thing I knew Kelly and Jesse were there, waiting for me, and the only thing that mattered was getting into that car with them.

We drove around for a while. I was absolutely giddy. The other guy was a friend from Elgin named Chad. He was a tall, lanky boy with short blond hair and devious eyes. I didn't like him. I hoped that we were going back to Elgin, and I hoped that meant we were going to drop him off somewhere soon. He had a crude mouth. He talked too much and too loud and seemed to resent me right off. I never said anything to him beyond a hello when we were introduced.

Around five o'clock I had Jesse take me to Jenni's house to get my stuff and thank her mother for letting me stay. I still hadn't thought up a plan as to why I was leaving her hospitality, but I was desperate to get back in Jesse's car where I felt safe and sure. The guys all waited in the car as I knocked on the front door. Jenni opened it with tears on her face.

"What's wrong with you?" I asked her, stepping into the house.

"Where have you been?" she asked me hysterically.

"I told you Kelly was going to bring me here," I told her sternly. "Why are you crying?"

"My mother wanted to know where you were, and then she made me give her your phone number."

"You didn't!"

She nodded and sniffed. "Now she knows I lied. You'd better come upstairs. She's on the phone right now." She turned and headed for the stairs.

"Great," I mumbled and followed her. Every fiber of my being was telling me to turn and run out the door, but I couldn't do that to Jenni, and somehow getting my stuff was important to me. Stupid.

When we walked into Jenni's large bedroom I noticed how in just two short days I had managed to scatter my things all over, mixed in with her things. I glanced at her mother sitting on the bed, holding a phone to her ear, and saw the look of disapproval on her face.

"She just walked in," she said into the phone. "Okay, hold on." She placed her hand over the mouth piece and looked at me. "Your mother has explained the situation."

"I'm sorry," I mumbled. "I didn't mean to lie to you."

"Just tell me where you've been. Jenni's been upset ever since she came home from school, talking about never seeing you again."

This was a side of Jenni I hadn't known. I turned and glared at her. "I told you I was coming back, didn't I?"

"I'm sorry, I was worried," she offered nervously.

But I was thinking that she was blowing everything out of the water for me. And then when I heard her mother describing the car in the driveway to my mother, I prayed for the earth to split and swallow me whole. This was not going as planned at all. I had to think fast because all at once the house was in a commotion, as we could hear Jenni's two big brothers yelling bloody murder from the first floor.

We looked out the window to see the guys standing around the car waiting for me, and from what I could make out of the yelling, Chad had decided to drop his pants and urinate on their driveway in plain sight. I was mortified. Everyone was in an uproar. Jenni's father and brothers were threatening the guys to get off their property before they called the police, and her mother was still on the phone trying to explain what was going on to my mother. Jenni looked shocked and disgusted, and I thought I would faint from the embarrassment. Here I was being held accountable for that lowlife and I didn't even care to know who he was.

"Your mother says you can either stay here or come home, she'll pick you up." Jennie's mother informed me amidst all the yelling. I was surprised that a full-on rumble hadn't broken out on the driveway yet. "I'll let you stay if you want but neither of you are leaving this house tonight."

My mind was racing. Neither choice sounded very good to me and the guys were seconds away from leaving me behind. Knowing that I couldn't make it to the Base to find them, I panicked and sighed dramatically.

I looked out the window to see Kelly and Jesse getting into the car while Chad still faced off with Jenni's brothers and father. I thought of how stupid he was and wished I could spit on him from up there. I noticed Jesse scanning the windows of the house, looking for me, while Kelly yelled at Chad to get in the car. I didn't care if they beat Chad to a bloody pulp, the longer he stood out there fighting with them, the better chance I had of getting to the car before they took off. And as long as my mother was on the phone no one could call the police.

"They won't leave without me," I lied, wishing in my heart it were true. "I'll have to go down there and tell them to go." I was inching my way toward the door.

Jenni gave me a curious glance as her mother said, "I don't think that's a good idea."

I didn't reply. I ran out of the room and down the stairs with Jenni behind me, trying frantically to keep up. "Jade, wait!"

The guys were already on the street, pulling away from the house slowly, waiting until the last minute to see if I was going to come running out of the house or not. Jenni's brothers were still standing on the driveway, puffing out angry clouds of winter air with their hands on their hips. I skidded past them on the ice-covered driveway and towards the car. They were too stunned to reach out and grab me, though Jenni was still calling my name and pleading with me to stop. I jumped into the front seat and slid down as far as I could as Jesse sped away. I felt awful about what I was doing to Jenni and her family.

CHAPTER FIVE

I heard from God today and she sounded just like me
What have I done and who have I become
I saw the devil today and he looked a lot like me
I looked away, I turned away

Wrong Side of Heaven by Five Finger Death Punch

It took a few minutes for me to realize what had actually happened. I was off in space thinking about the probability that Jenni's mom was still on the phone with my mom, when I heard Chad laugh from the backseat, and I snapped back to reality. I turned around and punched him square in the jaw.

"Whoa!" Kelly yelled, surprised. Chad instinctively lunged after me, but Kelly grabbed him, holding him back.

"Let go of me, man," Chad growled. "I'm gonna tear that bitch apart!"

Kelly's hold tightened as Chad struggled against him, but the look in his eyes said that the only person who was getting tore up was Chad.

"You stupid son of a bitch!" I seethed at Chad. "What the hell were you thinking?"

"I had to go!" he yelled back.

"You're not a child! If you have to go, you hold it! Don't you have any respect for yourself? I know those people for Christ's sake!" I was so mad I was trembling.

"Shut the hell up!" Chad screamed in my face.

"Watch it," Kelly warned, but Chad ignored him.

"For the past four days all I've heard is 'Oh we've got to find Jade. Jade this and Jade that.' You should be feeling pretty damned lucky right now." Kelly sat next to Chad, his fists balled up, his jaw set and clenched, while Chad babbled on.

"So, I get the honor of being blessed by your uncontrollable bladder?" I asked Chad sarcastically.

"Let's just drop it!" Kelly said angrily.

"No, I won't drop it," I said and turned back to look at Chad. "The next time you have to pee, pindick, I suggest you think twice before you whip it out, or I'll make sure you've got nothing left to use."

"Kiss my ass, bitch," was his reply. "You should-"

"That's enough!" Jesse finally yelled. He had pulled up to a stop sign and turned to face the backseat. "You can just shut the hell up, or you can walk back to Elgin."

Chad was astonished. "Oh man. I can't believe you, man! Some chick comes along and you just-"

"I swear to God, I'll hit you myself," Jesse interrupted. His voice was gruff and full of resentment. I stared at him in total silence. I wasn't sure if I should be happy that he was defending me or scared of how mad he might be at me, too. Jesse wasn't a big talker and I had never seen him angry before. He turned back toward the wheel and skidded on the ice as he pulled away from the stop sign.

"It's cool, Jade," Kelly was telling me from behind.

I still sat fuming, facing front, while Kelly started to rub my shoulders. He was the only one who knew how to calm me down when I was mad or upset. My biggest pet peeve was when people told me to calm down or chill out. It just made me madder. But when Kelly did it I just ignored him and let him rub my shoulders. He was the best at massaging. He did a killer job with those fingers of his, and I was forever putting my feet in his lap for one of his amazing foot rubs. I've never known how to relax as well as I did when Kelly gave me a massage. I lay back in my seat and let peace slip over me as Kelly continued to rub my neck and shoulders.

The best was when Kelly rubbed my head. I used to get real bad headaches and instead of taking an aspirin for it, Kelly would rub my head until it went away. It was amazing. Sometimes my headaches got so bad I'd crawl into a dark corner and cry. No one had ever been able to take away the pain like Kelly did.

I hadn't done much thinking of him since Jesse came along, but Kelly was always in the corners of my mind. We were listening to Queen on the radio sing "*My Best Friend*" and I felt this huge wave rush over me, making me want to cry. I knew that Kelly *wanted* me, but that he had always been okay with the way things were between us. I didn't want him that way, and I didn't mind Corie being his girlfriend, but still there was a part of me that did want him for myself and for myself only. I loved him uncontrollably and with no direction. It was not rational. He was a good-looking guy, not as tall or broad as Jesse, but taller than me. He had light brown hair that fell into his eyes and barely touched his shoulders. He had big, green, sparkly eyes and a huge smile with perfect white teeth. He wasn't big, but he was strong, his sinewy arms showed definition. I could see why so many girls swooned over him.

We drove on for a while, chain smoking and flipping through the radio. The tension was so thick I thought I would choke from it. Jesse apologized, but I knew it wasn't his fault what Chad had done. I figured I wouldn't be spending any more time at Jenni's house anyway.

I realized that we were on the outskirts of Elgin and I hoped were going to Chad's house. It didn't seem as though Jesse or Kelly wanted him around anyway. He got out of the car when Jesse pulled to a stop in front of a trailer much like his own, and Chad said something like, "Thanks, man. I'll catch you later." He said it so casually, as if no words had been spoken between them. I had a feeling that he wasn't going to be seeing Jesse anytime soon.

"Yeah," Jesse answered quietly. "I'll see you around."

He started driving again and I wanted to ask where we were going. I kept my mouth shut though because I could tell he was still in a bad mood. I wanted to ask him what kind of friend Chad had been to him, if they had known each other a long time, or maybe if he was important to Jesse the way

Kelly was to me. But I was determined to turn the mood around and kept silent.

It dawned on me suddenly how little I knew of Jesse and even Kelly at times like these. I had no idea where we were going or what to expect, because I didn't know where they went or what kinds of things they did when I wasn't with them. Usually they were in Deerfield with me, crashing in my basement, even in the bunker once or twice, and a lot of the time in an old, abandoned house we found in a cemetery in Lincolnshire. But it was too early to think about where we would crash for the night. It was only six-thirty.

"Where's Corie?" I finally asked.

"She's at home," Kelly said bitterly. "She's been there since Monday."

"Why?" I wanted to know.

"I don't know," he sighed. "We never found out."

"Well, let's go get her."

"We can't."

"Then I'll call her."

"Stop, Jade, alright?" He sounded defeated. "Just forget it. Maybe she wants to be there. Maybe she's happy there."

"No, she's not," I said, turning around to see him slumped down in the darkness. "Her father beats her, Kelly. Would you be happy going back to that? She's probably scared out of her mind right now."

"And you're not?" he argued with me. "If I had a family to go back to, don't you think I would?"

"No!" I guffawed. "You had plenty of chances to go back, and every time you did they gave you another reason to leave. I'm sorry if the truth hurts, Kel," I added quietly, turning back to face the front. "But I know you too well, and Corie is no different."

I didn't know where all that bitterness was coming from. Knowing him as well as I did I could only assume that Kelly had finally found a girl he really cared about, possibly even someone he could put above me if he ever figured out how to do that. But she was in her own chains and he felt helpless. What a mess of things we had made, to not even be able to drive back into Deerfield without getting arrested. And to think that we had come this far only to be short of our goal once again.

"Let her figure it out," was his reply.

I didn't want to let Corie figure it out by herself. It was so unlike Kelly to be defeated. I knew there was something battling in his mind, something that he felt he had no control over. He didn't ever expect to feel that way, but I thought for sure he really cared about Corie, which was all the more reason to go get her. She was the first of Kelly's girlfriends who didn't resent me, and I genuinely liked her back. I could see he was having a hard time dealing with these emotions. I felt it was important to go get her now. If we waited, we might be too late. Why give her father that chance? Living on the road shouldn't be the alternative to being abused, but at least there was no father around to hit anyone. At this point I realized that there weren't many choices that were fair.

In the short time that I had known Corie I found her to be a lot like me. She was someone who was looking for freedom and acceptance; to exist peacefully. That's what we all wanted really. I acknowledged that the guys had their own reasons; being disowned by family and police records, but choosing to leave society behind and live on the road was their own cop-out. Well, it was for all of us. We just had different reasons. All we wanted was to invent our own kind of society, with our own rules. No one to watch over us or tell us what to do, no one to slap our wrists or put us in jail. Whatever it may be, whoever the enemy may be, we'll just run from it. We'll leave them all behind to choke on our dust. No one could ever own us again. No one.

I still had no idea where we were going. I began to wonder what the big plan was now. Before it was just a game to me with the guys playing along, but now it was real. I had no home to go back to, no parents to fool. I had forfeited that when I ran out of Jenni's house. I had turned my back the same way Kelly and Jesse, and even Corie had. It hit me then that my reality was nothing to the guys. To them, there was nothing monumental about having me as a permanent fixture in their car, but I knew there wasn't any point in hanging around anymore. We had been driving in circles for a month and I had believed it was because of me, because I wouldn't commit. Now I knew that wasn't true.

We ended up at a pizza parlor where a guy we knew worked. Jason usually slipped us some free food when we came in, and occasionally hooked the guys up with a little something to get high with when he could. I had met Jason a few years before from my friend Tori, who used to date him, but I never knew him until I met Jesse. I didn't think Jason actually remembered me, which was fine because I didn't like him very much, free food aside.

We had been sitting in a booth for over an hour and finally out of total boredom I snagged a quarter off the table and ran to the pay phone. Corie was crying when she answered the phone and asked where I was.

"I'm at Jake's Pizza," I told her. "Are you okay?"

"You mean you're in Elgin?" She sounded relieved. "I thought you all were gone. Does that mean Kelly is with you? What happened to you guys?"

I realized that she had no idea what had happened with the three of us getting arrested at my house. That one day seemed to have set off a ton of other things. "Man, it's been a crazy week," I said. "I only just found the guys today. They heard you'd gone back home and didn't know what to do."

"I didn't want to come home," she said. "I was hanging out in the park with some people, waiting for everyone to come back, and the cops picked me up. My father hasn't taken his eyes off me since he dragged me home."

"Are you okay?" I asked again.

"No," she cried. "I'm scared as hell. He's already given me a black eye, he hasn't let me leave even to go to school, and he's been threatening to put bars put on the windows. He's crazy." She whispered the last part, her voice breaking.

"Why didn't you leave?" Surely, she'd had some opportunity to escape?

"I had nowhere to go," she wailed quietly into the phone. "I was too scared to run away again because I couldn't find Kelly, and I know, Jade, that my father will find me."

"Where's he now?" I looked back at the booth to see what the guys were doing. Jesse was watching me curiously, and Kelly was trying real hard to not pay any attention to me. Instead he was focusing on twisting straw wrappers together.

"He's just downed a fifth, so he should be crashed out about now," Corie said. "But if he finds me on the phone I'm dead. Where's Kelly?"

"He's with me." I bit my lip and put my back to Kelly. "Can you get out at all?"

"Yes."

"We'll come get you."

"No! The cops know Jesse's car. Just wait there. I can make it."

I hung up the phone and walked back to the booth. Sliding into my seat I stared at Kelly until he finally lifted his head to meet my gaze. "I told you so," I said evenly.

"Is she okay?" He looked worried.

"No, Kelly, she's not okay," I said roughly. "She's on her way over here. We're taking her with us."

"And where do you think we're going?" Jesse wanted to know. I stared at him straight in the eye.

For the first time I didn't lose my stomach when I looked at him. For the first time I wasn't consumed with thoughts of being close to him. I was angry and fed-up, and it showed.

"I don't know, Jes, but we're not staying here. I know you're not working, so it's not like you can go back to your probation officer, right?" He nodded slowly. "It's wintertime in Chicago, it's freezing outside, and all we have is a crappy old station wagon. Tell me, boys, why do you think we need to stay around here?"

"Where do you think we should go?" Jesse asked me with a tight smile. "Mexico?"

"Don't be stupid," I told him. I reached for a cigarette and Jesse produced a lighter.

"I just don't understand what you're trying to get at," he said as he laid the lighter back down. "What do you want?"

"We don't have any money," Kelly said.

"You manage to find money for your dope, and for gas to drive back and forth between here and Deerfield," I said pointedly as I blew a smoke ring at him.

"Why are you being like this?" Kelly sounded hurt. "You're being so mean."

"I am not."

"I guess we have some things to talk about," he surmised.

"Maybe we do, Kelly," I agreed softly, though I wasn't sure what about.

Jesse looked ill at ease for a minute, not knowing what to do. He got up and went over to

Jason to have a less stressful conversation, while Kelly had gone back to twisting his wrappers.

"Listen," I hissed at him. "I don't know what your problem is but stop taking it out on me."

He scoffed. "I thought it was the other way around." When I didn't say anything, he sighed and looked up at me, his eyes softer. "I'm sorry, Jade, I do want you here. It's just that...hell, I don't know. I'm just having a harder time than I thought I would, dealing with you being with Jesse is all."

I stared at him for a full twenty seconds. "Oh, puh-leeze!" I drawled and rolled my eyes. "You brought him to me. You said so yourself."

"I know I did!" he snapped.

"You just want to have your cake and eat it, too."

"I've never had the cake!"

"And what about Corie?" I demanded. "Doesn't she count for anything? Don't you care about her at all?"

"Yes!" he said angrily. "Does that make you feel better?"

"You better not be lying to me, Kelly."

I trotted off to the jukebox. Someone had been playing a terrible medley of country-western songs that could have bored a fly off shit. I was pretty sure they were gone by now, so I felt safe playing something else. I stood at the jukebox for a while, reading all the songs, when I had an idea. I made my way back to the booth and sat down with a wide smile.

Kelly looked up and said, "What's that stupid grin for?"

"Remember the time you and Kurt and Shannon took off for North Carolina?"

"Yeah," he shrugged. "So?"

"So," I said, stressing the small word. "You said you wanted to leave Chicago, do something different. You didn't even want to come back."

"What's your point, Jade?"

"You pitched a tent and lived at a camp ground for two months," I reminded him, my hands rolling for emphasis.

"You did?" Jesse asked. He'd returned and sat down next to me.

"Yeah," Kelly's eyes lit up. "It was cool, man. We used to swim in the river and have a fire every night."

"You guys survived like that for a long time," I reminded him with a nod of my head. "We can do that, too."

"You're really serious, aren't you?" Jesse asked me.

"*Why* are we staying here?" I stressed again. "Kelly, you do stuff like this all the time, none of it should come as a shock to you." He nodded in agreement. But the truth was I was tired of starving and freezing my butt off in a crowded car or sleeping in some abandoned house in a cemetery. I wanted out of Elgin. I wanted out of Illinois. I wanted to leave to know I was really free.

Just then Corie came in to the restaurant. She looked awful. Her face was bruised and tear-stained, and she looked exhausted. She carried a bag of clothes with her and slid into Kelly's arms at the table.

"Hi," she smiled weakly. "I'm back."

CHAPTER SIX

And we can run away
Swimming in the sunlight everyday
Paradise, it's in your eyes
Green like American money

American Money by Borns

The more we talked about leaving the more we thought of places to go. I felt it would be best to head south since it was winter, but the guys wanted to go west. I mentioned that if we wanted to survive we'd have better luck in warmer weather, and the south was a lot closer than California. Then they declared that we couldn't leave yet anyway because we didn't have any money. Jesse said he had a small stash, but it would be best if he used it to turn it over for a bigger profit.

"And what if you lose it instead?" I asked.

"I'm not betting on a horse," he said, as if I should know. "Trust me, it'll make a profit."

I knew what that meant. I wanted to be more included, play a more active role in moving us forward. I'd already spent sixteen years sitting on the sidelines, and here I was again. It made me feel completely dependent on them and I hated it. They did all the planning, they made all the money, and Corie and I just sat around and looked pretty. While the guys were out doing their manly thing, Corie and I were left alone a lot.

We did end up staying at the cemetery house. There really wasn't anywhere else to go, and we needed a few days to get ready. The only livable space in the house was one of the upstairs bedrooms. The kitchen and bathrooms didn't work, and the rest of the house was full of boxes and junk. It was weird. It was as if someone had dumped their stuff there and left in a hurry. Either that or they had packed up and then never came back for any of it.

The house was a small two-story, hidden behind large trees in the corner of the cemetery. The graveyard itself was small, set way back from the main road, clustered within a small wooded area with an old dirt road leading up to it. You couldn't see any of it from the highway. I wondered what came first, the house or the cemetery, because it seemed strange that someone would live with graves just twenty feet from their front door. It could have started as a private family cemetery and then over time the county used it to bury other people as well, but it definitely hadn't been in use in years. The state no longer maintained the grounds.

The money came in everyday, a little bit at a time, and we put most of it into a big jar. The guys wouldn't discuss with me and Corie what they were doing, but it wasn't hard to imagine. I gave them three days to do what they had to do. It was a very long, boring three days. Corie and I stayed at the house alone most of the time. During the day we played cards and napped. It was too cold to do anything else. The guys told us to stay in the house, but on that third day we were going stir crazy and decided to walk into town and get a burger.

We bought some more cigarettes and then headed to the arcade next door. I put our order in and Corie went straight for a game. I was watching her play Galaga when I heard a familiar voice behind me. I turned around and looked into pupils that were dilated to the size of dimes.

"Hey, Lisa," I said curiously. "What are you doing here?"

"I had some business to take care of," she said lamely. "You know how it is."

"You're not in school?"

"It's my lunch hour." As if that explained it all.

"That's a pretty long ride for your lunch hour."

"It's all good," she said with a flip of her hands. She swayed.

I stood looking at her and nodding my head. She stared back at me with a stupid, spaced out smile for the span of a minute, and I wondered what in the world she was doing. It occurred to me that I was looking at one of my closest friends and I had no desire at all in talking to her. It was as if she were a total stranger. Or rather, I had become the stranger.

Corie cursed at the game and spun around to face us.

"Who's this?" Lisa asked. She actually lifted an entire arm and pointed straight at Corie. She was wasted.

Corie scowled at her and took a step back.

"She's Kelly's girlfriend," I said, getting annoyed.

"Ahh, and where is that cat?" she looked at me knowingly.

I shrugged and offered her a tight smile. "I don't know."

"Hmm," she mused for another thirty seconds. "You know, Jade, I thought you'd be long gone by now."

"Why?"

"Didn't you read the clipping in the newspaper?" I shook my head, but I should have known better. We were always checking the police section of the paper for write-ups on people we knew who'd gotten arrested for various misdeeds. It just never occurred to me to look in there to see my own name.

"Oh man!" Lisa went on. "They wrote an article about you guys getting arrested at your mom's house and about the restraining order. They've listed you as a runaway and there's a warrant out for that other guy." She was snapping her fingers trying to think of his name.

"Jesse," I said.

"That's it. And knowing Kelly, well, I just know he's got to be in some kind of trouble."

"He's not," I informed her in an 'it's none of your business' way. Corie was getting impatient and started tugging on my arm. Just then I heard my name called; our burgers were ready.

"Sure," Lisa smiled her irritating little all knowing smile. "Well, take it easy, man. I gotta get back to the 'burbs."

"Yeah," I said absently and handed the guy at the counter a twenty. I waited for my change, grabbed the bag of food, and followed Corie out the door. We huddled into our jackets and started back toward the cemetery.

"What was she talking about?" Corie asked me through clattering teeth. The wind had picked up and it felt like it was blowing right down the back of my jacket.

I just shrugged at her. "She's tripping."

"What if she's right? What if she goes back and blabs that she saw you?"

I had to laugh, though I didn't really find any humor in it. "I doubt she'll even remember seeing me. Don't worry about Lisa. She may be obnoxious but she's still my friend."

It was still getting dark early. It was only five thirty when the sun had set and the cold crept in. Corie and I had given up on our never-ending card game and retreated to bundling up under some old blankets to keep warm. I don't know how long we slept before the guys came strolling in. It was pitch black inside the small room.

"Hey, girls, wake up!" Kelly was singing as he entered through the door. He was using the flame from his Zippo to see by and stopped to light a candle. Jesse followed in behind him and sat down on a big ratty chair beside the door. Corie and I sat up, rubbing our eyes.

"Did you bring any food?" Corie asked. Jesse tossed a white paper bag onto the mattress.

"What are you two doing sleeping?" Kelly teased as he flung himself to the edge of the mattress.

"Being cold and bored!" I yelled at him and stood up. "Where the hell have you guys been all day?" The two just looked at each other stupidly. "I don't like being left here for hours, not knowing what's going on or if you're coming back." I didn't realize how angry I was until I saw Kelly's smug face.

"Hey, Jade?" Kelly said in his patronizing voice. "We came back."

"We heard today that the police wrote about your arrest in the paper," Corie managed through a mouthful of fries. "They said all kinds of things about you guys. Is it true that there's a warrant out for your arrest, Jesse?" She looked at him with wide eyes and he shrugged back.

"Probably so," he mumbled.

"Wait a minute," Kelly said hotly and sat up. "Who told you that?"

I spun to face him. "We heard about it on our radio!" I said sarcastically.

"You guys went to town?" he asked me, disbelieving. "Man, I told you not to do that! What if the cops had seen you two?"

"We're not blind, Kelly," I reminded him. "I'm not worried about being seen by a cop. It's not like they've got our mug shots on the dashboard of every squad car. I mean let's face it, the two of you stand more of a chance getting busted driving around in that sand wagon all day!"

"We're busting our butts to get money, and you're gonna blow it!" Kelly roared.

I had never been so mad at him. I was used to Kelly's indifference to other people's feelings, but never mine. I expected more from him. I expected him to consider me more, like he always had. At that moment all I wanted was to leave. I didn't care anymore about all our big plans.

"Forget this!" I screeched.

"Where do you think you're going?"

"I need to get away from you!" I shot at him and started down the dark stairs. I could hear him laughing behind me, saying that I wasn't going anywhere. It was futile and we both knew it. I had no place to go. I thought about my options and knew that I had burned up all my bridges. Besides, leaving would take me away from Jesse and I couldn't do that.

I was halfway through the dark cemetery, tripping over grave markers, when I heard Jesse coming after me. He grabbed my arm and I tried to jerk free of his grasp.

"Will you stop?" he growled at me. I spun around to face him. "Jesus, Jade, where do you think you're gonna go?"

"Nowhere," I said, shrugging my arm free. I turned around and took two steps only to be waylaid by his grasp again.

"He's pissing me off," I said, pointing to the house. "As a matter of fact, so are you, Jes."

"I'm sorry," he shrugged.

I didn't say anything. Instead I crossed my arms and pouted, brooding. I didn't have anywhere to go. I didn't want to leave Jesse, but I didn't like this place we had all come to, this hiding out. We were still cold, still homeless. We were still doing the same things we'd been doing all along. Nothing had changed and I was tired of it. We hadn't even made it out of Chicago yet and I was wondering what in the world we were doing. For several depressing minutes I experienced that malcontent feeling of not wanting anything. I didn't want to be there nor did I want to go home. It was very disturbing to discover that getting what you want isn't good enough.

"I wouldn't have left you here," He had set his hands on my shoulders and looked down into my upturned face. "We've been through too much for me to just leave you somewhere. And how can you doubt Kelly like that? He's your best friend."

I shook my head, and said warily, "I know him better than you do. And he's never hidden stuff from me before." I didn't mention that the possibility of them getting arrested rather than just ditching us had been my main concern.

"Things are different now," Jesse explained. "Everything that we are doing, we're doing for you and Corie. You have to believe me."

"What does that mean? That you feel responsible for me? Because I can tell you right now that-"

"No," he interrupted with a tightening grip on my arms. "It's more than that. Jade, don't you know how I feel about you?"

I shook my head and waited to hear the words. How I wanted him to tell me how he felt. I needed to know if he wanted and needed me as much as I wanted and needed him. He could read it in my eyes. He knew what I was thinking and nodded as if I had spoken the words.

"I'm sorry, if you felt like I didn't care." There was a moment of silence as we looked into each other's eyes. "I am so *in* to you." His voice was low, gruff.

I nodded and offered him a small smile. My heart was beating out a cadence I was sure he could hear. His hands moved up my arms and he lowered his head to meet mine. With one hand clasped behind my head, the other held my jaw with one thumb reaching and finding the hollow of my throat, slightly stroking the soft depression. I was sure he would be able to feel my pulse beating on his thumb, the simple act creating a stirring in me. I reached my own arms up and placed my hands on two firm biceps. The kiss wasn't romantic, not even lusty. It was a connection between two people who needed each other.

Around midnight the four of us were laying around when Kelly stood up and announced that he was in the mood for a drive. He thought us girls were so stupid. I snorted, and he smiled devilishly as he pushed me into the car. "You know I love you," he whispered in my ear. We drove for about ten minutes before Jesse parked the car on a dark street lined with houses and trees. He turned to me and said, "Get in the driver's seat."

Before I could ask any questions, Kelly was getting out of the car, saying, "We're going to the shopping center down the street. Corie, you come with and stand at that corner." He pointed in the direction of the mall. She and Jesse got out, and Corie nodded nervously while I slid over behind the wheel.

They walked down the dark street and stopped at the corner, directing Corie to stand under a tree.

As she stepped up to it the darkness closed in around her and she disappeared. The guys continued walking around a bend in the road until I could no longer see them in the rearview mirror. Although Corie was only fifty feet away I couldn't see her, and I felt very alone.

It must have only been five minutes. I was listening to Gregg Allman sing about how he had nobody to run with anymore, when I looked into the mirror to see Corie running for the car. I could see her looking back and forth nervously between me and the direction the guys had gone. She jumped into the front seat and yelled, "Go! Go!"

"What?" I asked, confused. I looked into the mirror again, expecting to see Kelly and Jesse running toward the car, but they were nowhere in sight. Corie yelled at me again so I started the car and pulled out on the highway.

"What happened?" I asked.

Instead of answering she just mumbled. "You won't believe this. You won't believe what just happened."

And then I saw them ahead of me, jumping the side fence and running across the highway. By the time I was passing them they were on the other side of the road and waving their arms at me, telling me to keep going. Kelly was holding something in one hand he waved me on with the other. He was trying to shove it in his pocket as he ran; something shiny.

"A gun?" I yelled. I looked again to see that they had disappeared behind me as I sped down the highway. "A gun?" I asked again. Corie was on her knees looking out the back window. "Where did they get a gun?"

"I don't know," she cried, turning on her seat and sitting down to face the front. "I didn't even know they had one."

"Where am I going?" I yelled desperately.

"I don't know!" she wailed back, her head in her hands. "Back to the cemetery."

"Corie," I said as calmly as possible. "Did they make a deal in the mall parking lot, or not?"

"No," she shook her head. "I mean...I guess not. I didn't see them go in, but I think they robbed that convenience store over there."

"Great!" I sobbed. "Were there any cops around?"

"I don't think so," she sniffed. "They ran off before any came anyway. Maybe the clerk didn't have a chance to make the call."

"You don't mean?" I stared at her with wide eyes.

"No!" she said, shocked. "They didn't shoot."

"Well, then at least they had a head start," I mumbled.

We waited back at the cemetery house on pins and needles. We chain smoked and paced. It seemed like we waited with baited breath for hours until we heard Kelly and Jesse strolling through the cemetery.

"I'm gonna brag about it, I'm not gonna stay in school. Gonna rob and steal and break every rule."

I could hear them singing as they walked toward the house, their voices getting louder and clearer. Well, clearly slurred anyway. They were drunk. How they managed to get so sloshed in just over an hour was beyond me, but there they stood, each holding a Coke and passing a bottle of Crown Royal between them. They were swaying between the headstones and singing. We could hear them all the way from the entrance road of the cemetery. Real stealth these two.

Corie and I walked outside and waited for them, sitting ourselves on top of a large headstone.

"I'm gonna brag about it, gonna kill my mom and dad. Won't be sad about it 'cause they treat me so bad. I got a change to tell you off and I'm gonna use it well. Everybody, everywhere, you can all go to hell!"

They sounded so stupid as they slurred and tripped over their own feet. The two continued coming closer until they reached Corie and me, and then kept on singing right in our faces with droopy eyes and stupid smiles.

"I gonna brag about it, I flunked, I didn't pass. And I'm gonna kick somebody's ass. Because I'm a time bomb, baby!"

"You sure are," I said dryly.

CHAPTER SEVEN

Promises, where they gonna lead me to?
I still have wishes that haven't come true
Well I toss and I turn at what this life that can give
Yeah, I toss and I turn at how this life I should live

Are You the Answer by Collective Soul

So that's when we finally left. Not out of boredom, not for a vacation, but because the guys had held a gun to an innocent man and robbed his store. We didn't talk about it. Corie and I didn't ask any questions, and they didn't offer any details. But we knew.

It wasn't until the next morning that they realized what they had done and suggested it was time to go. They were too drunk the night before to think clearly and couldn't do anything besides sit on top of gravestones and sing the words to that crazy, ironic Ramones song. They sang it over and over again. I'm surprised they didn't break out with the Robin Hood theme song and try to fly through the trees.

We started out on I-94 and drove through the city toward Indiana. I had no idea where we were going but I hoped it would be some place warmer. I dozed on and off. Jesse drove with purpose, determined to get somewhere fast. When I woke up from one of my catnaps and saw a sign for Kentucky I couldn't believe it. We were really out of Illinois!

"Am I dreaming?" I asked Jesse quietly. He jumped slightly as if I had startled him. It was quiet in the car with Kelly and Corie asleep in the backseat. I looked over my shoulder to see them spread out next to each other, Kelly spooning Corie with an arm wrapped around her.

"Nope," Jesse answered.

"Where are we going?" I peered out the window and gasped at the sight of so many stars. I'd never seen that many at once in the Chicago sky.

"I'm not sure. Just gonna keep on driving."

He looked tired. He'd been driving for at least eight hours straight and no doubt had a hangover. I scooted closer to him and he moved his arm around my shoulders. I fiddled with the radio, picking up mostly static and horrible country music. Corie and Kelly slept a little bit longer, rocking with the motion of the car. When Jesse stopped for gas everyone woke up and got out to stretch. The sky was dark, but the air was already warmer than what we had left behind.

"I'm hungry," Corie announced sleepily.

"Me too," I agreed.

She kicked Kelly's legs off of her own and pushed herself out of the car, stretching her arms over her head and yawning. We found Jesse pumping gas under the bright neon light of the station.

"Grab something for me, too," were his orders as he plopped some money into my hand.

"Come on," I said and threaded an arm through Corie's. "There's a place across the street."

"Don't forget to get me something!" Kelly called after us.

"I'll get you the kiddie meal," I called back.

"I get the toy," Corie teased.

"No, you don't!" Kelly yelled.

After we ate the guys traded places and Jesse and I settled into the backseat. He laid his long frame over the width as best as he could and wrapped an arm around me, making a pillow for me with his other arm.

"Hey," Kelly leaned into the back seat. "Where we going?"

Jesse groaned and opened one eye. "I don't care. Just don't wake me up until we get there."

"How about Mexico, man?" Kelly asked excitedly. I didn't even bother to mention that we were going in the wrong direction.

Kelly had been telling me stories about Mexico for as long as I had known him. He made everything about it sound so great, like one wild party after another, and he always made it sound like he had just been there. I don't know when or if he'd ever been but one time he had shown me a book that he said came from there and was illegal because it had all these recipes for making homemade drugs. I just wanted something easy, so we found a recipe for banana peels. We scraped the white pulp out of the skins and baked them according to the directions in the book. That was it. That was the whole recipe. After we smoked the pulp we realized it was all a bunch a crap. It was disappointing because we were always trying to smoke one thing or another to catch a buzz. One time we smoked tea leaves because we were told it had PCP in it. What a crock that was. And I'll never forget the time we smoked potpourri. It tasted really good, but oddly there was no smoke when we exhaled. The best was when we bagged up the banana peels in a dime bag and sold it to some kids at school. Two days later one of them came running up to me, saying, "Have you got anymore? Man, that stuff was great!"

The next time I woke up it was daylight. I didn't know what time it was, but the heat in the car was strong and comforting from the sun beating down on it. We seemed to be in what appeared to be a state park. I looked around to see that Kelly and Corie were nowhere in sight. Jesse stirred next to me as I crept silently from the car.

It was slightly chilly but nothing like the temperature back home. As I stepped out of the car and stretched my arms, I could hear water running close by and followed the sound until I came to a small, thin creek behind a mass of trees. The stream was running swiftly, rolling over rocks with little white caps bouncing along. I sat down on a big, warm rock and lost myself in the sound of gurgling water. I mused that the stream must be a beautiful sight in the spring. Right now, everything was still on the brownish side though there was some new grass popping up, and a few trees had already started to bloom big, pink blossoms. The lullaby of the stream had me more relaxed than I had been in weeks.

I don't know how long I sat there. It seemed like a long time before I heard voices coming from the direction of the car. Slowly, I pulled myself up and headed back. Corie and Kelly had returned and woken Jesse up. I found the three of them sitting on top of a picnic table.

"Good morning, Sunshine," Kelly smiled at me. I gave him a quirky smile in return.

I plopped myself down on the bench between Jesse's knees, and Kelly said, "Check it out. There's a place back there were we can hide the car so when they patrol at night we won't be seen. We can camp out here tonight. There's even a fire pit and a grill."

"Oh joy!" I said. "Why would we want to camp out here, Kelly? I don't even see any bathrooms."

"You're such a city girl," he tisked at me. But when he saw that my expression hadn't changed, he said, "We don't have a choice. We can't afford a motel room every night and we need a better place to sleep than the car. It'll be fun. We'll have a cookout and roast marshmallows."

He was mocking me but we all started laughing anyway. Tough guy Kelly talking about roasted marshmallows. Imagine that. He might as well have said he wanted to go picking daisies.

Before the guys left to pick up some food and provisions, we moved over to our camping site and Jesse built a small fire in the pit. Corie and I spread a blanket on the grass and sat playing Gin Rummy while we waited for them to get back.

"Well, this is familiar," I murmured.

"What do you think is going to happen to us?" Corie asked.

I shrugged vacantly as I studied my cards. "I don't know."

"Here," she whispered. I looked up to see a big grin across her face as she lit a joint and passed it to me. "I've been saving that."

"Where did you get it?" I asked in awe as I pulled in and held the smoke.

"Secret," she squeaked. "Besides, you know they party when they're out doing their manly things, don't you?"

"I figured," I admitted. "Did Kelly tell you that?"

She snorted and took another pull before handing it back to me. "Kelly doesn't tell me anymore than he tells you."

We passed it back and forth until it was nothing but a lump of ash between our fingers. Corie had to pull out one of her hairclips and squeeze the roach inside so we could smoke it all the way down. The buzz hit me fast and I started to giggle. I looked at my cards and put one down on the pile.

"Hey!" I said suddenly, causing her to jump and then start giggling. "How are we gonna explain being stoned?"

Corie picked up my card and laid a different one down. "I'll tell them we found some wild peyote." She said it deadpan but within seconds we were both laughing hysterically.

"It'll never work," I declared. My cheeks were hurting from so much laughing.

Corie looked back and forth between her cards and the pile on the blanket. "Hey, is it your turn? Jade, go, it's your turn."

"Oh yeah," I said. I peered at my cards trying to remember what I was doing. I looked up at Corie and said, "Go Fish."

She started laughing so hard I thought she would bust her seems. I started laughing, too, though I wasn't sure what was so funny. You just can't watch someone else dying of laughter and it not be infectious.

"I have to pee!" she screamed through her laughter. "Stop laughing, Jade."

"I'm not, you are!" I laughed back. "What's so funny?"

"We're not playing Go Fish!"

By this time I was on my back laughing so hard I had to hold my stomach.

"Okay," I finally managed to say. I sat up and wiped the tears off my face. I placed a card down on the blanket as Corie ran to the trees, laughing the whole time she was in there. When she came back she picked up her cards and studied them. Then she looked at me and said, "Got any threes?"

When the guys returned all they had to do was take one look at us sprawled out on the blanket, staring at the clouds, and they knew. We looked up at them standing above us, upside down, and started giggling afresh.

"I don't believe this," Jesse drawled, still looking at me. "They're stoned." He laughed as he dropped onto the blanket next to me and propped himself on his elbows. "What's so funny, girls?" We laughed harder.

The next morning we packed up the car and drove on. Kelly said that we had spent the night in

Virginia, and he hoped to take us at least as far as North Carolina, which would be a much shorter driving day. I asked if we were going back to the same place that he had been with Kurt and Shannon, but he said no. He didn't want to go there, and anyway, there were plenty of other places just like it. As we made our way down mile-high tree-flanked highways, I couldn't help but sense that this southern state had a serene feeling all through it, and I wondered what it would be like to grow up in the country, away from all the hustle and bustle of the city.

We drove in contented silence most of the way. The trip to the coast was made in less than six hours. Before we knew it, we were looking for a campground to set up in. The guys managed to get a tent from somewhere and for a while the four of us-squeezed in at night to sleep. About a week later Kelly decided we needed some more space and came up with another one.

Staying in North Carolina was a lot like it had been in Chicago, only warmer. The guys started leaving us more and more as they went out and looked for a way to make money. The whole thing certainly wasn't as romantic as I had fantasized it to be, but at the same time I couldn't complain. I had gotten what I wanted, and anything Corie or I asked for they tried their hardest to produce it.

About two weeks after we arrived we took a trip to the shore to scout for a place to stay that was closer to the beach. It was a quaint, little sea-side tourist town, with the ocean right at our toes. Corie and I didn't have bathing suits but we didn't care.

We wore cutoff jeans and T-shirts and pranced down to the sand like we owned it. It was glorious for about a week; after that there always seemed to be sand in everything. Then one day Jesse announced that he and Kelly got a job on a fishing boat.

"How can you get a job?" I asked him. "Do you even know how to fish?"

"They're paying us under the table," he said. He didn't need to bother with my second question because I already knew the answer. Obviously, he hadn't gotten hired for his fishing skills.

"Sounds too good to be true," I eyed him suspiciously, causing him to laugh.

"You are a city girl," he teased, plopping a kiss on my mouth.

They worked for three weeks with their pockets getting fuller and smelling like dirty sea water and fish. Then one day they came off the boat after another long week of working and suddenly announced that we were moving on. Corie jumped up and started packing without any questions. I think she was bored with the guys spending so much time on the boats. Truth was, I was bored, too.

"What happened to your jobs?" I asked as Jesse started to break down the tent.

"Jade," he said calmly. "We weren't going to keep them." His voice said I should have known that.

"Yeah," Kelly said from behind me where he was packing things into a duffle bag. "We can tell you're getting bored."

"Well, yeah, I guess..." I said lamely.

"You said you wanted to travel, so that's what we're doing."

"You mean we're just gonna keep on driving...forever?"

"What should we do?" Jesse asked me. "Find a town and settle in, maybe get an apartment and a job? Go back to school? Do you really think that would work?"

"What's so crazy about that?" I asked him. Of course, I knew it couldn't happen, but I wasn't the one running away from a warrant, either.

He just looked at me crossly and continued to pack up the tent.

"What's wrong with you, Jade?" Corie asked me quietly.

"Something's up," I said. "Just watch them." Her eyes followed mine as we studied the guys. They were silent, determined, just like I had seen them once before. "They're running from something."

The car was packed, and we headed out on the open road once again. I was a bit confused and sulky at first, but once we started driving it disappeared. I loved being on the road. There wasn't a mile that went by that I didn't bask in the freedom it gave me. With nothing but the hum of the engine and the methodical rhythm of the tires on the pavement, ahead of us were endless possibilities. The sun was shining, the breeze felt warm coming in through the windows, the grass smelled fresh and new, and the clouds were perfect puffs of white against a deep blue sky.

"Where to next?" Kelly asked Jesse from the backseat. He was sitting behind me and had leaned over my shoulder, his head between me and Jesse. Corie was stretched out with one foot in his lap as she painted the toes of the other. She hummed along with the radio as she painted, occasionally throwing in some words.

"I don't know," Jesse said with a shrug. "It doesn't matter to me."

"Well, how about if we-"

"Cellophane flowers of yellow and green tower over your head," Corie sang.

Kelly threw her a quick glance, but she only smiled sweetly in return and went back to her toes, humming softly. He turned back to the front and continued.

"Well, we could get-"

"Newspaper taxis appear on the shore, waiting to take you awaaaaaay."

The two made eye contact again and I covered my mouth to muffle a giggle. Corie looked at him with mock innocence as she focused again on her toes, while Kelly cleared his throat and said, "Would you stop that?" He gave me a look like he wanted to strangle her.

"Anyway, I was thinking we should-"

"Climb in the back with your head in the clouds, and you're gone."

Her timing was perfect, even if the lyrics weren't in order, and I couldn't stop myself from bursting out laughing as Kelly slapped his leg in disgust and turned back to Corie.

"Will you stop? I'm trying to have a conversation here!"

But even he couldn't keep from laughing when she sat up and started singing in his face. "Lucy in the sky with diamonds! Lucy in the sky with diamonds!" She had a goofy grin on her face, and her voice got louder until she finally flung her arms out to the sides and started bellowing out the words. In the end she couldn't sing any longer when she started to laugh.

"I'm gonna get you for that, brat." Kelly teased.

After the laughter died down and he'd faked a punch to her shoulder, Kelly turned back to us. "I guess we don't really need a plan."

"Nah," Jesse replied.

No plan didn't sound like a very good plan to me. "What if we can't find a place to set up camp?"

"Oh," came Kelly's smug voice from the back. "We won't be camping tonight."

I caught Corie's eye and saw her raise an eyebrow.

"I think we deserve a little luxury, don't you?" Kelly went on. He was laying it on thick. His voice was so smooth I almost got a sugar rush. I saw him catch Jesse's eye in the mirror and the two exchanged a conspiring sort of smile. They obviously weren't going to tell me or Corie why they could afford a little "luxury", but they weren't afraid to let us know that they could. It was unnerving.

Corie and I played along stupidly, letting them think that we had never once questioned the money, the move, or the mysterious gun. We continued to bat our eyelashes and let them think they were our heroes.

We drove on for several more hours talking, laughing, singing along with the radio, and occasionally napping. Jesse and Kelly shared the driving, trading places every few hours as we crossed into Tennessee and then toward Mississippi until it got dark. So far it looked like cattle country to me. There wasn't anything around us for miles but a few farmhouses, occasional shopping centers, and a lot of dirt roads.

"Maybe we should have headed toward Memphis," I said, looking out my window at the darkness. I knew what I'd see if it were light out. Nothing.

"This is perfect," Jesse said. "It's quiet and secluded."

"It smells like cow dung!" Corie said, pinching her nose.

Several hours later we saw a billboard advertising a motel-truck stop ahead. When we got there, I decided it didn't look all that bad. It was a little rundown, but I wasn't expecting the Hilton anyway. It was a cottage-style motel with a restaurant and bar and laundry facilities.

"Look, everything we need is right here," Kelly said as we pulled up to a stop in front of the office.

The motel office was small and smelled musty. There was a high counter that ran the length of the room, separating the lobby from the owner's private quarters. On the far-left side against a wall one could pass though where the counter top lifted on hinges. I could see a doorway leading through the office, and then another one that stood open to reveal a living room. It looked very lived in, and within seconds the proprietor himself was walking through the two sets of doors.

He was a short, plump man with a balding head and sparkly eyes. Little white puffs of hair stood out on his head and went in every direction as if he'd just come in out of the wind. When he smiled I could see his yellowed, uneven teeth. He looked unsure of us, a little skeptical, but signed us in anyway.

"Business is slow," he said, as if that was why he allowed us to rent a room. "Where y'all headed?"

Jesse was signing the registry and looked up at the man slowly. "Grand Canyon," he replied simply.

"Is that so?"

"Yep."

"Well, I'll be," the old man said. "Y'all look real young to be going out there by yourselves. But I'm old." He chuckled at himself. "All you young-in's look the same to me."

The room cost more than I expected. The cheapest place I had ever been was Motel 6 back home and that was thirty-five dollars a night. It didn't stop Kelly from getting a second room, and the owner didn't even bat an eyelash or ask for any identification. He just accepted the money and handed over the keys.

"The diner'll be open for supper for a while longer yet, and if you decide to stay on longer just give me a holler."

Outside, Jesse handed me the key to our room. "I'm gonna pull the car over and then you can get out what you need."

As he and Kelly slowly drove down the row of cottages, Corie and I read the numbers on the doors.

"Which one you got?" I asked her. I looked down at my own key and saw the number sixteen printed on it.

"Fifteen. We've got the two rooms on the end."

The guys were ahead of us, already parked and lounging against the car. Jesse looked so good that saliva started to pool under my tongue. All this time we'd spent together and we'd never really had a chance to get close. The five weeks we spent in North Carolina had been weird, almost like a getting to know you time, and with him and Kelly gone all the time and then coming back dirty and smelly, well...we just had very little time to be together. And I wanted more. I wanted all the time in the world.

I slowed my steps and pulled on Corie's arm. "Where do you suppose they got the money?"

"I don't know," she shrugged. "But I've been thinking about what you said back in North Carolina and I think you're right. The money came from that boat."

"Well, maybe they won't tell us how they got it, but I'll bet we can make them spend it," I smiled mischievously.

When we reached the car, the guys were waiting. I went to the back hatch and opened the door. Corie followed and grabbed for her knapsack as I slung my own bag over my shoulder.

"You two walk like snails!" Kelly ragged at us.

Jesse followed me as I unlocked our door and stepped inside the room. It wasn't very big, just enough room to house a double bed, a chest of drawers, two night tables, and a TV on a rickety stand. All the wood was the same, the room set in dark pine that looked worn and scarred. The carpet was brown, the walls were a bare white, and the bedspread was a splash of faded pastels in a vain effort to brighten the room. There were vertical doors on the far wall, presumably the closet, and the door leading to the bathroom next to it. It was tiny with green and white-checkered tile, and white towels stacked on metal shelves.

"A bath tub!" I exclaimed as I spun around to see Jesse fiddling with the TV. "I haven't had a real bath in forever." Suddenly the TV screen came in clear as the glow illuminated his face.

I flung myself on the bed next to him. He took my feet into his lap and started unlacing my sneakers. "Take a bath," he said. "We'll get some dinner later."

I watched him from where I lay on the bed, my hand propping my head up. "Jesse, what happened in North Carolina?"

He looked at me and took his time answering. "It was just time to move on."

I shook my head at him. His answer wasn't good enough, especially knowing he'd already made me his getaway driver once.

He carefully laid my shoes on the floor, then he turned fully to me and said, "I won't lie to you, but I think it's best if you and Corie know as little as possible."

"Why?" I asked. I sat up now, taking my feet off his lap and sitting crossed-legged in front of him. He was already shaking his head when I said, "You don't think you can trust me, is that it? Is that the way it's always gonna be then?"

He took my hands into his and was rubbing his thumbs mindlessly over my palms. "You have to trust me. The less you know the safer you will be."

I doubted that. I'm sure the police in Lake County wouldn't see it that way, either. But I knew that in Jesse's mind he was protecting me. I knew he thought that I could never be held accountable for anything he might have done. I thought it was weird that he would choose to shelter me when we had all screwed up somehow. We were all responsible for our actions. What did it matter in the end if I knew what store had been robbed, or which house they'd broken into, or which guy had his pot ripped off of him? I was willing to bet that there was some fisherman in North Carolina right now still wondering where his stash went and how he got hustled out of his wallet at the same time.

CHAPTER EIGHT

I'll dive in deeper, deeper for you
Down to the bottom, ten thousand emerald pools
Under water time is standing still
You're the treasure dive down deeper still
You're all I need to breathe
All I need is you

10,000 Emerald Pools by Borns

I didn't ask any more questions after that. Jesse was Jesse and had always been tight-lipped. If he didn't want to talk then there was nothing I could do about it. He was as stubborn as Kelly, I could tell. I left him on the bed, staring at the TV, and headed for the bathroom. I filled the tub with hot water and eased in, letting the steamy water cover me. I closed my eyes. I must have been in there a while, not realizing the time. I was enjoying the bath so much that I dozed off and woke up to the sound of Jesse beating on the door, scaring me half to death.

"Jade!" I heard him yell. "You still alive in there?" He opened the door and stepped into the small room.

"Don't worry," I assured him. "Your banging on the door could wake the dead."

He stood there smiling at me, shaking his head.

"Do you want to take a shower?"

"Yes. Hurry up and get dressed so we can go get some grub. I'm hungry."

The four of us walked past the office and across the small parking lot where the diner stood. It was bigger than it looked from the outside and more modern than the motel. There were booths rowed all along the walls, and tables in-between those and the counter, which was lined with stools. All the tabletops were white, and the seats were red vinyl and chrome. It had an authentic diner appeal to it. A waitress winked at us as we walked in the door, an unseen bell chiming at our arrival, and told us to find a table. Several of the customers turned to stare at us. I felt out of place but Jesse and Kelly walked right past the gawkers and sat down in a booth without a care.

There were no menus, just a large chalkboard that hung on the back wall over the counter with the daily specials on it. It was definitely a country style diner that boasted all of the South's favorites such as southern fried chicken, chicken fried steak, meatloaf with gravy, hamburger steak with gravy, shrimp burgers, Brunswick stew, okra and collard greens. I had no clue what half of the items listed on the board were, and I had never heard of people who ate bar-be-queued pork as a sandwich with vinegar and coleslaw on it, which several of them were doing now.

I was thinking I might just get something safe like a salad, and then remembered my plan to see how much of that money I could get the guys to spend. I leaned closer to Jesse and playfully asked him, "Whatcha gonna get?" I was twirling my hair and smiling up at him.

"I don't kn-" He stopped speaking and stared at my fingers working my hair. I don't know why it mesmerized him like that. I found it funny that for the strong and silent type that he was, he could be so easily seduced.

"Well, I was thinking about a steak," I said. It was the most expensive thing on the chalkboard.

"Okay," he replied, still looking at my hair being flipped this way and that.

"You know, Jade, they don't have prime rib here," Kelly said in a snotty tone.

"You be quiet," I told him. I dropped my hair and looked back at the menu.

"She's been spoiled," I heard Kelly stage-whisper to Corie. "She only eats prime rib and filet mignon."

"Kelly!" I snapped at him. "Shut up!"

"Whoa!" He held up his hands in mock defense. "Maybe you should have the snapper!"

"And maybe you should have the..." Quickly I scanned the menu for something fitting. I looked down at the counter and my eyes rested on a large jar. I turned to the others and said quietly, "Eeeew! There's a jar of pig's feet over there!"

"Gross!" Corie said. "What's that for...decoration?"

"People eat them," Kelly informed us. He had a big smile on his face as he watched me and Corie turn green.

"Yuck," I said. "Well, that's what you can have, buddy."

"No thanks," he laughed.

We ate our steaks served with mashed potatoes and collard greens. At least now I knew what they were. When I had asked the waitress if there was something I could have in place of the greens, she said I could have fried okra. I raised my eyebrow at her and asked if they had anything that wasn't fried. She said yes, the collard greens. What the hell, I didn't know what okra was either. But damn if half the menu wasn't fried. Even the fish was fried. It was a miracle these people weren't already dead from the cholesterol. And everything else was cooked well done. It was as if they were afraid to eat anything rare, causing an eyebrow in return when I asked for it. She looked like she didn't understand, and it was obvious the cook didn't either.

When we were done the waitress appeared to whisk away our plates. Then she flashed us a pearly white smile and drawled, "Y'all want some dessert? We got banana puddin' and pecan pie."

Her voice was grating on my nerves, and so was the way she was drooling all over Jesse. It was so obvious. I hated the way she pecan like *pee-can*. Up North it was pronounced *pacon*. She rested her hands on the table and leaned toward Jesse, showing her cleavage, and said, "*Pee-can pie*."

Jesse ignored her as she leaned into him and ran down the dessert list. He pulled out a cigarette and lit it, all the time staring straight ahead as if she weren't even there. I smiled up at her as if I didn't know what she was doing, but I could tell Corie was giving me a funny look.

Finally, Jesse looked her square in the eyes. I could tell she was holding her breath, expecting at least a smile or some kind of encouragement from him. But instead he quietly said, "No." He continued to hold her eye a moment longer, making his point, then went back to his cigarette as if dismissing her.

She was undaunted. Still leaning over, hands bracing her palms flat on the tabletop, she purred, "You sure? It's homemade. I bet y'all never tasted pecan pie like this up North. Say, where y'all from anyway?"

She wasn't fooling anyone as she swept her eyes over the rest of us. Her waitress uniform was so tight that her short skirt was riding up her backside, giving off a pretty view to the booth next to us. I was biting my lip, trying to control the urge to slap her, when Corie burst out laughing right in her face.

The waitress looked confused but smiled, and said, "What?"

"You stupid bitch," Corie cackled. I put my hands over my face and dropped my head to the table, but my shoulders were shaking with quiet laughter. Jesse just continued to sit in silence and stare at his cigarette. I could tell he was assessing the situation and thinking about what to do.

"Excuse me?" The waitress stood up straight and drawled at Corie. "You are a rude little girl!" She had her hands on her hips and her bottom lip pouted out. I didn't know who she was putting the act on for. Surely, she knew that Jesse wasn't coming to her rescue.

"Oh please!" Corie drawled back at her. She gestured to me and said, "Did ya think that was his sister?"

The waitress eyed me and a *pfft* escaped her mouth. I gave her a dirty look, but when I looked over at Jesse I saw that he was smiling at me. Somehow it drew a giggle out of me.

Kelly had been digging his wallet out of the back pocket of his jeans, and finally spoke up. "Look," he said evenly, staring straight at her. "You've done your job, now give me the tab and go away."

She sniffed, plopped the bill on the table and flounced away.

Jesse stood up and held a hand out to me. I took it and slid out after him. As I stood up he looped his arms around my waist, and with twinkling eyes said, "Wanna dance, little lady?"

The bar was also bigger than it appeared from the outside, and I could tell that there was a door behind the bar that led to the kitchen in the diner. It seemed that we had lucked out when we found the motel. The diner and bar brought in a good size crowd between the truckers and the locals.

There were two rooms. The first had a long bar that ran half the length of the room, circling around in a crescent shape. There were TVs at either end, and booths and tables took up all the remaining space. The second room was a game room with pool tables and arcade machines, a jukebox, and dart boards.

Jesse walked up to the bar and ordered drinks. The bartender eyed the rest of us and said, "You guys staying here at the motel?" Jesse nodded. "Okay, what'll you have?"

The bar started to fill. It was getting later, around midnight, and by then we'd all had quite a bit to drink. Corie and I weren't big tequila drinkers, so the shots hit us faster. From where I was sitting the guys looked completely sober and I was looking stupidly buzzed. I never did like hard liquor much, and after a while I switched to some sweeter drinks. After some time Corie and I started to get rowdy. The bartender was loving it and started giving us weird shots like B-52's and Woo-Hoo's. I had no idea what was in them but they were sweet and tasted like liquid candy. When I asked the bartender why the drink had such a funny name, he replied, "Because after you drink it, you say 'woo-hoo'!"

At some point I looked up and noticed the busty waitress standing behind the bar. I guessed she was done for the night because she was taking off her apron and letting down her hair. She caught my eye as she passed in front of me to pull a beer off the tap, and we stared at each other stupidly for a full twenty seconds before I turned on my stool and put my back to her.

Corie noticed her, too, and leaned over to whisper, "There she is. I wonder who's next on her list."

I watched her out of the corner of my eye as she made her way down the row of booths, toward the game room. She walked with an exaggerated sway and a saucy twitch of her hips, coming up short where Jesse and Kelly sat with their backs to the wall and their legs stretched out in front of them on the booth seats.

"Apparently, she isn't finished with her last prey," I said casually.

Corie leaned back and looked at where the guys were. The waitress had turned toward them with a wide smile and placed her hands on her hips playfully. She had her head cocked to the side and was running a tongue over her lips invitingly. I didn't know what she was saying to them, but I could tell she was trying real hard to erase from their minds what had happened earlier in the diner.

"That girl is trouble," Corie said, looking back at me. "I can't believe her nerve."

I called the bartender over and said, "What is that girl's name?"

Joe looked over at the booth and saw who I meant. "Who? You mean Charity?"

"I mean Miss Busty Flirt over there."

"Yeah, that's Charity," he said in a knowing voice.

"*Charity*?" Corie and I asked together. Joe laughed and nodded as he wiped out pint glasses with a bar rag. I looked at Corie and tried real hard to suppress a laugh.

"Well, that explains a lot!" I managed to squeak.

Corie was already laughing so hard that she was literally banging her head on the bar. When she finally looked up she had tears in her eyes. "So that's what she's doing. She's being *charitable*! Come on, Jade, you can't blame her for that, can you? After all, it's her namesake. It's her job!"

Joe looked amused as he watched us laugh and joke. I finally calmed down enough to ask him if she flirted with strangers a lot. He leaned over the bar to get a better view of the booth. One good look at Charity posing, running her fingers through her hair and jiggling her leg, and he knew what I meant.

"Yeah," he sighed. "She's bored. You would be too if you lived here."

"I don't know what that means."

"It means she's got her eyes on your men and she doesn't care about you. She knows you will be gone in a day or two."

"That's terrible!" Corie gasped.

Joe shrugged. "If she knows about you then it's just more of a challenge to her."

"She does know," I informed him.

"Then be careful. She doesn't play nice."

I looked over at the booth and watched them a minute longer. Jesse and Kelly were definitely paying attention to what Charity was saying, but neither of them looked very interested. Both of them nodded and responded when necessary, but I knew when Kelly was interested in someone or something, and this was not one of those times. Still, I was getting madder by the minute watching her fawn all over Jesse, and when she turned her head during a giggle and caught my eye, she winked.

"Oh, hell no," Corie muttered and hopped off her barstool.

We made our way slowly over to the table. Charity had her back to us and didn't notice that we were standing a few feet behind her. I looked at Kelly and he rolled his eyes in a painful way. I could tell that he'd had enough, but short of telling her she was pure trash, she wasn't getting the message. Jesse wouldn't look at me but the small smile on his lips said he was thoroughly amused.

"So, what are you two doing tonight?" Charity drawled in her come-hither voice. "I know a really great place for an afterhours party."

Jesse nodded noncommittally. "Maybe."

"We'll have to see what our girlfriends want to do," Kelly enunciated.

"Well they don't have to come," she said smoothly. "I mean, if they're too tired or something. But I don't see why y'all can't go with me. It'll be fun. Just the three of us."

It was the most bizarre conversation I'd ever heard.

"I don't think so," I said from behind her. She whirled around, startled, gaping for something to say. "Why don't you go fling yourself on someone else? No one here is interested in sexually transmitted diseases."

She glared at me hatefully, and with as much honey as she could muster, she drawled, "Well, I'm sure these men are capable of deciding for themselves." She was a real piece of work. I'd never come across someone like her in my life.

I shoved past her and sat down next to Jesse. "No, I do all his thinking for him."

She stared a minute longer, noticing how readily the guys had made room for me and Corie to sit down when they had made no such gesture toward her in the course of their conversation. Unable to believe that she'd been rejected and insulted yet again, she turned away from the table quickly.

Jesse looked like a little kid who'd gotten caught with his hands in the cookie jar, and I looked pointedly at him. "What?" he asked with a nervous smile.

"Really?" I said dryly. "You actually let her stand there and coo in your ear for twenty whole minutes."

"I didn't," he said. "You did."

"Oh, what is this?" I looked back and forth between him and Kelly. "Some sort of test?"

Jesse laughed and leaned over to shut me up with a kiss. "I just love seeing you in action," he said when he'd pulled away.

"You've never seen me in action," I told him. "But you," I pointed to Kelly, "have been talking about me, I see."

Kelly smiled big and held up his hands. "I can't help it if I'm proud."

Pretty soon it was closing time and the guys suggested we get a bottle from Joe and head back to our rooms. As they were settling up at the bar, Corie and I were finishing up our drinks and heading for the door. For some reason I looked over at the far corner and saw Charity sitting at a table with three other men. She was leaning into one of them with a coy smile on her face. He was a big, burly man, about six feet tall with extra wide shoulders and short, curly dark hair. She whispered something into his ear, and the two of them turned and looked our way briefly before turning back to their private conversation.

Corie was already outside, unaware that I hadn't followed her, and the guys met me at the door. Jesse slung his arm over my shoulders and walked me out.

Around four in the morning we started to wind down. There was still a third left in the bottle but no one seemed interested in finishing it. Kelly said that he'd had enough, and from the looks of Corie, she'd had enough hours ago. She looked like I felt.

I was lying on the bed, snuggled up to Jesse, as Corie and Kelly started making out on the floor in front of the TV. I listened to the two of them make wet kissing noises as I tried to focus on something in the room to keep my head from spinning. Suddenly the slurping from the floor stopped, and Kelly sat up to announce that they were going to their room. He reached down and helped Corie stand.

"See ya," Jesse said, not caring one way or the other. "Lock the door." A hand slipped back in to turn the lock and the door clicked softly behind them.

"You tired?" he asked me.

I shook my head. "Dizzy," I confessed.

"You sure drank a lot," he smiled at me.

"I didn't realize," I said.

He looked at me for a moment, and then slowly started to rise off the bed. I watched him as he pulled on his shoes and asked where he was going. "I'll be right back," he assured me.

I waited on the bed, taking deep breaths, and then realized that the spinning was getting better and I wasn't feeling quite as nauseous as before. Jesse came back and handed me a honey bun.

"It's all they had in the vending machines besides candy bars," he said.

"Thanks." I sat up and opened the plastic wrapper. I wasn't really hungry but figured the bread would help soak up some of the alcohol in my stomach.

Jesse went into the bathroom and started up the shower. A few minutes later I followed him into the small room to brush my teeth. From inside, I heard him ask me, "You want to come in?" I pulled off my jeans and shirt and stepped inside the small area. Turning around, I felt the blast of hot water spraying me. Jesse was slicking back his hair, and he smiled.

"Something about a shower always sobers me up," he said.

We stood there for a few seconds, staring at each other. He finally raised a hand and placed a palm on my wet cheek, his thumb moving in small circles, then lowered his head to meet mine as we kissed. The water was streaming down around us as our two naked, slippery bodies touched. His other hand came up to take its place on the other side of my face, claiming me, as his kisses became more demanding. Returning his request, I lifted my arms and held him close to me, my hands running over his smooth, slick back. With the steam engulfing us, I pressed back against the shower wall, pleasantly crushed by the weight of his body. He kissed me everywhere he could reach, and I found myself taking his head into my own hands and guiding his mouth to the places I wanted it the most. When I thought I couldn't stand it any longer, he lifted me up and fit himself beneath me.

We held each other tightly as we moved together. A burst of sensation ripped through me and I gasped. I had never experienced anything in quite the same way as I did at that very moment. I had done this before, yes, but sex to me was always something that you just did. It had never served the same purpose as it seemed to now. With Jesse it became beautiful. My emotions came pouring out of me, and I was grateful that we were in the shower so he would not notice the tears on my face.

After we dried off and crawled into bed, we lay watching the early morning sun peek through the curtains. I hadn't realized that it was almost dawn. Jesse lit two cigarettes and handed me one. We lay silently, smoking and thinking about everything that had happened that night. It felt like a turning point.

"How do you feel about sticking around for another day or two?"

"Do we have the money?" I asked. I wasn't trying to get him to tell me what I knew he wouldn't, but I thought it was a reasonable question. He nodded and dragged hard off his cigarette before snuffing it out in the ashtray. "Fine, but I don't want to see Charity any more than I have to."

"Charity?" He looked confused, and then chuckled when I said, "The bimbo."

"Is that really her name?"

"I would have thought she told you that."

"I thought it was an offer," he said, and I laughed.

We slept through the morning and woke up around two in the afternoon. I guessed that Corie and Kelly had slept late as well because they never even knocked on the door. I roused to find Jesse gone from the bed, and I could hear water running from inside the bathroom. When the water stopped, he appeared with a towel wrapped around his waist and water dripping from his hair and chest.

"Good morning," he said as he reached for a pair of jeans.

I looked at the clock and said, "You mean afternoon."

"Ah, but the day has just begun for us," he teased.

I lit a cigarette and squinted at the light streaming in from between the curtains. Jesse continued to get dressed as if he were late for a meeting. He had his back to me and was drying off his legs with the towel. It was intoxicating to see that he had no insecurities about standing naked in front of me.

"What are you doing?" I finally asked.

"Kelly and I have some work to do."

"Work?" I hated the way those two made plans and didn't bother to tell me and Corie until the last minute. "When did you guys plan this out?"

"Last night. We met some people at the bar who said they could hook us up."

"Hook you up?"

"Jade, we need money to survive, you know that."

"Fine," I said. "What are Corie and I supposed to do while you're gone?"

"I'll leave you some money and you two can go get something to eat, go to the bar, do whatever you want." Oh, the options for entertainment simply made my head spin.

Kelly came by fifteen minutes later and the two left with the car. Neither one of them gave me or Corie any further explanation. It was the same old story.

"He just dropped it on me like a bomb," Corie said, exasperated. "Just fifteen minutes ago he said that he and Jesse were taking off to make a score."

"I know," I nodded my head. "Jesse did the same thing to me."

"Did you ever try talking to him about North Carolina?"

"I tried," I sighed. I was collecting our dirty clothes, figuring now was as good a time as any to get them washed. "He told me it was better if I didn't know anything."

Corie rolled her eyes at me. "Kelly would either tell me to shut up or not to worry my pretty little head."

"And who says chivalry is dead?" I joked.

We walked down to the laundry room with our bags of clothes, and quarters in our pockets. The room was empty, with the exception of one machine already in use. We set to work, each taking two machines. I hoped that no one else needed to do laundry very badly because there was only one washer left. I was determined to get this chore over with as quickly as possible. When the machines were humming rhythmically, Corie and I sat on top of two of them and smoked.

"I've been thinking," I said slowly. "What if we made a score? Something big enough to make those two beg like dogs and stop treating us like damsels."

"That would be a sight," she laughed. "What kind of score?"

I shrugged.

The door opened and Charity walked in. She stopped short when she saw us and then slowly approached the washer that was running when we came in. She lifted the lid and started to pull out the wet clothes, placing them into a dryer.

"You live here?" Corie asked her roughly.

Charity turned to face us and said, "For your information I am washing the diner uniforms."

"Thanks for the *information*," Corie said back, just as rude as before.

"Hateful girl!" she hissed back and walked out quickly.

When we finished washing, drying, and folding the laundry, the guys still weren't back and we were getting hungry. We decided to forego another encounter with the waitress from hell and went into the bar to eat. We figured Joe wouldn't be spitting in our food anytime soon.

CHAPTER NINE

Brakes on, the car is running empty
Downhill, Head on
This crash is comin' slowly
Move, or watch the slow death of your way of life

Science of Fear by The Temper Trap

There wasn't anything for us to do after we ate. It was way too early for a bar crowd, and Jesse and Kelly still weren't back. Joe said he was taking a break before he started the night shift, and he was closing the bar down for a few hours. He asked us if we had anything to do, and with bored looks we said no.

"Why don't you come back to my place for a while?" he suggested.

At first, I thought the offer sounded strange, but he explained that his roommates would be there and that there was always a party going on. I trusted that he didn't have any ulterior motives, knowing that Jesse and Kelly would be back soon, and agreed to go. Luckily Joe lived only a few blocks away and we were able to walk the short distance to his doublewide. When we walked in there were several others there. Aside from the three roommates there were four other guys and two girls, who were dating two of the roommates.

Led Zeppelin was playing loudly as people scattered around the small living room. There was a stash of beer in a cooler on the floor in a corner of the kitchen and empty bottles everywhere. The room reeked of pot smoke, and I noticed people kept going in and out of the back bedroom. We sat down on the couch with our beers and talked to Joe and another guy named Aaron. Occasionally one of the girls would sit down and talk with us for a bit before going into the back room for a few minutes. They never stayed in there long, just a few minutes at a time. I glanced at Corie and she gave me a knowing look.

Charity's name came up between the other two girls and they laughed, making off-color remarks about her. I told them that I didn't like her very much, and one of them said, "When she goes into a vegetable garden it's like a family reunion, bless her heart."

"You girls want a bump?" Joe asked after a bit. He'd already been in the back more than once.

"We don't have any money," I said.

He smiled and held up his hands. "You're my guests," was his answer. He reached for my hand and I tugged on Corie's arm, pulling her up with me.

Joe knocked softly on the door, and when it was opened by a big guy named Pete, a large, choking cloud of smoke filtered out to us. He nodded slightly and stepped aside to let us enter. The door closed behind us. There was only one other person in the room, the other roommate, Josh.

"Hello, girls," Josh said invitingly. "Sit down."

We sat on the bed. Corie and I tried to remain calm but there was more cocaine in that room than I had ever seen in my life. My only assumption was that they were major dealers in these parts. Large, plastic bags of the stuff were taking up the small table. There were two scales, one big one for weighing the kind of big bags they had, and a smaller one for ounces and grams. Little baggies, seals, and twist-ties were all over the room.

I looked around trying to appear nonplussed, and saw several mirrors lying around. They all had traces of powder on them, some with blades waiting to be used again.

"Catch them up," Joe instructed to Josh, who sat with a mirror on his lap, chopping up little rocks. Josh looked up at us and then at Joe, who said, "Don't worry about it."

Josh shrugged, clearly not worried about anything. Joe left the room and Pete continued to stand by the door, his large arms crossed.

"What are you, the bouncer?" Corie asked.

Pete chuckled and said no.

We fell silent again and watched Josh cut up the rocks into a fine powder. When I looked up at Corie, she caught my eye and whispered, "Bingo." I didn't understand what she meant and gave her a questioning look. There was no way we could pull it off. We couldn't afford it, which would defeat the purpose anyway, and we sure as hell couldn't steal it. People like them would kill you for taking their dope. It wasn't a game.

Josh cut out two long lines and held the mirror out to me. I gaped at it for a minute, and then slowly reached out to take it and set it on my lap. These lines were fat and long; too long to be free. But from the looks I got from Josh and Pete it appeared they couldn't care less how much I did or didn't do. When I was done, the back of my nose burning and my eyes watering, I handed the mirror back to Josh who started to cut two more for Corie.

"So where you from?" Pete asked as Corie picked up a rolled twenty and held it to her nose.

"Chicago," I said. He nodded, still standing by the door. "Could you sit down? You're making me nervous."

"I can't," he said after a pause. He flashed me a boyish smile that I did not expect from such a huge and rough looking body. Josh laughed as he busily weighed out grams and folded them into paper seals.

"He's too wired," Josh explained. "He gets like that. It's just easier to stand."

"But he's so still," Corie said, awed. I agreed. What difference did it make if you were standing or sitting? Either way you're going to twitch.

Pete just shrugged and laughed. At least it broke some of the tension and we were able to relax more.

Corie had finished her lines and handed the mirror back to Josh. She lit a cigarette and leaned back against the headboard.

"You ready for another?" Josh asked me.

"In a minute," I said, surprised. I didn't want to go overboard but I knew if he continued to offer I was going to take it. He set the mirror at my feet and told me to take it when I was ready.

"What are those for?" I motioned toward the small pile of seals he was working on as I lit a cigarette.

"Business," was his reply. "We'll take them out to the bar later."

"Were you there last night?" I was wondering if these guys were the same connection Kelly and Jesse had made.

"No, we went to Memphis and hit some of the big clubs. Ever been there?"

I shook my head. Corie nudged me and I looked at her. She nodded toward the mirror, telling me to take the lines so she could get more. I picked it up and saw Josh smile as I held the bill to my nose.

"What's this cut with?" I asked him, holding my nostrils closed for a second.

"It's clean," he assured me. "You're probably used to crap that's cut with aspirin."

"Gah, I hope not," I said.

"There's some kind of a B complex in there," Corie said suddenly. "I can taste it."

Josh raised his eyebrows at her but said nothing. We watched as he folded up some more seals, then cut Corie her two lines and hand it to her.

"How'd you like to make a profit tonight?"

"What kind of a profit?" I was skeptical. Maybe it was the high, but my first thought wasn't on the cocaine.

"Whatever you want," he shrugged. "Cash, dope, whichever."

"If everybody's selling, who's left to buy it?" I asked, meaning the eight people in the next room.

"Oh, they don't sell," Josh said. "Just Pete and Aaron."

"So, what's the deal?" I was very curious about this opportunity that had just been dropped in my lap. It couldn't have been more perfect.

"You two can go run the bar with Aaron. Pete and I need to be somewhere else. It's simple. The baggies are a gram and the seals are half grams. No quarters, no eights."

"Do we get a cut of it, or what?"

"I can either cut you a rock now, or I can give you extra seals. You can sell it or keep it. Give the money to Joe and he'll have your rock."

"Sounds fair," I said. "What kind of a cut?"

"How much do you want to make?" he asked. "I'm giving you enough seals and baggies worth two grand. Anything over that is yours plus the rock."

"How much?"

"A hundred for a gram, fifty for half." He said with a smile, "I think you'll do okay."

Aaron drove us all back to the bar, letting Joe out at the front door before parking. We sat in the car for a minute, sorting through our stash and dividing it up.

"It may seem like a small bar," he said. "But the people here are big buyers. You won't have any problem getting rid of what you've got very fast. And I'm sure some of those drunk guys will pay just about any price you give them. But remember, you need to make at least two grand. If you need anything come get me."

We nodded and I handed Corie half of the seals and baggies. When we got close to the door I stopped Corie, and said, "You realize how much we could make, don't you?"

"Maybe," she said. "But this isn't Chicago, Jade. Obviously, these people aren't used to higher prices. I'm not willing to get the crap beat out of me by some angry, wired guy."

"We can try," I suggested. "Like Aaron said, they've never had girls doing the running before."

"Just be careful," she warned me.

"It's simple," I said. "Just open one for freebies, and they'll pay an extra twenty. We'll have enough to cover it and still walk out of here with four grams on top of our rock. That'll do the trick with Jesse and Kelly, don't you think?"

"Yeah," she smiled. "Three and a half eights ain't too shabby. Hey, I wonder if they're back yet."

"Remember, Corie, it's a surprise."

"Yeah, but I'm *wired.*"

We got a beer from Joe and headed in separate directions. We'd met a lot of the locals the night before, so it was easy to walk up to a group of people and start up a conversation. I still felt uneasy about letting it known that I was holding and went to find Aaron after a fruitless thirty minutes.

"How's it going stranger?" he asked from where he sat at the bar.

"Funny you should say that. Just what are the chances of me selling to the wrong person?

He thought for a moment. "I'll tell you what. I'll send the first few to you, okay?"

I didn't know where Corie was, or how much luck she was having either. And at least I hadn't seen Charity either, but it was getting close to midnight and I knew that was unavoidable. I asked Joe if he'd seen Kelly or Jesse and he shook his head from the other end of the bar. I swallowed a shot for courage and set off for the game room.

About ten minutes later I was playing pinball when two men approached me from behind. "Aaron said we should talk to you," one of them said nervously. I could tell he was uncomfortable dealing with a stranger, and a girl to boot.

"What are you looking for?" I asked them, keeping my eyes on the pinball game.

"A quarter-pounder with cheese," the other one said.

"That's all?" I looked at them quickly. I was a little surprised and suspicious that this was a set-up. I thought the locals already knew the deal since Josh made it so clear to me earlier. "McDonald's is down the street, boys. I can only get you a Big Mac."

The two stared at each other and I assessed them with my eyes. "I can tell you'd be back anyway," I said, looking at their large frames.

"How much?"

"Two for two," I said, turning back to the game. It was quiet behind me for a full thirty seconds before I heard, "Fine."

And so, the rest of the night went. After the first few that Aaron sent to me, it became easier and word got around who was running, so more people were looking for me rather than vice versa. Aaron even went as far as telling people that Corie and I were his cousins, visiting from the Big City. It only took me another hour after that to unload, and I figured we'd earned at least two grams on top of our rock, providing Corie hadn't done any worse than me. But I was wrong. She had a way about her that made men want to jump in front of trains for her. She wasn't afraid to approach anyone and make a sale, or to offer any price she saw fit. She told me that she even got one really drunk guy to pay her a hundred and twenty for a gram. We'd been there about two hours when I ran into a guy named Rex that I'd met the night before.

"You just get here?" I asked him.

"Yeah, I was in around ten but there wasn't any action, so I went to a party. I hear you're holding."

"Not anymore, but you can talk to Aaron."

He shook his head. "I'm not looking. I just wanted to make sure you were handling it okay. Some of these guys can be pretty rough."

"All is cool."

"That's good. Jesse asked me to keep an eye on you."

"Jesse?" I blinked. "When did you see him?"

"When I was in here earlier. He said to tell you that he was in room four if I saw you."

"He's been in room four all this time?" I asked, surprised. "What's he doing there?"

"Party," Rex said simply. "You've probably supplied them with most of their dope tonight."

"Really?" I said dryly. "Who's there?"

He shrugged. "People you met last night. You know, mostly locals, a couple of waitresses from the diner."

I walked away from Rex and looked for Corie. I couldn't see her in the small, congested crowd, and sat down at the bar. I felt ready to go to the bathroom for another fix. I had taken the rock to our room earlier but I still had a gram on me. I looked up to see Charity walk in the door with the same burly man she was cooing to last night. They came up to the bar and ordered drinks, standing right next to me. She gave me a sidelong glance and I asked her how room four was, pretending as if I had known all along that she had been there with Jesse.

"It was lovely," she purred. "Only half a revenge to go."

When I responded with a dirty look, she leaned closer to me and whispered, "I always win."

"You must be a very unhappy person," I said to her evenly. I got up calmly and walked away, but not before I noticed her huge friend leering at me in a dangerous way.

I finally found Corie playing Galaga and dragged her to the bathroom with me. We went into a stall and I opened my seal, sticking my longest fingernail into it and sniffed it up my nose.

"Guess where the guys have been all night?" I loaded up my nail again and put it under her nose.

"Where?" she asked, holding her eyes shut for a second.

"At a party in room four with Charity." Corie's mouth fell open as I told her what Charity had said to me just a few minutes ago.

"He wouldn't," she shook her head. "I've known Jesse for years, and you have to believe me when I tell you that he wouldn't, Jade, not to you. I've never seen him the way he is with you." She dipped her pinkie into the seal and stuck it in her mouth.

"You keep doing that and you'll be drooling instead of talking," I told her, which sent us both into a fit of giggles.

We walked out of the bathroom, swaying a bit, and I blindly followed Corie through the crowd. She walked deliberately up to Charity and poked her finger into the surprised girl's shoulder.

"Did you get my man all warmed up for me, too?" Corie poked her two more times.

"Stop!" Charity screeched.

"Who the hell do you think you are," Corie leaned in close and sneered at her quietly. "Coming on to other people's boyfriends in front of everyone like some whore?"

Charity eyed her back carefully before replying, her voice low and threatening. "Who do you think you are, coming into my town, my bar, running cocaine like you belong here. You don't need to worry about what I'm doing. You'd better worry about yourselves."

The threat was clear, and even though she was whispering toward Corie's ear, Charity was looking directly at me.

I grabbed Corie's arm and pulled her toward the door. We wandered down the lane of cottages, stopping in front of number four. There were still several people in there, their voices and music filtering out. I hesitated, wondering if we should go in or not. I looked at Corie who shrugged back at me. Neither of us cared. There didn't seem any point in going in. What was done was done, and either way we'd probably look foolish going in.

We walked the rest of the way toward our rooms and ended up on the hood of Jesse's car, smoking and talking. There was a light on in my room, and I couldn't remember if I had left it on or not when I went in there earlier to stash the rock. It was getting close to closing time, but from the sounds coming from the bar, everyone was still going strong. We watched the door to room four where neither Jesse nor Kelly had emerged from yet.

"Let's go get a Coke," I said. "I'm seriously thirsty."

"I found a closer machine," Corie said as she hopped off the car. "It's just around this corner." She stepped past the last cottage and disappeared into the darkness. I thought the vending machines were in the other direction because I couldn't see a single light illuminated past the wall of black. The only thing on this side of the motel grounds was a huge field that stretched all the way to the highway.

"I can't see anything," I said. There was no reply. "Corie, turn around. Let's just go to the other one by the office." And when I did, I turned into a big, burly chest.

Large, strong arms grabbed me, pinning me to my sides, and I was picked up and dragged away from the parking lot. I bucked and kicked, squirmed and tried to scream. He flopped me over, clamped a hand over my mouth and held his other arm around my waist, with my back to his stomach. He warned me to shut up and carried me as if I were nothing more than a baby. I bit his hand. It tasted salty and dirty. He let go just long enough for me to let out a long, terrified scream. He plunked me on my feet, turned me to face him, and backhanded me across my face.

Winded, I felt blinded as he picked me up again and threw me over his shoulder as if I were nothing more than a rag doll, which wasn't far from how I felt. It seemed he only took a few more steps before throwing me to the ground. My head hit the earth with a dull thump, and I lay there confused for a second before my instincts told me to start fighting.

He had gone down on one knee, fumbling with his belt with one hand, and holding me by the neck with the other and cutting off my screams. The pressure was severe, and I couldn't tell if I was breathing or not.

"Stop!" I croaked and gasped. "No! No! No! Stop!" My arms flung out in front of me, trying to gain purchase on anything, to scratch, to claw, hit, even slap, but I couldn't reach him. It seemed as if his arm was a mile long.

I could hear the buckle loosen and the zipper go down, but he had yet to remove any of my clothes. I noticed that my right leg was between his left knee and right foot. Quickly, I brought my leg up as hard as I could. I was hoping to make contact with his groin but was only able to catch him off guard. I used my feet and legs to push up as hard as I could, his middle landing on my head as he fell forward. Not the best position for me. I tried to push him off me, wondering if I had enough strength to grab him by the balls and squeeze real hard. All I wanted was to get away from him but everything was happening so fast and he was so big.

I squirmed until I felt his grasp slacken and I tried to sit up, but before I could get my legs out from under him and scramble away, he grabbed my arm and jerked me back. I screamed as loud and as long as I could before he brought his elbow down on my stomach, causing me to fall back and gasp for air.

He was grunting and calling me a stupid whore as he crawled on top of me again. I pummeled him with my fists while he groped for my zipper. I was a gnat fighting an elephant. He grabbed both my wrists, held them firmly in one hand and flipped me over effortlessly onto my stomach. If I'd had any chance of escaping before, I had zero now. I could feel him yanking my jeans down, burning my legs. I tried to scream again but it sounded more like a croak to me. I wasn't sure if I was actually making any noises besides whimpers.

"You're gonna get what's coming to you, you little bitch," he growled in my ear.

I felt the most deadening fear that I had ever experienced in my life. I closed my eyes and sobbed uncontrollably, my face pushed into the ground. Then I heard a *thump* and the burly man slumped over on top of me.

The weight scared me. I couldn't see, I couldn't breathe, and I had no idea what was happening. I started screaming in a panic. Even after the weight was pushed off of me and I was suddenly alone and afraid of what was going to happen next. I struggled to get up. I looked over and saw the huge man's form at my side, still and motionless, and I skittered, crab-like away. He wasn't moving. A second later I felt hands on me and I screamed, flinging my arms and legs, in a vain attempt to protect myself.

"Jade," I heard Jesse's desperate voice. "It's me!"

He picked me up and ran for the motel. I was shaking, whimpering, as I felt myself being juggled around in Jesse's arms. He shushed in my ear and said soothingly, "It's okay, Jade, I've got you."

I could hear Kelly and Corie yelling as they ran toward us. They stopped short at the sight of Jesse carrying me, dirty, ripped clothes, and sobbing in his arms.

"What the hell did that bastard do?" Kelly stormed. "Where is he? Jesse, where is he?"

"She's fine," Jesse told him gruffly. "I got to him before he could...he's back there." Kelly glared out toward the large, darkened field. He didn't understand what Jesse meant by *back there,* and turned questioning eyes on him, but Jesse only carried me into our room and placed me on the bed.

Kelly rushed over and went down on his knees at my side, wiping my tears away. "Oh, my God, Jade," he said. "Are you okay?"

I looked at Corie, who had turned white and stood by the door, looking frightened. She rushed over to the bed, her face tear-stained and puffy. "I turned around and you were gone," she said in a fearful voice. "By the time I heard you scream I could barely see. I started yelling for help and the guys heard me from in here. I am so sorry, Jade!"

"It's not your fault," I said. I could tell she was blaming herself, but I meant it. It could very easily had been her had I been leading the way to the vending machines in the dark. Besides, I knew who was to blame.

"I would have killed him," Kelly said vehemently, his face close to mine. "You know that, don't you? If I had gotten there, I would have killed him." I nodded, knowing it was true, but glad that he hadn't.

From the other side of the room, Jesse said quietly, "I think I did."

CHAPTER TEN

I've seen an ocean run away
I'm torn from the truth that holds my soul
I'm down in the grave where I belong
Oh, what a ride
Identified my devil
Wings to the sky on the run from trouble

Don't You Cry For Me by Cobi

The next thing I remember was waking up in the car. It was still dark outside and I had no idea where I was or what day it was. I lay in the backseat with my head in Jesse's lap and a blanket spread over me. With the exception of the motor humming as we drove, it was silent. It seemed to me that I kept fading in and out of sleep. My lids wouldn't stay open, my tongue felt thick in my mouth and my limbs too heavy to move. Jesse had an arm around me protectively as he sat upright with his head leaned against the window, his eyes closed and breathing deeply as if in sleep.

I woke up some time later to see a faint light peeping through the clouds. The car was warm from the early morning sun, and aside from Kelly who was driving, everyone else was asleep. I tried to sit up, the effort exhausting me, and I laid back wondering why I felt so spent. My arms hurt as if I had done too many push-ups, my legs ached like I had ran too fast, and the skin on my neck burned. It wasn't as if I didn't remember what had happened; I just had no concept of time.

I must have been in shock. I kept thinking that it had all been a horrible dream, yet the nightmares persisted. More than once I woke up screaming, wet with sweat, and crying, only to hear Jesse's soothing voice telling me that I was safe with him. Every time I woke up we were in the car. It seemed as if we'd been driving forever.

When I finally awoke in complete clarity I was in a motel bed. For a moment I thought we were still in Mississippi, and I truly believed it had all been a dream. But as I looked around, I noticed that I was in a strange room. It was bigger than the last one, and brighter. All alone and frightened, something in me snapped and I panicked.

"Jesse?" I yelled, sitting up and holding the sheets in tightly clenched fists. The bathroom door flew open and he came running out, dressed only in jeans. He grabbed me in an embrace as I flung myself into his arms.

"I'm here," he said softly.

"Where are we?"

"Oklahoma."

When I stopped shaking, Jesse pulled me away from him just far enough to look into my eyes. "You're okay. I won't let anything like that happen to you again. I promise."

He left me on the bed long enough to draw me a hot bath, and then came back to help me into the tub. I saw deep bruises all over my arms and legs, and noticed that he kept his eyes on mine, nodding encouragement. But his lips were tightly set in an even line. He told me to stay in the bath and relax and then later we'd get something to eat.

"Jesse, wait," I called to him. He paused halfway out of the door and looked at me. "What day is it?"

"It's been two days. You had a fever and slept the whole time."

From behind the bathroom door I could hear him talking on the phone. "She's awake. She's asking questions." There was a pause. "I'm keeping her calm, but I don't know how much she remembers." Another pause. "Well, she's been through a lot, Kelly! I'm no doctor but I'm sure she'll be fine."

I wasn't sure what they were talking about. I mean, I knew they were talking about me, but Jesse sounded impatient with Kelly. There was another moment of silence before Jesse yelled, "They what? Get her and come over here now!" The phone was slammed down and I could hear him muttering and pacing the small room. Thirty seconds later I heard a knock on the door, and Jesse opened it to let Kelly and Corie in.

"Where is she?" I heard Corie ask.

"Taking a bath," Jesse growled. "Why don't you explain how Kelly found bag of cocaine?"

"Where did you find that?" Corie gasped, her voice indicating she'd been wondering where it had been, too.

"I found it in a pair of jeans," Kelly said. "I picked them up when we were leaving Mississippi. When we left we were just grabbing everything we could."

"Well?" Jesse demanded.

"We earned it that night," was Corie's answer. There was silence for a few minutes, and I could tell she was getting a stare down from both of them.

"What does that mean?" Jesse sounded almost accusing.

"Joe's roommate is a dealer, and he asked us to run the bar for him. The rock was our payment." She sounded scared, her voice trembling with the threat of tears.

"You were dealing in the bar?" Kelly asked her, getting just as heated as Jesse.

I knew where this was going and I pulled myself into a sitting position. I dropped my head as blackness darkened the room, but a few seconds later my eyes cleared and I stood up slowly, reaching for a towel. I started to dry myself off as I heard Corie say, "We couldn't pass it up."

"You put yourself and Jade in danger to earn a rock?" Jesse yelled at her.

"I can't believe this!" Kelly stormed at the same time.

"Now wait a minute!" Corie said defensively. "Selling had nothing to do with what happened to Jade." I had wrapped the towel around my body and opened the bathroom door to find Jesse's and Kelly's backs to me. Corie was facing the bathroom, her arm raised to Jesse as she pointed accusingly at him, and yelled, "It happened because of that *wench* you and Kelly were partying with all damn night!"

"What are you talking about?" Jesse sounded dumbfounded.

"Charity," I said. The guys whirled around, and all three of them stared at me. "Charity promised to get revenge on us and every time I saw her it was with that man. I saw him looking at me a few times."

Kelly stood like a statue, turning red and clenching his fists. Jesse came over to me and said quietly, "Get dressed. We'll talk about it later."

Kelly and Corie silently left the room, saying they'd meet us in the lobby in a bit. I pulled some clothes out of my bag and laid them on the bed, while Jesse sat down at the small table by the window and lit a cigarette. I finished getting dressed and went back into the bathroom to let the water out of the tub. The whole time I brushed my teeth, my hair, and attempted to cover my ashen face with makeup, Jesse sat quietly. Finally, when everything was done, I sat down on the bed near him and waited.

"Jesus," he finally said, lowering his head into his hands.

I reached out and circled one of his wrists with a hand, slowly rubbing it with my thumb. He looked so worn down and tired. I missed the laid-back person I had come to know and hated that I was the reason he'd become so defeated. He didn't say anything else for a few minutes as we both pondered over what had taken place, where we were, and having no idea what to do next.

"I could hear you screaming," he finally said. "Corie came in freaking out, saying that someone had grabbed you. I just got up, grabbed the gun, and ran outside. I just followed the sound until I found you." He stopped and I waited. "I didn't even think about it. I just hit him on the head with the gun and he fell over. I didn't even care if he was dead."

I didn't care either, but that didn't mean we were safe from murder charges.

"I wasn't with Charity that night," his voice was harder now, determined.

I looked up at him and saw the conflicting emotions on his face. Neither of us had expected to be here. This had all started out as a joyride, and now we were dealing with much stronger feelings. Neither of us quite knew what to do with this. I opened my mouth to say that it didn't matter, but he interrupted. "It's important." So, I nodded and let go of his hand.

"When we got back to the motel it was around nine and you guys weren't there. We went into the bar for a drink, but the only people in there were Rex and a few others. We talked for a little and Rex told us there was a party in room four. We knew most of the people and figured word would get around and you'd find us. We were really only in there about three hours. Charity showed up and started hanging all over me, trying to pull me into the bathroom, and whispering all kinds of crazy stuff to me, talking trash about you and Corie. Kelly and I didn't want to be around her anymore, and you could tell she was making a lot of people uneasy, so we left. Honestly, Kelly and I went back to the room and were there the rest of the time."

I'd never heard him say so much at one time before.

"I believe you," I said. "I guess I thought you'd come looking for me. I didn't even know you were there until I saw Rex, and by then Charity had come into the bar. She was still wiping the drool off her chin and made a point of telling me how *lovely* you were. She said she still had half a revenge to go."

"Well, it was a lie," he growled low. "The closest she got to revenge was setting that bastard rapist for hire loose on you."

I didn't say anything. Part of me was relieved, hearing from him that she had been lying. I knew it deep down, but there was no reason for Jesse to reject her other than because it was what he wanted. I didn't have any claim or hold over him. I didn't even know if I had that right.

*   *   *

After we fled Mississippi we left behind any more talk about the cocaine and the possibility that Jesse had left a man for dead out in a field. Over the next few days I also realized that Jesse was probably in more trouble for his probation violation than I had previously thought. I didn't have any clue whether either he or Kelly had been identified in the store robbery, but the warrant alone was enough to keep Jesse away from Elgin for a long time. He didn't say it. In fact, neither of them spoke about any of it. Ever. But I was sure he understood what he'd done when he drove out of the state, and eventually he'd have to deal with it. He may not have decided to run forever, but if that was what he had to do, he wasn't expecting any of us to run with him. That much I knew.

"No!" I yelled at him. "I'm not going back!"

"I'm not telling you to go back," he said. "I'm just saying you should think about it. I think all things concerned it might be the best thing for you."

"You're asking me to leave you."

"Jade, I know what it'll mean if you go back," he said it calmly but his voice was strained. "But if you stay for me, you'll be ruining your life."

I shook my head in denial. Part of me knew he was right, that if he chose to continue running, I'd have to accept becoming wanted as well. The other part of me was too afraid to leave him and return to the unknown. If I left, I would never see him again.

"What about Corie and Kelly?" I wanted to know.

"They have their own decisions to make. Besides, I think you have the most to lose."

"You have more to lose," I reminded him, thinking of his freedom.

"That's not what I meant," he sighed. "Look, I'm not trying to push you away. In a perfect world we could both go back and everything would be fine. But that's not possible."

"Fine," I agreed. "If you aren't pushing me to go then let's agree that whatever I decide will be my choice, and mine alone." He agreed, though I couldn't determine if he liked the arrangement or not.

I knew why he was doing it, but it hurt. If I was willing to stay, why couldn't that be enough for him? He'd already admitted that if the choice were his, he'd want me to stay. The only reason he didn't is because he knew it was selfish and he didn't think he was worth it. I did think about going home. I knew what the right thing was to do; the responsible thing. And I knew that he cared enough to let me walk out of his life forever if only it could save mine, but I couldn't do it. I was the truly selfish one. I'd always been. I may have been living in a fantasy, but I was still determined to have it all. I just knew there had to be a way to keep him in my life. I hadn't made up my mind to never go home; at least not consciously. But one thing I did know was that until I figured out how I could with Jesse, then I wasn't going at all.

He could see it in my eyes and it scared the hell out of him. He knew it would never happen. Even if he really wanted it too, he knew that he'd never be accepted by my family. There would never come a day when he could walk up to my parents' house and ring the doorbell. The idea was foreign to him, but I still held to the belief that anything was possible.

We stopped in Texas and set up camp again. I think the guys wanted to stay in warmer weather but hopefully get us lost in the largest state possible. It was a lot like being in North Carolina with the campground hookups, bathhouses, and pool. Off the pool area was a game room and a grill that sold pizza and burgers and other snack foods. There was also a small store where you could buy toilet paper and things if you needed it bad enough and didn't mind paying five dollars for something you could get for two down the street at the grocery store.

There was something about the familiar routine of cooking over a campfire and sleeping in the tents that I found comforting. I was eager to get back to the ways things were, but Jesse and Kelly weren't the same. They watched me a lot. Sometimes it felt like I was under a microscope. They weren't very good at hiding it. More than once I yelled at them to get over it. If I was okay, why weren't they? It was like they were waiting for me to have a nervous breakdown or something.

Their whispering and creeping on me when they thought I wasn't looking was only the beginning. Jesse was pushing me away whether he knew it or not. Convinced he was going to have to go it alone, I could only wonder what his next move would be and what that meant for Kelly and Corie as well. From the way he spoke to me about leaving, I got the impression that he and Kelly had been talking privately about making lots of changes. At first, I thought it was because they were worried about me recovering from nearly being raped, but as time went on I realized that it was just an excuse for them.

Sometimes I'd watch Jesse, too, when he wasn't looking. He looked sad, like he knew something the rest of us didn't. He smiled for me, still held me, kissed me, but he was fighting something and I couldn't help. I knew none of this was easy on him. In my mind everything would be fine if we both just accepted where we were and that we were in it together. But he couldn't do it. He was fighting between two evils, and we were both losers in this war. Whoever would have thought beneath that rough exterior stood a humble and ethical person?

Those were the thoughts that occurred to me, though they gave me very little comfort the morning I woke up alone. At first, I thought Jesse had gotten up to use the bathroom, but after a while he still didn't come back. I went outside and lit a cigarette, sitting on top of the picnic table. The sun was just about to come up, the morning light still soft and grayish pink. I looked around me as I smoked, my eyes landing on Kelly's tent. I could hear the faint noises of people breathing inside. An alarm went off inside of me, and it wasn't until I looked around me again more carefully that I realized why. The car was gone. I willed myself to stay calm as I remained sitting and smoking. I told myself that there were several reasons why Jesse might have taken the car so early. Maybe he went to get us breakfast. Maybe he was just out of cigarettes. Maybe Kelly was with him and they were getting supplies or finding a score. Maybe.

My theories started to crumble after another thirty minutes went by, and then completely crashed when Kelly unzipped the front of his tent, crawled out, and made his way over to a tree to relieve himself. He joined me on the table, lighting a cigarette for himself.

"Mornin', Sunshine," he said. "You're up early." We just looked at each other for a moment, his features becoming quizzical at my silence.

"Notice anything different around here this morning?"

"What?" he looked around.

"The car is gone."

"Yup," he nodded. "I see that."

There really was no clinging to any hope now. Kelly wasn't surprised, which means he knew it was going to happen. Which also means he agreed to it. Which means he didn't tell me. Kelly had never lied to me before. I don't know why things were different between us now. It wasn't just the feeling that he betrayed me over keeping Jesse's confidence, though a part of me could argue that Kelly and I went too far back to justify his change in loyalties. It was the whole thing, starting with the way he and Jesse had approached everything from a provider standpoint. Corie and I never asked to be taken care of. Maybe I was stupid for thinking things would be the same as they had been back home. Had I been ignorant to not know what it would require of them to keep us fed and safe? I didn't know anymore. But I knew this; I didn't like what this trip had done to us.

The tears were threatening to spill, and I willed them to stop, angrier than anything else. Kelly was silent, staring at the empty parking spot. He swallowed hard and dropped his head.

"You mean, you knew he was going to leave me, and you didn't say anything? Why, Kelly?"

"It's not like that. Honest, Jade," he said, but he wouldn't look at me. "I didn't know he was going to leave last night. I just…hell. I'm not surprised is all. He thinks he's doing the right thing by you. By all of us."

"Damn," I muttered, wiping at my stupid, weeping eyes. "If you knew something, you should have warned me before he left me sitting here like a fool."

"Well, we all look like fools with a bunch of tents and nowhere to go," Kelly said with a weak smile.

His attempt to lighten the mood failed as I dropped my head into my hands and bawled. A minute later I was stumbling for my tent, pulling the flaps closed and zipping them tightly. I pulled the blankets over my head, taking in deep breaths of Jesse's scent that still lingered on the pillow. I was going to sleep. There was no point in doing anything else.

Time ceased to exist. I don't know how many days I slept. Every time I woke up it was against my will, and I'd lay there until sleep took over again. Sometimes there would be light in the sky, sometimes it would be dark. One time it was raining. Once I found a bottle of Coke and a turkey sandwich wrapped in plastic near my head. Another time I saw a bottle of water and two large, white pills. I didn't know what they were but they made me feel really good until I slept off the effects and woke up again.

Kelly came in, crawled up next to me, and lay down with his arms around me. It was like old times. "We need to move on," he was saying.

"No," I croaked.

"We're out of money. We can't stay here."

So, this is what will become of us. The three of us walking with our blankets and tents strapped to our backs with no direction, no money, nothing. And we'll have to steal to survive; possibly even worse. Because at least before when we had a car and a decent, albeit criminal, start, we could have made something out of our lives. But now we couldn't. I wondered if that was how Jesse felt all along. Like my grandiose ideas of making a home somewhere, having an honest life, just seemed too far out of reach for him. He said it would never work and now I understood why. I'd been so stupid. And yet, I'd do it all again just to be with him.

"You go," I whispered at Kelly. I was still lying in the same position I felt like I'd been in for days. My back was against him. I didn't even look at him.

"I'm not going to leave you," he promised.

"It's okay," I said, tonelessly. "I don't care."

He was quiet for a minute. I prayed for sleep to take over again, but then I heard him say, "One more day. And then we go." I didn't respond and after a few more minutes he slipped back out, zipping the tent up behind him.

CHAPTER ELEVEN

Shame, such a shame
I think I kind of lost myself again
Day, yesterday
Really should be leaving but I stay

Dissolved Girl by Massive Attack

Two days later we packed up and walked west.

We scouted the town, the bars, the shopping centers, looking for some ideas, thinking about what we needed to do next. For me, the hardest part was figuring out what I even wanted. Kelly's goals hadn't changed. While Corie worried about where we'd sleep, what we'd eat, and how we'd shower, Kelly's only concern was making his next score. Me, I didn't care.

Since we were out of money we had to be creative about where we slept. We couldn't put our tents up just anywhere. I hated this feeling of being homeless. I didn't care if we were camped out in the woods, or sleeping in a car, or even in an abandoned house. It was better than not having any clue at all about where to go. At least back home we were in familiar surroundings. Here in Texas, we just had to trust that a suitable place would present itself.

Kelly led us through the nearest town. We spent our last bit of money at the grocery store, buying protein bars to sustain us in case we had to go without food for a day or two. Corie suggested we try to make some kind of score right away. I agreed to do whatever I had to do. They thought I was being helpful, but really, I was just numb. And I wanted to stay that way.

There was a strip of bars and restaurants. Everything seemed to be busy, which was good because that meant there would be lots of men to scam. Easy pickings. Kelly didn't like our plan but we out-numbered him, and for once he didn't have anyone to back him up. While he found a safe place to store our camping gear, Corie and I used a public bathroom to freshen up, change clothes, and put on some makeup.

I could see her watching me through the mirror as I applied lip liner. I tried to ignore her, but she said, "It sucks. I can't believe he did it." As if that was supposed to make me feel better. It didn't. When I didn't reply, she said, "I mean, did you know he was going to leave us like that?"

I finished filling in my lips with color, and said, "I really don't want to talk about it."

As far as I was concerned, this was it. We were in Texas of all places, though we could have ended up anywhere and it would have been the same. I'm sure we had other options but at the moment I just couldn't think of any of them. I meant it when I told Kelly he could take Corie and leave. I knew he wouldn't do it, but I meant it nonetheless. Whatever I had to do now, it was on me. I shut my feelings off and stayed focused on scoring. What I scored didn't matter.

We left the restaurant and headed for the closest bar. The bouncer eyed us and I stared back at him, determined he let me in. He stood aside and waved us through. Lots of eyes wandered my way. Most of the men stared, even some that were with their girlfriends. I didn't think I was particularly beautiful, but I knew when I looked like a piece of meat, and that was my angle for the night.

Corie and I perched on bar stools, and it was only a matter of time before guys were buying us drinks. She intended to remain in control, I could tell by the way she only asked for a beer. I ordered a shot of tequila and threw it back. My new friend, Steve, was encouraged by this and bought me another one, taking a shot with me. After my third shot, Corie nudged me in the ribs with a look on her face that told me to stop. I turned on my stool to face Steve, putting my back to her.

I could feel the alcohol. It'd been a while since I'd done straight liquor, and I'd barely eaten anything all day. Steve's hand found my thigh, his thumb putting pressure on my leg as he slid his hand higher toward the opening of my skirt. We looked at each other and I swung my leg out a little wider. He scooted his barstool closer to mine, his hand further up my skirt. I said I needed another shot.

It felt good in a dirty, desperate way.

Every time thoughts of Jesse popped into my head I pushed them away. I glanced behind me and saw Corie talking to the guy who had bought her a beer. He said something and she laughed loudly, as if he were the funniest person on the planet and placed her hand on his arm. Just a few more maneuvers and she'd have his wallet in her pocket before he could even suspect she was ripping him off.

Steve's hand was warm and probing. I was deciding how far I wanted to take this. I needed a moment to think before I got too deep into something. Images of Mississippi flashed through my head and I jerked away suddenly.

"You alright?" Steve asked.

"Yeah," I said quickly. "Just gotta use the bathroom. I'll be right back." I tugged Corie's arm discreetly as I slipped off the barstool and headed for the bathroom. Assuming she would be right behind me, I went in to find a single stall. When I came out she was there, waiting. She stepped into the small space with me.

"You got it?" I asked her and she nodded.

"I gotta get out of here before he notices," she said. "You score?"

"No, but I can if I go back."

"It's not worth it," she said. "Two wallets gone and the whole bar will know it was us."

"Okay."

"I've gotta pee. Slip outside and wait for me back at the diner, and then we'll go find Kelly."

As soon as the door was shut behind me, Steve was there taking me by the arm, smiling. He led me out the backdoor into an alley, lit only by the full, bright moon. I barely had time to allow my eyes adjust before he had me slammed against the brick wall, one hand over my breast, the other up my skirt. His mouth was sliding over mine.

I couldn't do it. I had no idea where his wallet was and I wasn't as good as Corie anyway. I thought of Jesse again as this strange tongue was probing into my mouth, and I felt an instant rush of guilt. I tore my head away from his and pushed at his chest.

"No," I said. "I can't do it."

"What?" His voice said he heard me but his hands did not. A second later he was kissing me again, his groin pushing into me, pushing up, while his hands slid my skirt up higher, his fingers searching.

"No," I said again. This time I was panting, whether from lack of air or fear I did not know. He was relentless as he continued to kiss my neck, feel my crotch, squeeze my ass. "You have to stop."

"Oh, you're a little tease, aren't you?" he murmured, pushing his fingers into my panties while he reached for the front of his jeans. "Come on, sweetie. We both know what you're looking for."

His tongue was in my mouth again. Somehow, I couldn't fight both sides of the war raging inside of me. I heard the zipper of his jeans, felt him tug them down, all the while the other hand was pulling my panties aside. A second later he was shoving himself inside of me. And I knew what I'd just done.

"Jade? Jade!" Kelly was yelling my name.

Startled, I pushed him away from me. He tripped back, confused at first, then angry. I was shaking my head at him as he came back toward me. "No, no, you can't," I whispered fiercely. The tears flooded instantly. He was still reaching for me, trying to get back inside.

143

"Jade!" Kelly yelled again, followed by Corie's voice, somewhere further away. They were looking for me. It would only be a matter of time. And I couldn't let them see this. I didn't even want to admit what I'd just done to myself, let alone them.

"What the hell is your problem?" Steve yelled at me. "You can't just stop!"

I was trying to scramble away from him, adjusting my clothing, and saying, "Just go away." He was grabbing for me again, trying to keep me against the wall, when I saw Kelly come around the corner and sprint across the alley towards us.

"Get off her!"

"Hey, it's cool!" Steve was saying. His hands were up and his pants were down around his ankles, as he backed away from me. Kelly wasn't one for reasoning and threw a punch without further discussion. Steve landed on the pavement, clearly confused.

Corie came running up behind Kelly, yelling, "Jade! Jade! Oh, my god!"

I looked over at Steve, who was still on the ground. He was feeling his jaw, his eyes were blinking rapidly, and I could tell he was out of it. Kelly grabbed my arm to pull me away, but I quickly squatted down by Steve and pulled the wallet from his jeans.

"Hey!" he said, sounding drunk. "Hey, you bitch! Give that back!"

I opened it, took out the cash, and threw the wallet back down at him. "Payment," I hissed at him. Turning, I grabbed Kelly's hand and he pulled me away as we ran behind Corie.

We ran several blocks and didn't stop until Kelly told us to. He'd found a good sized wooded area and had stashed our things there. We knew we needed to keep moving but we were exhausted. It was hard to know when it would be best to try and get out of town. Would we be bigger targets right now, only minutes after our crime, or tomorrow during the day when we'd be more noticeable? Who would identify us anyway? I was willing to bet neither Steve nor Corie's bar friend would recognize us in the light of day without all that makeup on our faces.

We couldn't risk starting a fire, but Kelly set up one of the tents and we all climbed in. He said he'd get some provisions early in the morning, and if we needed to we'd find a thicker spot to pitch the tent. If we laid low for another day, we should be able to walk out of town unseen by the next night. All I really wanted was to take a shower and clean off the filth I felt crawling all over my skin. But that filth was inside of me and nothing I did was going to be able to erase it from my memory. I decided it was penance for every horrible thing I'd ever done and did my best to push it to the back of my mind.

It wasn't working. One minute I'd be in happy denial, the next I was sobbing into my pillow, ashamed. Kelly and Corie assumed I was still depressed over Jesse leaving, and at that moment I blamed him. If he hadn't left me none of this would have ever happened. But it didn't matter, did it? He was gone. We'd all left the last place we were together. There was no going back now. Besides, it had been days. He could be in Mexico by now for all I knew.

It was a good thing Kelly's plan was for us to stay put all the next day and rest up before we packed up and headed out of town after dark, because I didn't want to move. I barely managed to crawl out of the tent to pee behind a bush before making my way back into my sleeping bag. Kelly had gone to the store at first light as promised, bringing back food and water. I didn't want to eat. I didn't even want to brush my teeth. Nothing would suffice until I could stand under a hot shower. I'd even settle for a river or a lake to submerge myself in. Until then I didn't want anything.

They were worried. I could hear them talking about me outside. They thought I'd been through too much, what with two sexual assaults. That I was in shock. Little did they know. The more they speculated the more I thought about Steve and his grimy, greedy hands all over me. His mouth; his tongue in my mouth. His body inside of mine. I wanted to throw up but there was nothing in my stomach to bring up. Instead I cried until I couldn't stand it anymore and then I started screaming.

"Jade!" Kelly yelled, diving into the tent. Corie was right behind him. He gathered me in his arms as I stuffed a pillow into my mouth, muffling the screams. "You have to stop!" He was worried about someone finding us, and I was worried about never finding myself again.

"Oh, Jade," Corie said sadly. "Kelly, maybe we need to think about going home. I think she's done."

"I'm fine!" I cried, my body wracking with deep sobs. "I'm fine!" Then I pushed Kelly away and got out of the tent to breath some fresh air.

"You're not fine," he said carefully. He crawled out of the tent and stood in front of me. I couldn't read the expression on his face; trepidation mixed with anguish. "Jade, I...I can't believe I let this happen to you. I can't believe this is what we've become."

It hurt. It really did. Because he and I had been friends for so long. We'd done so many crazy things together, had so many stupid little adventures. But this was taking things too far. I didn't blame him. Neither one of us could have known how this would turn out. And even through my anger at Jesse for leaving, I knew the only person I had to blame was myself.

*   *   *

Kelly seemed to have a plan of some kind. We packed up and started walking well after dark, intending to make it out of town unseen. His choice of direction and destination wasn't as arbitrary as he probably wanted it to appear, but Kelly was never very good at bluffing.

The dark highway stretched out before us. Luckily the moon was still full and high as we trekked mile after mile on the field flanked road, because there was no other light to see by except for when cars and trucks passed us. We walked for hours. I was never a very athletic person, and Kelly definitely wasn't. His idea of running was dashing into the store for a pack of cigarettes, and I'd always said I'd only run when being chased. We walked slowly though, so it was more of an endurance thing than a race thing, and we didn't seem to be in a hurry anyway.

"I can't walk anymore," Corie complained. We'd just passed a road sign stating that the next town was eleven miles away. "Can't we hitch a ride?"

"No," Kelly said. "We need to keep to ourselves." But he let us sit and rest for a bit.

Corie dug out a few protein bars and passed one to each of us. We sat and chewed quietly. We shared two bottles of water. I was thirsty but I was also relieved because carrying water is heavy. No one spoke, though I wouldn't have said anything anyway. It was about four in the morning, so I knew by the time we reached the next town it'd be after sunrise. That would help as far as finding a place to set up camp and scout the town. We still had a little bit of money left over from the two wallets. Not much after Kelly bought food and water yesterday, but enough to either buy us all a really good meal, or a campsite. I didn't really see the point in paying for a place to pitch our tents, especially if we'd have to pack up the next day, but Kelly said we'd find the money to stay one way or another. It was interesting how there were certain rules he lived by, though I guess it all came down to what you were willing to get caught for. Stealing was survival. Getting busted for camping on private property was just stupid. Unless we had absolutely no choice, of course, and even then it was rare because we were better off on a park bench.

We dragged our tired, dirty selves into a diner and sat down wearily. We probably looked as bad as we felt. Corie had taken to braiding her long hair to keep it cleaner and out of the way, but mine was only shoulder length and I hated wearing it up, so I'd tied a bandana on my head. I was glad Kelly was insisting on finding a campground because I needed a shower in the worst way. We drank hot coffee and ate biscuits and gravy. It was cheap and filling.

The waitress came by to refill our coffee cups, and Kelly asked her where the closest campground was located. I was surprised but didn't say anything. Corie didn't seem to care as she practically licked her plate clean.

"It's about three miles up the road," she said, pointing to the back wall of the restaurant. "When you leave out front, turn right at the light. You can't miss it." He thanked her.

I was so exhausted I was sure that if my life depended on it I wouldn't have been able to walk another mile. The only thing that spurned me on was the thought of putting up my own tent and sleeping the rest of what was my life away. It had been over a week since Jesse left. It felt like an eternity.

*　　*　　*

"Jade, are you ever going to get up?" Kelly asked me. It was later that night. Or maybe it was the next night. I didn't really know.

"No," I said.

He'd unzipped my tent and crouched just in the entrance, holding a paper bag. It smelled like a burger. My stomach rolled and growled.

"So, you're just gonna sleep forever and expect me to bring you food every day?"

Sounded like a plan to me. Besides, my plan to contribute didn't exactly work out so well. I honestly didn't know how I'd be able to help without completely spiraling downward, because there really wouldn't be any other direction for me to go if I ever had a repeat of the other night in that dark alley. I didn't answer him and he made a *piffling* noise. What did he expect? I'd told him to take Corie and leave and he'd said no. I never made any promises. Yeah, I got up and walked. I put on some slutty clothes and whored myself for sixty bucks. That didn't mean I was okay. I'd never be okay again.

Maybe he and Jesse had been right all along about me. Maybe they had known from the start that I wasn't capable of thieving or lying. I mean, I knew somewhere inside myself that what happened with Steve wasn't necessary in order to steal his money. The position I'd put myself in came from needing something else anyway. I knew that. Running the cocaine was easy because in a way it was honest. Those people were willingly handing me money. I wasn't slipping my hand into back pockets like Kelly and Corie could with ease. So maybe the truth was that I needed to be taken care of, that I was useless. And now I was nothing more than a burden.

"I like this place," I finally said in a sleepy voice. "Let's just stay here."

"What, like forever?"

Forever was just a word. It could mean years, but for all we knew we only had days. The way we were going the odds were not in our favor. And since we didn't have anywhere else to go it made sense to just stay where we were. At least until we got chased out of town anyway. Which would eventually happen, I was sure. I just shrugged in reply.

"Jade," Kelly said, concerned. "I don't know how much longer we can do this. I mean, maybe…" he sighed. "Maybe you need to go home."

He wasn't saying the words he was thinking. The same words I was thinking. I didn't know why not. Kelly had never been afraid to say whatever he was thinking to me. But we weren't the same anymore and neither one of us knew how to put this into words. The thing is, there was no real reason to go home. It was just a place that we were familiar with but going there wouldn't make any of this go away. Life wouldn't be easier. In fact, I was positive things would only be harder.

"This is home," I said.

I woke up sometime later to the sound of a car door banging shut. I blinked my eyes and sat up to stretch, not sure if I had imagined it. It was nighttime, my little tent dark as I felt around for my lighter. I used the small flame to find my bearings and unzipped the doorway. The fire pit still glowed with small flames, but it was unmanned. Kelly and Corie were nowhere in sight. I rolled the flaps back, tying them in place, and left only the mesh netting down, allowing some fresh air into the tent. Then I lit a cigarette and lay back down. I heard footsteps a minute later and thought maybe it was Kelly coming back from the bathhouse, but when I heard a voice say my name it wasn't his. I started and peered through the mesh at the person standing on the other side.

"Jesse?" Now I knew I was bad off. I was hearing and seeing things.

"Jade," he said again. "Come out here."

"No," I said, fearfully.

"Why not?"

I just shook my head, afraid that I had made him appear because I'd wanted it so badly. Even though I could see and hear him, I was sure it was a hallucination. He didn't look real standing there on the other side of the netting with the faint glow of the fire and smoke rising up behind him. I reasoned that he couldn't be real. He had no idea where we were and we had no idea where he was.

"I'm coming in," I heard the voice say. I closed my eyes and waited for the moment to pass, waited to wake up from this very real dream. I expected that when I opened my eyes he would be gone. But I heard the zipper and someone was crawling in next to me.

I blinked and moved further back into the tent. There was nowhere to go. He must have seen the fear on my face, the uncertainty, because he stopped just short of the entrance. Slowly, my eyes focused on his familiar face, and I inched closer. A hand went out to touch his cheek, to feel that he was really there in body and not just in my imagination.

"How?" was all I could think of to say.

He didn't want to tell me. He swallowed as he worked the words around before explaining. Something he and Kelly had agreed to before he left. Some kind of arrangement that if he decided to come back he'd have an idea of where to find us. It was the second time Kelly had lied to me. If he had been in front of me I would have slapped him. As it was, Jesse's face would suffice. He didn't even blink as my palm cracked across his cheek. Then I started to cry.

"Damn you!" I said. "Why?" There were so many things I wanted to say, to ask him, but mostly I just wanted to know why he bothered leaving in the first place if he knew he might come back. Because I knew that if I forgave him I'd never survive him leaving me again.

"I hated it, knowing what I did to you," he started to explain.

"You left!" I sobbed at him, pushing. "You said you wouldn't let anything happen to me, but then you just...abandoned me!"

He closed his eyes, taking in a deep breath. He knew he had no excuse. It would have been one thing if I never saw him again. Dealing with that was hard enough, but now he was here, and I had no defenses against him.

"I had to leave," he finally said.

He was trying to come back to me, but I was so angry all I could do was scream, "You can't come back! I'm not the same! It's too late!"

I was spazzing out and he grabbed my arms, forcing me to look at him as he growled back at me. "I know I've been a real bastard, Jade! I can't take it back, and I can't explain it so you'll understand, and I know that no apology will make it better!" He was angry, gripping my wrists, and shaking my arms as he spoke. I stared back at him speechless as he continued. "Listen to me because I am only going to say this once. I don't expect you to be able to read my mind, Jade. I know I hurt you, and I'm sorry. But you need to know that I love you. It doesn't matter if we are together or not. You need to remember that always, understand?"

I nodded, the tears falling freely now. I hated the way all I ever did was sob and crumble anymore. I hated the words he was saying, as if he knew someday he'd leave again and I needed to be better prepared for it. Is this why he came back? Because the guilt of sneaking off was too much for him and he wanted to make it right? I didn't want this love if I had to be in it alone.

I still hadn't moved, though the pressure on my wrists slackened. Maybe I looked as terrified as I felt. He sighed and pulled me closer to him, whispering, "I'm sorry."

He felt so familiar, he smelled just the way I remembered. I couldn't help the sobbing that choked out of me because I was so afraid that he was leaving again, afraid of what it would do to me if he did, afraid to give in to him even a little, afraid that if he ever knew the truth about me he'd hate me as much as I did.

"I'm not the same," I said again, weakly. He still held me against him.

"I know," he said. "I'm sorry."

CHAPTER TWELVE

I remember when we used to sing
And go dance outside in the pouring rain
We lived like we would never wake up
From a dream that we shared, just the two of us

Not Too Late by Moon Taxi

We slept. I awoke the next morning to hushed voices outside. Kelly and Jesse were talking about me. I figured Corie was still asleep by the way they were whispering. Jesse was asking questions about the past week, about our journey from where he'd left us to where he found us, about me. Kelly didn't want to say too much, I could tell. He wasn't the kind of person that liked to hash things out anyway, but maybe for a minute he realized how much he'd lied to me and was considering how far he was willing to stretch my confidences.

"She keeps saying she's not the same," Jesse said.

"She's not," Kelly sounded sad. "I don't know what it is, man. It's just…everything."

"And she still won't go back?"

I didn't hear Kelly answer so assumed he was shaking his head. Then I heard him say, "Going back wouldn't fix anything." There was a brief silence, then, "Why'd you come back? You know you can't do this again."

"I know what I'm doing," Jesse told him.

"I'm just saying, she barely survived the first time. I hope you found what you were looking for," Kelly said.

There was a long silence before I heard Jesse say, "I did."

There were lots of things left unsaid. I had so many questions that I knew I'd never ask. It didn't matter. Since he was back I had to assume some of the answers and forget the others. It was frustrating but entirely typical of a conversation between two men to finish with so little actually said.

With Jesse back, we decided to move on. They spent the rest of that day scouting the area, looking for a way to make one last, good score before we left. Corie and I stayed behind, just as usual, and sat around the picnic table playing cards. We hadn't done that in a long time.

"I'm so glad Jesse came back," Corie said absently. "Part of me knew he couldn't just leave us behind." She had more faith in him than I did. I didn't say anything as I puffed on my cigarette and dealt the cards. "You look like you're getting back to normal," she observed.

I knew she wanted to talk about it, about anything really, because some of the worst parts about being on the road with the same limited group of people is that it can get so lonely. But also, because Corie was one of those people who liked to voice her observations, as if that helped make everything clearer. I think she also believed in the fairytale idea that happy ever after was possible, and she wanted it for her friends as much as she did for herself. I used to think that way, too. But I couldn't satiate her and say what I was feeling, or that I was happy that Jesse was back. It didn't matter if I was glad he'd come back. I couldn't give in to it because I knew he could leave in the middle of the night again at any time.

"You're still angry," she said several minutes later. I shrugged, still looking at my cards. "I don't blame you. I was mad at him, too."

Somehow that didn't comfort me. I didn't know if it was that I was still angry so much as I'd been trying to sift through the disappointment. There was really only one thought forefront in my mind, and since it had always been a major contributing factor from day one where both Jesse and Kelly were concerned, I found myself saying honestly, "I don't know if I can trust him." *Them.* I didn't know if I could trust *them*, meaning Jesse or Kelly, which was a really hard pill to swallow after everything Kelly and I had been through together. But I didn't say that.

Corie looked at me sadly. "Oh, Jade," she said. But what could she say, really, that would change my heart? That she knew Jesse better than I did? That she knew he wouldn't disappoint me again? That if I just forgave him I'd see that I could trust him? I'd already given away all the parts of me that I could, and they'd all come back damaged. What was left to offer?

When the guys came back they were in a hurry to pack up and get on the road. I took that as a bad sign. They may have managed to fill their pockets with money, but it seemed like we were always running. Corie and I had already packed everything up and broke down the tents, so all we had to do was get in the car and wait for Jesse and Kelly to store it all in the back. I sat far over on my side of the front seat. Jesse looked at me a few times while he drove, his face unhappy, but he didn't say anything.

We drove for hours. The sun came down in front of us and I knew we were driving straight through the state, but to where I didn't know. I didn't ask either because the guys usually didn't have a destination in mind. It made sense to go west as opposed to back the way we came though. Jesse stopped the car at a Denny's when we all became hungry. Instead of taking a break and letting Kelly drive like he normally did, Jesse got back into the driver's seat and started the engine. It was only about an hour later when we spotted a sign for a KOA and he pulled in.

He went inside the office, rented our space, and came back out to drive over to the spot. When we got there we all climbed out of the car, each of us automatically doing the same things we always did. Jesse and Kelly started putting up the tents while Corie and I unpacked the bedrolls and blankets. We sifted through our bags and took out the things we wanted to keep in our tents with us, and once they were up, we'd take everything in and organize it while the guys collected wood or whatever they needed to do to start a fire in the pit.

I came out of my tent to find Corie finished setting up her own and sitting on a log near the almost ready fire. Kelly was using his lighter to start a few twigs and sticking them in the bottom of the tepee of logs. I had my toothbrush in hand and decided I might as well search out the bathhouse. It wasn't hard to find since the closest one was back at the main building. Most newer KOA's were pretty much all the same. I fiddled in the bathroom for as long as I could, brushing my teeth, my hair, washing my face. It was weird how desperate and lonely I felt after Jesse left, and now that he was back I only found comfort alone. But that was my doing anyway.

I came out of the bathroom and saw him waiting for me. He was leaning against the railing that separated the bathroom entrances from the pool area. His hands were in his front pockets, one ankle crossed over the other. We looked at each other. I knew that if I walked away from him now it would be over, but some sort of gravity I couldn't control pulled me closer to him. We stood only a few feet apart.

"You have to forgive me," he said.

I nodded, blinking hard.

He sighed and stepped closer, placing a hand on my cheek. His eyes searched mine for several seconds, apparently finding nothing. "Where have you gone?" he asked.

I could only shrug, though I could feel the back of my nose stinging as my eyes threatened to fill. I swallowed it all back down and looked blankly back at him. My hands were clenched into fists. It was taking everything I had not to throw myself in his arms.

"Please come back to me," he whispered.

It wasn't him, it was me. But I couldn't form the words; give an explanation. I so badly wanted him to understand why I'd pulled into this shell, to get some kind of validation from him, but I knew I'd never speak the words. Some secrets were meant to be buried. I'd have to live with it; it was no one else's burden but mine. The only thing that truly mattered was that Jesse was standing in front of me, admitting that leaving had been a mistake, that he couldn't do it, and saying things I never thought he would. This roller coaster of a relationship between us had evolved into something much deeper than I had anticipated. I still didn't have the words for it, but I knew a strange sensation pulling from my heart, something that went beyond lust or dependency. And the only thing that felt right at that moment was stepping into the circle of his arms, feeling his warmth.

The next afternoon was warm and sunny as Corie and I walked slowly around the roads circling the campground. Jesse and Kelly had left for a while, doing whatever it is they do. I was hoping more than anything that whatever it was they did it inconspicuously, because I really wanted to stay in one place for a while. With a place to sleep and showers at our disposal, I still clung to the belief that we could make a better life for ourselves somehow.

"Corie," I said, as we strolled under the canopy of the tree-lined road. She made a sort of humming noise in return. "Do you ever think about Mississippi?"

She threw me a cautious glance. "What do you mean?" she scowled. "How could I not think about it?"

"Well," I started carefully. "Don't you want some answers?"

"We're all pretty sure about why that guy attacked you. What else is there to know?"

"If he's dead for one," I said. I was a little irritated because it surprised me how no one else talked about it at all, like it didn't happen. "Don't you want to know?" I asked her when she gave me a horrified look.

"No," she shook her head adamantly. "I don't give a damn about that guy."

"Well, I don't either! But don't you want to know if Jesse killed him or not? I mean, if that guy is dead, chances are we're the suspects."

She stopped walking and turned to face me. "Stop trying to scare me."

"I'm not," I said. "But you know as well as I do that it probably looked fishy how we all took off in the middle of the night, and there's this guy passed out in the field with his zipper down and a big knot on the back of his head. Whether or not he's dead, people will ask questions, and Charity for sure will open her big mouth and blame it on us."

"Oh, god," Corie's face went pale. "She would." Then she shook her head, and said, "It's too late to plead self-defense, you know. We're better off not knowing. No good can come from it."

"Not if people are looking for us," I said logically.

"Let it go," she advised. "If the guys aren't worried, we don't need to be."

Truth was, neither one of us knew if the guys were worried about anything because they never shared those thoughts with us. For all I knew that was the last straw that made Jesse leave. He was already running from a warrant back in Elgin. Attempted manslaughter was the cherry on top. No wonder he thought it was best to go it alone.

We'd reached the store near the front of the campground by now. Corie ran in to get some toothpaste and I stood staring at the pay phone. To call Joe, or to not call Joe? Would contacting him make us look guilty? I hated loose ends. I had so many questions about everything. Maybe it was best to just put it all behind me.

For the first time in two months I thought of my mother. I mean, really thought of her. Not in the regretful kind of way. Not in the 'I wonder what she's doing?' kind of way. Not even to suspect that she was sorry for ignoring me, misunderstanding me, and possibly even missing me. It was weird and uncomfortable, actually, because I couldn't identify what I felt when I thought of her. And I realized that I should probably feel guilty, because no matter how I rationalized it, I was the one who'd run away. On some level they had to be concerned.

Before I knew what I was doing, I dropped some coins into the machine and dialed the private number Anne and I shared. The voicemail came on and I felt a rush of relief. It took all that to realize that I didn't really want to talk to anyone back home. I didn't want to know. I wasn't ready yet.

The voicemail beeped and I stumbled, still unprepared, still unsure about what I was doing and why I'd even called. "It's me," I said. Then my voice sped up. "I'm fine. Tell them if they care." And then I slammed the phone on the hook. I turned around and saw that Corie had come out of the store and was watching me curiously.

"Why did you do that?"

"I have no idea," I admitted.

*   *   *

We had a few days of calm. Jesse and Kelly stayed close to the camp with me and Corie. I guess that meant we had enough money to tide us over, but I learned long ago not to concern myself with those details. Each day they went off to buy more ice for the cooler, and anything else we needed or wanted. We slept if we wanted to, played cards, listened to music, drank beer, got high, played hide and seek in the dark. We were lazy, we were unconcerned, we were careless.

Corie and I never spoke of Mississippi again after that. Just like everything else that went unsaid, those two days were swept under the proverbial rug. Jesse didn't talk about the time he was gone, and we definitely didn't either. Other than that first morning I heard him and Kelly talking about it, Jesse never asked anymore questions.

Every once in a while, Jesse or Kelly would come up with some pot or some pills. I never quite understood how they did that. The money made sense because you could find that lots of places and in lots of ways. But drugs...it was just weird. But

164

then again, I didn't know what they did when they went out to work an area. More than once they left Corie and I at night for a couple hours to scout a club or two. They were obviously scoring somehow, and Kelly was still the sneakiest con artist I ever knew.

When the weekend came so did the party. So far this was my favorite place. On either side of us were groups of people near our age, partying. It seemed as if this place was to the locals what the Nike Base had been to me and Kelly. Corie and I walked around aimlessly, looking at the people milling about. They were waving at us, saying hi and come on over and smoke a joint or have a beer. We just waved back and kept walking, waiting for the guys to get back from the store.

Jesse's car appeared behind us as we strolled back toward our own lot, and Kelly leaned out the window and whistled. Corie laughed and jumped on the hood of the station wagon just as Jesse pushed on the gas and pulled into our parking spot. I continued walking the remaining hundred feet or so, seeing them get out of the car, each carrying a grocery bag. The radio was still on and Corie was dancing on top of the hood, singing along with the music.

Kelly was dumping ice into the cooler, unpacking food, and watching Corie with an amused smile. Jesse was building a fire. Then Kelly walked over to us holding two cold beers and handed me a pill.

"What is it?" I asked. Corie didn't question as she swallowed hers and drank one of the beers, still dancing.

"What is it?" Kelly parroted me, flipping open my can of beer for me. "It's *gooooood*, that's what it is." I shrugged and swallowed.

It hit me fast. Within twenty minutes I was on top of the car singing and dancing, too. It got dark and Kelly fixed some burgers, but I found that I wasn't very hungry. It felt too weird. I was chewing and I could feel it, but it didn't seem as though my mouth was attached to my body. It was like I could visualize the whole process from the chewing, to the swallowing, the food passing down into my stomach, yet I couldn't see it. I couldn't explain it though I still tried. I was so obsessed with how strange eating felt that I couldn't stop talking about it. They all thought I was crazy and just laughed at me.

"Forget it," I said, disgusted. I tossed the burger aside. "I can't eat this thing. It's too weird." They howled with laughter.

Music was coming from all directions. At some point I realized that all the radios had been turned to the same station, so the entire section of our block was jamming to the same songs. People were walking around, holding beers and red solo cups, stopping at other campsites, saying hello and sharing joints. It seemed to go on forever. At first the guys were friendly and polite, but as the night wore on Jesse could see my tolerance waning. He took me by the hand and quietly led me away from the others. We walked toward the RV side of the campground, where there was barely anyone stirring. I'm not sure we'd ever walked together like this before, holding hands.

We didn't talk. We just walked together. The quiet surrounded us in a peaceful, calming way, and this contentedness was what I'd been looking for all along. After a while he turned to me and placed his hands on either side of my face, kissing me deeply. I didn't think about anything else in those moments. There was no room to consider home, or Mississippi, a gun, or anything else because every bit of space inside of me was consumed with Jesse. When he held me and kissed me like that I could feel that empty space inside of me filling up.

"Did you bring me out here to seduce me?" I teased him.

"You're damn right, you little hussy," he groaned back huskily.

An involuntary thought crossed my mind then and I stiffened for a second. Regaining my composure, I tried to play it off, but I'd pulled back just enough for him to notice.

"Jade?" His eyes searched mine. "What happened? Is it because of Mississippi?"

I clung to him. I still wanted him. That wouldn't change. Not even if that man in the field had finished what he'd started. Not even one, solitary action made in an alley. It didn't change the way I felt about Jesse. It only changed the way I felt about me.

"Do you ever wonder about him?" I asked, meaning the man in the field.

He was quiet when he said, "Not anymore."

I didn't know what that meant. I didn't know how to respond. I only knew that I wanted to put everything behind me and start over from here. All I needed was him.

"I miss seeing you smile. I wish you were happy again."

"I'm happy when I'm with you," I told him.

"But it's not the same." He didn't say I wasn't the same, because really, none of us were.

"I did things," I whispered.

"I know," he nodded and swallowed. "We all have."

"But you don't know."

"Because it doesn't matter."

That's how I knew Jesse wasn't going to turn away from me. I didn't have to confess to him. I needed to make peace with myself the same way he'd needed to make peace with himself for the things he'd done. What made it easier was knowing he accepted me regardless, just like I had accepted him.

"We could do this," he was saying. "I get it now, what you wanted."

I blinked. That was almost funny because I couldn't remember what it was I wanted. As long as his hand still held mine, nothing else mattered. I had given up on the ideals of a normal life. We could live in tents forever for all I cared.

We made our way back to Kelly and Corie sitting around our fire pit, and when Jesse handed me a lit joint, I didn't question it. It tasted funny, and I must have made a face as I exhaled because he and Kelly laughed.

"What's wrong with this?" I asked, passing it back to him.

"It's special," he said and pushed my hand back. "You'll like it, I promise."

"Really?" I puffed again. "You'll take care of me?"

His eyes clouded for only a second. Then he smiled. "Forever."

I was high in a way I'd never been before. Everything was heightened. The moon was larger, fuller, and brighter. The fire was hotter, it crackled louder, and the sparks were glimmering. The music was better and it was always my favorite song. Jesse's hands felt like heaven. His lips made fireworks go off in my head and a swarm of butterflies erupt in my stomach.

Corie and I were on a whirlwind. The music was loud and the beat was strong. She laughed and grabbed my arms. We spun around crazily. The stars were whirling around above me as I threw my head back. Everyone was whizzing by as Corie and I continued to spin. The blazing fire would disappear to my left and then reappear on my right. I could see Jesse and Kelly standing off to the side, watching us and smiling. Corie let go of my hands and I kept on twirling around and around, while the fire, the people, and the colors continued to swirl in front of me. I could hear Jesse laughing, his deep voice sounding safe to my ears. I'm happy! I'm happy! I wanted to shout to everyone. The colors, the colors! Do you see the beautiful colors? And they were beautiful. Colors of red, blue, and white flashed before my eyes as I kept on spinning and spinning.

CHAPTER THIRTEEN

Memories are just where you laid them
Drag the waters till the depths give up their dead
What did you expect to find
Was there something you left behind
Don't you remember anything I said

Hemorrhage in My Hand by Fuel

I sat in the small private therapy room near the nurses' station with Brenda, one corner softly lit by a lamp, the mood suppressed in the dim light. She was attempting another therapy session with the help of a staff doctor who claimed to be some sort of hypnotist.

"I'm going to say a few suggestive words," he was saying. "Hopefully it will help restart your memory."

He said he didn't want to hypnotize me, that he wanted me to remember for myself. I didn't see how it mattered one way or another. They could just tell me and I might stop the temper tantrums. Apparently, they didn't see it my way. I didn't really even see what it was they were trying to make me remember. All I wanted were the blanks filled in as far as how I'd gotten separated from the others and where they were.

When I said as much, Brenda replied with, "We can't tell you that because we don't know. We only know where you were right before you came to us."

"Which was where?"

She shrugged. "In a police escort. It was Phillip who alerted us to your coming. I can only assume this was something he and your parents worked out together."

I didn't say how unlikely that seemed and yet here I was of all places. She couldn't know what my parents were like, how status hungry they were, both professionally and socially. My mother would deny I was her own child before she'd ever let our dirty secrets be known to the world.

"Then I can't help you," I told them both. "Because I don't know what happened either."

"What's the last thing you remember?" Dr. Forrest asked me.

"We were in Texas somewhere. I really don't know where. We'd been moving all over the place. I think we'd been in this one place for about a week."

"What do you remember about the surroundings? Any road signs, street names?"

"Not really," I shrugged. "We didn't stray far usually."

"Stray far from what?"

"The campsite."

"So, you never went anywhere?"

I thought about it. I remembered the diner, but no, that wasn't right because Jesse wasn't there. Then we packed up and moved to a different place. It was the last campsite we were in before everything went hazy and I woke up here alone. I shook my head.

"Okay," Dr. Forrest said thoughtfully. "Tell me about this campsite you were at."

I only looked back at him blankly. They were all pretty much the same. Images and brief memories invaded my head, but I knew even then they were not in any kind of chronological order, and nothing was sparking anyway.

"What color were your tents?"

I could feel my eyes widen, not sure I'd heard him correctly. Was he serious?

"Kelly's was red, I guess. Mine was blue, I think, or green."

"Who stayed in your tent with you?"

"Jesse."

"What did he look like?"

"He's tall, dark hair, broad shoulders. Quiet. Beautiful." I heard my voice getting wistful and I snapped myself back to reality.

"Sometimes you say his name in your sleep," Brenda informed me. Not that I was surprised at this, but I was angry. I'd been here two weeks and it was the first she'd mentioned it, which meant she knew who I'd been looking for.

"That's not helpful," I told her coldly.

"Actually, it could be," Dr. Forrest said. "It would seem you dream about him often. And the others. Perhaps your subconscious is trying to tell you something."

"Perhaps it's just me wondering where he is and how I got here!" I seethed.

Brenda was nonplussed. "You mean you can't remember what happened to him at all?"

That was a tedious question and I bared my teeth at her before I realized the implication. Dr.

Forrest shot her a questioning glance, and I looked back and forth between them.

"What *happened* to Jesse?"

"I didn't mean-"

"Liar!" I screeched and pounded my fists on the arms of the chair. "Did something happen to him? Do you know? What aren't you telling me?"

"That's enough for now," Dr. Forrest concluded quickly.

"No!" I screamed, standing up when he did. "Tell me!"

Brenda stood up as well, while Dr. Forrest seemed to skitter away. She faced me and put her hands out, but I stepped back, shaking my head.

"Jade, you need to calm down," she was saying. "Let's just sit down and talk some more."

"No!" I could feel the hot tears building up. I couldn't control it. "You know something you're not telling me. Please," I begged. "Please tell me what it is."

She shook her head and attempted to get me to sit back down. "Jade, you've-"

"No!" I yelled through my tears again. "Just tell me what I need to know!"

"No." She said it calmly.

I stared back at her in frustration, my chest heaving, the hysteria rising up in me as I sobbed freely now, afraid of the truth; afraid that Jesse was not coming for me, that he couldn't. I opened my mouth and screamed. I didn't care if I gave myself an aneurism as I kicked the lamp over. Brenda was shrinking away from me as I grabbed whatever I could and throw it. A book, a cushion, a chair. I could hear Dr. Forrest on the intercom yelling out "Code 44! Code 44!" I knew what was coming but I didn't care. I continued to scream and throw things, kicking and stomping the lamp until I felt strong arms grab me, pulling me into my cell and strapping me into the bed. Then I screamed more, louder, even after the door was shut and I was left alone. Tears streamed down my face as I struggled against the restraints. I knew I wasn't getting out of here on my own but somehow driving the leather deeper into my wrists and ankles felt good, because for once since I'd gotten here I found a pain I could control. And then I kept on screaming until someone else came in, approaching me with a syringe, poking it into my arm. Then the screams started to fade as blackness overcame everything.

* * *

I liked it here. The light never seemed too obtrusive or too dim. There were flowers everywhere and fields of the greenest grass I'd ever seen. And it was soft. So very soft that it felt almost like a fuzzy blanket. The temperature was perfect. No chill, no breeze. As I walked my feet bounded my body upward with each step, a foot coming down to meet the grass periodically to propel myself forward again. It was almost like flying.

Jesse was there, smiling at me. He held his arms open to me and I felt true warmth in his embrace. I could feel his arms around me, his hands sliding over my back, his lips in my hair. I could smell him, breath in his scent. I could *feel* him.

When he spoke, he said, "Where did you go?"

"I don't know," I replied.

"Come back to me."

And then I could feel this pulling on me, dragging me away from him. Our arms still outstretched toward each other, grasping and trying to hold on as hands slid down arms, until fingertips barely touched. I struggled to stay with him, crying out, and he looked at me confused, saying my name, saying don't go. But I couldn't stop the force pulling me away from him.

"Stay with me," I pleaded.

"I can't," he said as I moved further away from him.

And then I woke up.

My wrists and ankles were bound. My arms ached from being held up over my head for so long. They were cold, as if all the blood had drained from them. I fought against the waking as the fog cleared minute by minute until I knew I'd been in a drug induced dream. And it had been so much better than anything real.

I was feeling so desperate. I couldn't do anything but cry. I thought about the week that I'd believed Jesse had abandoned me, remembering the numbness, the wish to sleep forever, to forget. I had truly stopped caring about anything then. This was different. Even if I could control all the crying and screaming I wouldn't. It was all I had to remind me that there were still things I cared about. That there was still hope.

It wasn't long before a tech named Joel came in and unstrapped me. He was nice so I didn't freak out on him right away like I would have Brenda.

"Slowly," he said when I started to sit up. "You've been out a whole day."

The blood rushed to my head, down my arms and into my hands, the tingling sensation turning into a thousand stinging pinpricks inside my arms. It was a rushing feeling, causing my eyesight to go dark for a few seconds. Joel stood nearby just in case I fell over or something. I pushed myself off the bed and stood up. We looked at each other.

"Think you could eat?" he asked. I only shrugged back. "Come on, breakfast just started."

I followed him into the dining room where the rest of my unit sat at tables of four, which were arranged in neat rows on one side of the room. On the other side was the same setup, those tables for another unit of patients that shared our floor, their wing on the opposite side of the nurses' station. No inter-unit communicating was allowed. Several of the kids from my unit watched me curiously as I shuffled into the room, found a tray of food and sat down wordlessly. Others didn't pay any attention to me. I suspected they were over my theatrics. So was I, actually. It was all so draining.

I picked at my food, not really interested in eating. The others at my table continued in their conversation, though one of them, a kid named Jason whispered to me, "Are you okay?" I lifted my eyes to his, mostly to make sure he'd been talking to me, and then just returned my attention to my eggs.

After breakfast the room cleared and everyone gathered into the common room for our morning ritual of hell therapy. I sat down in a large stuffed chair, exhausted, as the room filled up. Brenda and Lori came in, sat down and began the session. I put my head back, looked at the ceiling, and tried to drown out the voices. They were all talking about their feelings, about their goals and how they felt they were progressing. I was thinking about my dream with Jesse, the feeling of his arms around me, the pressure of his body against mine, his smell. It had been so real. I felt so alone. The emptiness in my stomach had taken over once again.

"Jade?" I heard someone say my name, and I lifted my head to see everyone looking at me. I waited. "We're having reflection now," Brenda said to me. "Anything you want to say?"

That was a pointless question considering I'd been there two weeks now, hadn't said a word, and everyone knew where I'd been for the last twenty-four hours. The fact that the techs continued to pull the others' attention toward me only made me madder. If they really wanted to help me maybe they should stop playing these stupid games.

I just leaned my head back and ignored them.

Finally, the ones who went to school were excused to gather their books and line up at the rear door that led down to the classrooms on the basement level. I hadn't been there yet because I was still in hospital robes, but I knew that kids from all the different units went there together, so their rules against patients interacting was kind of moot. The rest of us who were still waiting for that privilege, either because we were high risk patients, or because their home schools hadn't started sending in any work yet, were to stay in the common room. It was so boring. The techs would give us stupid assignments to do that had little effect on our therapy or our education, or they'd continue with some sort of group therapy, sometimes even breaking us up into one-on-one sessions. I noticed that while most of the other kids did this, the techs never put me with another patient. Most likely because they knew it wasn't going to help whoever they stuck me with.

Dr. Forrest came in then and gestured for me to follow him into another room where we could speak in private. I sat down in a chair opposite his and waited.

"How are you feeling?"

I shrugged. "Tired."

He nodded. "That's to be expected." When I didn't say anything else, he asked, "Have you been able to recall anymore memories?"

"No."

"Have you been dreaming about your friends again?"

"Yes."

"What are your dreams like? Do they take place in Texas?"

"No. They're not real."

He mused over that for a minute before saying, "That must be very difficult for you."

I shrugged and looked away because no amount of psychology or pretend sympathy was going to make me do what they wanted. He sat still looking back at me, waiting for me to say something. I could play this silent game all day, and he knew it by know, but there was one thing I really wanted to know.

"Have any of them tried to contact me?"

"Jade, you know only family can call or visit you."

"That doesn't mean they haven't tried," I reminded him.

He just looked at me blankly and said, "No. No one's tried to contact you." I couldn't tell if he was lying or not, so instead I nodded in resignation.

"Do they even know where I am?"

"I can't say," he replied. I believed him. Not because he wouldn't say, but because he really didn't know.

"I'm tired," I said again. He nodded and took me back to my cell, allowing me time to rest before lunch.

I did sleep some, but mostly I wanted to be alone to think. I tried to remember every detail that I could, but the only real thing I could recall was the dream that had felt so real when Jesse held me close to him and whispered those words. They were the words he'd said to me after he came back, when we were standing near the pool at that last campground we stayed at before I woke up here. Except for the part when he said he couldn't stay. That part left me feeling hollower than waking up alone. I had to face facts and realize that if I were here, it was unlikely the others were all free, looking for me. That meant Jesse could be in jail somewhere. And then I remembered that awful week he was gone and the things I'd felt, the things I did. How he tried to come back to me; how he said he understood what

I'd wanted all along and he wanted it, too; how he'd promised to take care of me forever. As much as I thought about Kelly and Corie and where they were as well, there was only one true thing missing from my life.

Sleep came and I gratefully grabbed on to it, hoping desperately for a dream of Jesse. I needed something to cling to. Even if it was in my dreams, I'd rather have that than a reality of void and unanswered questions. Scenes of our time together flashed in front of me like a movie, though in no particular order of actual events. Kelly was laughing, which was always what he did best, in his infectious way. Corie danced. Jesse smiled quietly, holding his hand out toward me. I reached for it.

*   *   *

"How are you today?"

I sat in the private therapy room with Joel, surprised that he was the tech assigned to be abused by me. Usually it was Brenda, who was one of the oldest, more experienced techs. Joel was young. He was sweet though, and cute in a boyish way, and I wondered if this had been some ploy designed by the techs to get me to talk.

"Can I ask you a question?" I said instead of answering his.

"Sure."

"Why do you work here?" It came out a little more bluntly than I had intended, but I'd only been given permission to ask one question when really, I had many.

"I'm an intern," he replied after a brief pause. "I study psychology. Well, forensic psychology, actually, but I needed work related experience for my degree."

I nodded. "So, you're in college?"

"Yes," he smiled. "Does that bother you?"

On the contrary I preferred him over all the other techs, though Brenda was the only one I really disliked. I didn't feel like Joel was one of them. He was closer to me in age and seemed to have a more down to earth grasp of what the patients needed. I only shook my head in reply.

"Let's get back to you, shall we?" He reminded me of my last session with Brenda and Dr. Forrest, and how I exploded and had to be restrained and even drugged. I nodded, agreeing that it happened. "I need you to focus on anything you can remember right before you came here. Anything at all. Who was with you, what were you doing, that sort of thing. Do you think you can do that?"

"I can try," I said.

"Good. Let's get started."

He asked questions that pulled memories to the front, made me describe in as much detail as I could what the campground looked like, what I remembered last doing there and who with. I pushed the dreams away as I focused on what was real, but it was all too blurry.

"Everyone keeps asking me to remember that last day, but I don't. I don't know when was my last day." I was extremely frustrated because all the memories were only fragments, images of Jesse and

182

Kelly and Corie, but those could have been images from any memory, not just my last ones.

"It's okay," Joel reassured me. "You don't have to have all the answers right now."

"I do!" I said desperately. "Something is wrong and I need to know now!"

"Well," he said calmly, "that's what we're trying to do. So, let's just go at it again, alright?"

I agreed but it was redundant. He used suggestive words, descriptive words, often using the same ones I had previously, trying to trigger something, I suppose. Sometimes they invoked a new image or feeling, but mostly they weren't revealing. I described the layout of our campsite, the ones around us and how many people had been there, wandering around listing to music, laughing, drinking. I described Jesse's car. I closed my eyes and brought his smell to the front of my memory and described how it made me feel, being alone in the tent after he left me, and then how filled the pit in my stomach became after Jesse came back. I described Kelly's big green eyes, his electric smile, and how I missed the sound of his laughter. I described Corie's energy and how she was always up for anything, how she always had my back, how we held on to each other's hands and spun around and around…

My eyes snapped open and I sat up quickly. Joel jumped a little in his seat.

"I remember," I said fearfully. My eyes felt the size of saucers as they glazed over and I reached back into time and tried to play it out in my head once again.

"I was high," I whispered. "I was so high. Corie and I were spinning and I could hear Jesse and Kelly laughing. And then there were these lights…just all these bright, flashing lights. I couldn't see anything else."

"And then?" Joel prompted quietly.

"And then I was running," I said, feeling my brows furrow because this was strange. I didn't remember this before and I didn't understand why I'd be running. "Someone had grabbed my arm and was pulling me quickly."

"Who was pulling you?"

I shrugged. I didn't know, but it only made sense that if something was happening Kelly would grab Corie and Jesse would come for me. I envisioned the running, the pulling on my arm, the disorientation, the fear. And then I was there.

I could see the lights flashing all around me as if I were really there. I looked at the hand holding mine as we ran, at the ground flying past beneath my feet. We were headed toward the trees, away from the others. This wasn't Jesse's hand. That wasn't Jesse in front of me. The person stopped and instructed me to stay put, hide behind the trees and wait. I could hear someone yelling my name. I thought it was Jesse's voice, but sometimes it sounded like Kelly. The voices would get close and then far away again as if they were running around in circles, searching randomly for me. There were noises everywhere, people running, voices yelling out for others. The person who had brought me to the woods turned and ran off, calling out names of people he was looking for. I tried to yell out, but my tongue was swollen, my mouth frozen. In frustration I got up and started running back toward the lights.

Cars were everywhere, stopped and parked on the road, blocking everything. I could hear Kelly's voice, yelling angrily, and I went straight for it, calling his name.

"Jade, no!" he yelled. I saw him then, standing between two police officers, struggling against them as he stared at me in horror. "Run!"

"Jade!" Jesse's voice came faintly from somewhere behind me. I turned and saw Corie crying, heard Kelly yelling at the police to let her go.

Someone was grabbing me again, pushing me into a police car. I was screaming, fighting, crying, yelling out for Jesse. I could still hear him calling my name but I couldn't see him. All I could see were the lights and the ground as I was being forced into the back of the car. Corie was screaming, too, and I caught a glimpse of her slapping a police officer before he shut the car door on her, caging her inside.

"Jade!" It was Jesse, closer now. In my struggle I turned to see him coming out of the woods, running fast, yelling and threatening the cops to let me go. "She didn't do anything! Let her go!" And as I was being pushed down into the car I heard a gunshot.

Pandemonium broke loose all around me. I could hear Corie scream out in anguish and Kelly cursing. I pressed my face against the glass and saw him turn and punch the cop holding him in the face.

I was sobbing hysterically as Corie wailed and beat on the window of her car next to mine. Jesse lay on the ground, a pool of blood spreading out beneath him.

Kelly had gone to his knees. His arms were bound behind him and he fell, defeated. His head hung low and I could see his shoulders shaking violently. I kicked at the cage-like divider as hard as I could, repeatedly, while screaming Jesse's name over and over. A cop came over and shouted at me through the window to stop. I placed my hands over my ears and screamed as long and as loud as I could until finally a paramedic came over, and with the help of two officers who held me down, injected me with something. As I wandered off into a dark, dreamless sleep, I could hear Corie's sobs and Kelly's cussing fading away slowly, until there was nothing.

I opened my eyes. Joel was looking at me tentatively. If I had ever believed he knew something of this, I didn't now. I sat there trembling, unable to voice my deepest fear, unwilling to accept the memory for truth. If I had felt desperate and alone before it was nothing compared to now. The emptiness was taking over my entire body and I hugged myself as I balled up in my chair and sobbed.

CHAPTER FOURTEEN

Wait, I feel you coming now
The chase is all you care about
I fake hating the things you made in me
I love the pain

Mind Games by Colours

Listen to me because I am only going to say this once. I know I hurt you, and I'm sorry. But you need to know that I love you. It doesn't matter if we are together or not, you need to remember that always, understand?

Jesse's words haunted me constantly. I had no pictures of him, no letters, nothing. Just the memory of his deep and passionate voice, his dark and stormy eyes. Did he somehow know it would come to this, or did he simply accept that at some point we'd be torn apart? I would have gladly gone home, walked out of his life forever, if only it meant he'd still be alive. He had so much more to offer than anyone ever realized. How could this person no longer exist?

For several days I wandered around the unit in a daze. I didn't talk to anyone, though I did what was expected of me for the most part. We had a routine. Get up, eat breakfast, gather in the common room for a group therapy session, go to classes if you were allowed or sit around and pretend to be constructive, eat lunch, go back to class or be forced into some sort of psychoanalysis therapy with one of the babysitters, do exercises (I hated this the most), quiet time, dinner, then more group therapy. Weekends were worse because there were no classes but twice as many therapy sessions. On any given night someone could get a visitor, family only, and Saturday mornings were a special kind of hell because there was always a family therapy session scheduled with every patient on the unit and their parents all in one room. The psych techs and family members sat in chairs that lined the walls of the room while all the lowly patients sat inside the circle on the floor. All was bared for everyone to hear.

My parents never came.

So, I followed the routine, going here and there when it was expected. I listened to the other patients in group therapy talking and pouring their hearts out on the carpet for all to see while I stared at the walls. Their words were mumbles to me. I had no real desire to listen, to give feedback, or to talk to anyone about anything, and I often found myself staring vacantly at something, or sometimes at nothing, while I was supposed to be doing something else. I was just going through the motions.

The other patients did try to be friendly at first. They'd invite me into a group discussion or a game, or even just try to talk. But even as I sat among them I found that I couldn't participate. Eventually they left me alone and I remained in my cocoon. The psych techs told me I wasn't trying hard enough, that I wasn't going to benefit from my treatment because I never socialized or spoke in group therapy. But I had nothing to say. I didn't see how being locked up with fifteen other juvenile delinquents could be considered treatment.

Time crept by and every day I was in here was another day the others were getting further away from me. I refused to eat and they constantly threatened to send me up to ICU where they could force feed me. I faked it by pushing the food around my plate, nibbling when they watched me, and hiding bits in my napkins. I just didn't care.

I was scared; I was angry. They wanted to know why I refused to speak, but that wasn't entirely true. I answered direct questions and I asked for things when I had to. It was ridiculous really. We couldn't even take a shower without clearing it with someone first. We were supposed to be learning to control our impulses, but if that was their main goal they were definitely falling short with me. Of all the reasons I could have been locked up for, they wanted to focus on training me to ask if I could pee. It was stupid. Most days I was numb. Unresponsive. Then there were days the techs would try to force me to talk, causing me to cry, scream, and throw things. The only way I could be subdued was to be physically picked up and strapped into my bed.

"You certainly are a drama queen, aren't you?" Brenda said as she stood over me. I struggled with my restraints and hissed at her. "You think you're the first person to come in here with real issues?"

I glared back.

"You've been in here long enough," she continued. "It's time you give it up."

I screamed then to shut her up. I couldn't listen to her voice for one more second. I didn't want to hear her patronizing, condescending, assuming words telling me that I needed help. I didn't want her help. I wanted out. And I continued to scream until she turned off the lights and left the room, leaving me alone in the dark.

I had a lot of dreams. I wouldn't say they were nightmares but I usually woke up with a start in a cold sweat. Sometimes I'd choke on a scream just as it was tearing from my throat, and other times I'd be crying. I was terrified of something but it wasn't the cliché monster under the bed sort of dreams. Not even the feeling of being grabbed and pulled into the darkness as I had been once before. These dreams were scary in the way that I felt an irrevocable void. I just didn't know what it was.

There were days I swore I didn't even know the date. It just didn't matter. The only real break in our routine was on the weekends when the bulk of the family visits came, and I felt like we were just sitting around, waiting for the tourists to come through and check out the freak show. My days were monotonous. I thought I would literally go crazy if I had to sit through one more group therapy session, ask to go to the bathroom, or even fill out another damn menu for my meals the next day.

They didn't bother me at first, the techs, once it came out that I'd remembered all that I could, and what had happened. I honestly still didn't know how much any of them knew, how much my revelations surprised them, but I didn't care about that anymore. Even though I still had no idea what had happened to Corie and Kelly, it didn't carry nearly as much weight as knowing that the three of us were still alive and Jesse wasn't.

When Phillip came I was angry. I didn't say it at first. He sat down in a chair next to me in the common room. It was the middle of a weekday so there were very few others in there with us. We sat off in a corner while the remaining high-risk patients put puzzles together on the large table. I watched them for a minute, thinking of how our time spent in here was such a waste of time. But when I considered the alternative, I knew that I'd rather stay here. Locked up, away from the real world. Away from anything that would trigger the pain and the helplessness.

"So, how are you holding up?" Phillip asked me. My eyes moved from the puzzlers to his face, where I held his steady gaze. Sighing, I looked away, bored. "I understand you remembered some very troubling things. Do you want to talk about it?"

"Are you serious?" I snapped at him. "I wanted to talk to you about this a month ago. You promised me you'd come and tell me how I got here, and you didn't! I have nothing to say to you."

"I understand the things you're feeling," he said to me. "But taking it out on me won't help you heal."

"It might!"

"You're not really angry with me. But I recognize that you are very angry, and rightly so. So, I want to do an exercise. Are you up for it?"

"What's that?" I asked sarcastically. "Punching a pillow? Role play with an empty chair so I can say goodbye? You don't know how I feel! You lied to me."

"That's not fair," he was saying. "Your parents didn't want me to say anything to you. And the doctors here agreed that you needed to remember as much as you could on your own."

"My parents?" I screeched. "Oh, that's right. That's why I'm here. Because of them. Did they make you pinkie swear to never tell another living soul about all this embarrassment for them, or did you have to draw blood?"

"Jade, stop this nonsense!"

"You're not even my doctor," I ranted. "You're their friend. And in case you haven't noticed, they've not come to visit me once since I've been here. They're too ashamed. So, they expect you to fix me and then send me home with a pretty bow on top of my head."

There was silence as he considered what I said. He wanted to argue my every point, but what purpose would it serve? I was right at least about him helping them, getting me admitted into this psychiatric hospital he worked with. Had it not been for that, there was no telling where I'd be right now.

"Do you want them to come visit you?" I shook my head. "I was under the impression they were giving you space. Time to heal first. And then they'd come when you were ready."

I snorted. "They don't ever consider me first. Ever. And I don't want them to come, either."

"Jade, I may not be your official doctor, and yes, I am friends with your father, but I do care about your rehabilitation. So far, you've sat in here a month and accomplished nothing. It's time to start doing things, to begin working toward healing. You need to attend AA meetings. You need to start participating in your therapy. You need to heal so you can return to your life."

I heard it all, knew it was what I was supposed to be doing all along, but I couldn't even fake caring enough to do it. I could sit in this hospital and rot away for all I cared. There was nothing waiting for me. There was no life to return to. And when it hit me like that, I started crying again.

"There are other programs available to you," he said carefully as he handed me a box of tissues. "You need to learn how to grieve for all your losses. We can help."

"You can't help," I sobbed. "There's nothing there." I was pointing to my chest. "It's just a big hole and I can't…I can't breathe."

"But you can feel."

"Make it go away," I said to him. "I don't want to feel anymore."

*   *   *

I'd been sitting on the floor in the long hallway. At one end was the nurses' station, past that were the elevators which led to freedom, and on the other end was the common room. All along the hallway on either side were all the private rooms that the patients lived in. Each one housed two beds, a nightstand in between, two wardrobes, a sink and mirror, and a small table with two chairs. I was still in hospital robes, living in one of the two restraints rooms that were through the common room. I didn't know if they were punishing me for not doing anything; if they kept me in robes and in the cell as a way of keeping me in place. I'd seen plenty of patients come and go in the month I'd been here and all of them were assigned to a regular room right away. Even the ones who came in robes. And usually they were in their own clothes within a week.

I watched with half interest as a new girl came in. She was standing by the nurses' station in a robe, looking terrified. Others were peeking out of their doors, or standing in the doorway of the common room, watching as well. It was the same every time a new person came in. They were all speculating. I didn't bother wondering what her story was. Considering why most of these kids were in here, as some sort of punishment from their parents, I knew it would only be a matter of time before this new girl was gone again. There were only a few others that had been in here long enough for me to realize who had real issues to deal with. Mark was one, who was still here and probably would remain for a long time, though I had no idea why. There was a girl named Karen who appeared to be very well adjusted, though after several months she was discharged and came back via ICU within a week with a gash the length of her forearm, down to the bone. Another boy, Jed, who was in and out, back and forth between here and ICU, so I rarely saw him. Of course, other than Mark I never spoke to anyone. He was the only one who couldn't care less if I ever spoke or not, but interestingly enough was not afraid to approach me.

"What's up, Cool Cat?" he said, plopping down next to me on the floor. He'd been calling me that since the night I met him. I grunted something in reply and we both stared down the hall at the new girl being processed. "Looks like a new addition to the zoo," he commented, which brought a small smile to my face. We thought alike.

We remained in silence, watching the new girl. She had a tear-stained face and turned her back to all the gawkers. I'm sure it was mortifying being sent here and then having to be on display. Sometimes these other kids could be heartless the way they made such a big deal about newcomers, like they hadn't ever been in the same boat. I was lucky coming in unconscious. I'm sure that was a great disappointment to the rest of them, having to wait days to get a good look at me, and then even more curious because of all my screaming fits behind closed doors.

I went back to scribbling in my notebook. I had pages of it. Since I didn't have anything to say to anyone, I just randomly scribbled to keep my mind from wandering. It didn't help much but sometimes it was better than just staring off into space. Mark opened a book and started to read. We did this often, sitting quietly together, though I rarely initiated it.

After some time a pair of feet approached me and I looked up to see one of the nurses standing above me. "You have a phone call, on number one."

That surprised me. I'd never had a call before. I glanced at Mark to see if maybe the nurse was speaking to him, but he only shrugged at me.

"Who is it?"

"It's your brother, Johnathon," she said. Of course, it was, since only family was allowed to contact me.

I stood up and followed her back toward the nurses' station. The hallway jutted off to the left here, which led to the other unit, the one we shared a dining room with but were not allowed to speak to. On the wall where the two hallways met were four pay phones. I really had no idea who'd be calling me. It was unlikely my brother even knew where I was, and even if he did, he wasn't likely to call.

I picked up the phone and held it to my ear. Cautiously, I said, "Hello?"

"Jade!" a relieved voice called out through the phone.

"Kelly?" The name came out broken as I immediately choked on a sob. The tears were falling already at the familiar voice, and I was comforted and frightened at the same time. "Oh, Kelly, how did you find me?"

"I called Anne," he said it like it should be obvious. "She told me to use your brother's name. Don't worry, she won't tell anyone."

"Where are you?"

"I'm in a half-way house in Elgin. Are...are you okay?"

"Oh, Kelly," I sobbed. "I hate it here. I miss you so much."

"I know how you feel," he said. "Just hold on, babe. It's not forever."

"Kelly," I whispered. I had to keep saying his name. It was the first real thing I'd experienced since being in here. "Where's Corie? Is she okay?"

"I...I don't know," he said quietly. "I hope so."

"What do you mean?"

"I'm not allowed to know where she is. I'll never see her again. Neither of us will."

"I'm so sorry," I cried. By now the patients were lining up in the hallway, getting ready to go to dinner, and they had all shifted their attention from the new girl to me. I turned my back to them and clung to the phone.

"What for? This isn't your fault," he said.

"Yes, it is," I insisted. "It's all my fault. Everything that happened is because of me, because I pushed for us to leave in the first place. And because I wouldn't leave when Jesse wanted me to."

"No, Jade," Kelly said sadly. "It's not. You can't blame yourself. I don't blame you."

"Oh, my god!" I wailed. "Is it true then, about Jesse?" He was silent. It was all the confirmation I needed. My shoulders were wracked with sobs. I couldn't breathe. I covered my face with my hand and hid from the onlookers as I gasped for air.

"All he wanted was to get to you," Kelly finally said. "That's all either of us wanted. To keep you safe."

"Everything is so different now," I bawled. "I can't deal with this, Kelly. I just can't. I don't...kn...know how."

"Yes, you can," he said sternly. "We can get through this. Me and you, we've been through tough times before."

"Not like this!"

"I know, but we are survivors. We always have been." He had more faith in me than I did.

"When I leave here they are going to send me home."

"I know. It'll be okay, Jade. It's time for you to go home. It's time for you to finish this with your parents and get your life together."

"What about you?"

"Don't worry about me. No matter what, I'll always be there for you. You're going to be fine."

I started coughing, choking on my tears. I sobbed and heaved until I thought my stomach was going to come right up through my throat.

"Jade," his voice sounded pained. "Please say something. Are you okay?"

"I never told him that I loved him. I never...I never told him," I whispered.

"He knew." But I was shaking my head violently. Jesse had such a hard life. Even his own mother didn't want him. How could he know when people truly cared? Even I pushed him away. I hoped more than anything he went knowing that I had loved him with my whole heart. But I couldn't know for sure. It was my greatest regret and I knew it would haunt me forever.

"I miss him so much."

"I know you do, babe," Kelly said. "Listen, I hate leaving you like this but I have to go. I just had to make sure you were okay." He paused, and when

I didn't answer, he said, "It's just you and me again. I'll always love you."

"I love you, too."

"Take care of yourself now. You're going to be just fine. I know you will."

Panic set in when I realized he was saying goodbye. "Kelly?"

"Bye, Jade."

"Wait!"

The phone went dead in my hand, and I stared at it disbelieving. I yelled his name again only to hear the pinging of a disconnection. Angrily, I slammed the receiver down on the hook, then picked it up again and slammed it some more. A nurse popped her head around the corner and told me to stop beating on the phone.

"No!" I screamed, sobbing. "I won't!" I started pummeling my fists on the wall, tears still streaming uncontrollably down my face. I yelled, "I won't! I won't! I won't!" And once again my arms were pinned down at my sides as large hands clamped around me, picking me up.

This time they didn't put me in restraints. Instead I was pushed into a quiet room, the door locked behind me. These rooms were just like the restraints rooms only there were no beds. It was an empty, cold room with hard, white walls and floor, and bright florescent lights above. The only window was the small observation pane of glass in the door. I don't like small spaces and I was having a hard enough time breathing through all my crying. I turned toward the door and pounded on it, screaming at them to let me out.

"I can't stay in here!"

"I'm sorry, Jade," Brenda said from the other side. Liar. "You need to remain in there until you calm down."

"Let me out! Please, let me out of here!" I kicked at the door. She didn't reply.

I don't know how long I sat in there, curled up on the floor in a corner of the brightly lit room. I missed dinner. No one seemed to care, but I wasn't hungry anyway. I could hear the others coming back from the dining room, talking about me as they passed through the hallway.

"Is Jade still in there?"

"Must be," another replied. "If they can't control her she'll be sent upstairs."

Upstairs was ICU. I didn't know what that meant or what happens up there. Visions of *One Flew Over The Cuckoo's Nest* popped in my head, and I couldn't help but wonder if that was my future. Maybe it would be better.

When the door finally opened, Joel stood on the other side. I lifted my head from where I rested it on my arms, propped up on my knees, pulled up against my body. He smiled.

"You hungry?" he asked. I shook my head. "Come on out then."

I pulled myself up slowly. It felt as though I hadn't walked in days. In truth I'd been eating very little and all my energy was expended between the tantrums and the crying. I wobbled a little and stepped toward the door. He held out a hand as if to steady me, but even I knew they weren't allowed to touch us unless we were being restrained. As soon as I started walking my eyes blackened and I felt faint.

"Easy," he whispered, catching me. My arms braced myself against the fall, against his chest, and I could feel his arms go around me.

"You're not supposed to," I whispered faintly. And then it went black.

I woke up in my bed. It was dark and quiet. I had no idea how long I'd been asleep, but it was clear it was late and the whole unit was down for the night. I opened my door slowly, looking for the night nurse. She wasn't in her usual place, monitoring the hallway. Instead, Joel sat in the common room, long past his normal working hours.

"Hey," he said. "Are you okay?"

I nodded. "I need to go to the bathroom."

He only nodded and gestured toward the hallway. Down at the other end near the nurses' station, I saw the night nurse keeping watch on the regular rooms from her desk. When I came back into the common room, Joel stood up as I walked back toward my room.

"Feeling better?"

I nodded again. "Did you carry me in before?"

"Yes."

"What happened?"

"You fainted," he said. "It's no surprise with everything you're dealing with. But you need to start eating, Jade. It worries me."

That took me aback. I never heard any of the techs getting worried over the patients. They looked at us as a job, nothing more. But then again, Joel was different anyway.

"Are they going to send me upstairs?" I whispered from my doorway.

"I don't know," he admitted. "I'm not sure that's what you need."

"I need anything that will help me forget," I told him sadly. Then I closed my door and went back to bed.

CHAPTER FIFTEEN

I had all and then most of you
Some and now none of you
Take me back to the night we met
I don't know what I'm supposed to do
Haunted by the ghost of you

The Night We Met by Lord Huron

I spent my seventeenth birthday behind locked doors. I hadn't felt a breeze or breathed fresh air in over two months. I finally got my clothes. Anne brought them to me when Phillip conceded and allowed me to shed my hospital robes. It was part of an agreement that if I were to try harder, he'd put me in a regular room and let me go to school. I just wanted regular clothes. I couldn't care less about school and sharing a room with someone hardly appealed to me.

I didn't completely ignore the bargain. He said I needed to start talking, he didn't specify to whom. The only person I had ever really spoken to was Joel, and I figured Mark was a decent person to start with since he seemed nice and we had a weird sort of friendship anyway. I still wasn't ever going to open up in group therapy, so it seemed a worthless goal to me.

I went to AA meetings on the third floor where the drug and alcohol addicted kids were housed. Next to them, I found out, was the unit for kids who had eating disorders. There was even a children's unit on the first floor for kids as young as four. I couldn't imagine what a four-year-old needed to be locked up in a mental ward for. The rest of the units were for kids between the ages of thirteen and nineteen. My unit and the neighboring one were for behavior disorders. Clearly there was no defined unit for someone like me.

I spoke very little in the meetings, though the others were more compassionate than the kids on my unit. These kids had a better idea of what a life of using was like, and how complicated things could get in the aftermath. These were people who had a better reason for being here, I thought. Not like my unit. That was more of a daycare for kids who'd skipped too much school, or broke curfew too many times, and their parents didn't know what else to do with them. At least down here, no one stared at me, or waited to see what I would do or say next. I could talk if I wanted, and if I didn't, I kept silent.

AA was on Wednesdays, which was also the night that our unit held family circle meetings. These were sort of a tagalong to the Saturday morning family sessions. Kind of like that middle of the week church service. Since my family never came, and I had no desire to sit through these sessions and listen to other people's problems, I always opted for AA. It got me away from my own unit and allowed a few minutes of quiet in the elevator. Most times Joel escorted me and retrieved me after.

"Have a good meeting?" he smiled at me in the elevator. I shrugged. "Do you even talk in there?" he chuckled as he asked.

"No," I admitted.

"Then why do you go?"

"I like to get away from my house." That's what the units were actually called. Each one had a name. Prairie House, Town House, Manor House. Mine was Country House. It made me think of some children's book where all the characters were mice. Joel only nodded in reply. We were silent the rest of the way to the fourth floor.

As the elevator doors opened and I started out toward the hallway, I glanced back at Joel. He stood, waiting for me to go ahead of him, and our eyes locked just for a second. I couldn't explain it. I'd never looked back at him before. Somehow, I felt safer around him. I trusted him. He just smiled and I looked away, heading toward the common room.

Brenda approached me in the doorway of the common room, and said, "Pack up. You're moving tonight."

I stalled. I wanted to ask if I were going to ICU, but that didn't make any sense. I had normal clothes now, I'd been going to AA, I hadn't had a breakdown or temper tantrum in weeks. I was even talking to Mark now.

She pointed to a room behind me, three doors down the hallway. I was finally going into a regular room. My new roommate stood in the doorway, staring at me as if her worst nightmare was coming true. It was the new girl, Carly, though technically she wasn't new anymore. I just nodded and grabbed my clothes and things, taking them into the room. I could see which bed and wardrobe mine would be immediately, the one closest to the door, and started to put things away. Carly sat on her bed and watched me.

"I'm not going to smother you in your sleep," I said, my back still to her as I folded my clothes before stacking them on the shelves in the wardrobe. "You can relax a little."

"I heard you never speak," she finally said.

"Well, clearly I can."

"I know that," she said with a roll of her eyes. "We've all heard you screaming, and you yell out in your sleep." It wasn't said rudely, but I had no reply for any of it. "Who's Jesse?"

I turned and looked at her. It would be nice to get along with someone, to have a friend in this place, it really would. But I wasn't going to tell anyone about him. Ever. It was my heart I was holding onto. My very fragile wall of emotions to hold together. These burdens were mine alone to carry.

"I'm sorry," she said sincerely. "I have no right to pry. It's just that you always look so sad. I thought maybe talking about it would help."

"Did the techs put you up to this?" I demanded.

"No," she was shaking her head. "I just…heard that your boyfriend was shot, and I-"

"You *heard*?" How on earth had she heard this? Did that mean everyone knew? In anger I spun away and out the door.

I had nowhere to go. My privacy had been ripped from me the moment they decided to move me into a shared room, and I realized then it was just another ploy to mainstream me whether I was willing or not. I couldn't go into the common room where most of the other patients were. I tried to keep back tears of frustration as I strode toward the nurses' station.

Joel looked up as I approached him sitting at the desk. He smiled at first, but it faded at seeing the look on my face. "What is it?"

"Put me in the quiet room," I said between clenched teeth. My whole head hurt as I tried to keep the tears from flowing and remain in control.

"Why? Jade, what's going on?" He stood up now, concerned.

"Now, please!" I whispered fiercely. But then a sob escaped, and I said desperately, "I have nowhere to go! There's nowhere to go in here!"

He shushed me and ushered me into the private session room. Since it was getting later in the evening no one would be using it. Most of the patients were settling down, getting ready for bed. He guided me with a gesture of his hands, a safe distance remaining between us, and we sat down next to each other in arm chairs.

"Did moving into a room bother you this much?"

"No," I shook my head, wiping at my face. I was so angry that it never took much to get me bawling. It was like I had no self-control anymore at all. And I really did want to stop. "It was something she said to me. She said she knew Jesse was shot."

I looked up at him then. His face was pale and he swallowed. "I'm so sorry," he finally said. "That must have come as a shock to you."

"How did she know? Does everyone know?" He could only shrug, clearly as confused as I was. "Who is talking about my business with the other patients?" I demanded.

"I don't know, Jade, honestly," Joel said.

"Brenda!" I growled and stood up. He shot to his feet and held his hands up at me.

"Jade, I will go get her, and you can talk it out rationally. But you can't just go storming out there and cause a scene."

"Why not?" I yelled. "She clearly doesn't care about how I feel!" I turned and yanked open the door before he could stop me.

Storming into the common room, Joel following me anxiously, I approached a startled Brenda. There were still a handful of patients in the room, but it only took a few whispers to get the rest of them peeking out of their doorways.

"What is it, Jade?" she said in an intolerant voice.

"You have no right to tell people anything about me. It's my life!"

"What are you talking about?"

I could feel Joel's hand on my arm, trying to get me to stop, but I only jerked my arm free of his grasp. He didn't push it, knowing I'd either go ballistic, or someone would question why he was touching me at all. The only thing he could do was sigh and stand by the intercom just in case I was going to end up in restraints.

"Don't lie to me!" I yelled at her.

"Jade," she started calmly. "You may not realize it, but you have a lot to offer these people.

208

You could really help some of them if only you would open up and start healing."

"Really?" I yelled back, exasperated. "What will they learn, Brenda? How to mourn your life away? How to lose everything? What?"

"You can't keep it all inside forever," she replied.

"So, you decided my story was going to help someone else? You condescending bitch, you had no right to discuss my private business with anyone!"

"Go to your room, Jade," she said. "Now!"

"Or what?" I said back angrily. "You'll have me restrained? There's something new."

I gave up then. Screaming at her in front of other people wouldn't accomplish anything. She had the power to do what she wanted. If she wanted me locked in the quiet room, or restrained in my old cell, even sent upstairs, all she had to do was snap her fingers. But I knew she would have denied everything had I confronted her in private. I wasn't even trying to get her confession. I already knew she was the one with the big mouth. I only wanted to call her out in a way that would prevent her from doing it again, and I'd accomplished that. I turned away from her then and went into my room, pushing the door shut as hard as I could, which wasn't really possible because the doors were all on pneumatic hinges. So, I had to wait until it was nearly shut and then slam it the rest of the way. Carly looked terrified as I stomped over to my bed and flopped down on it.

"I'm really sorry," she said.

"I'm glad you said something," I told her. I lay on my back staring at the ceiling. "Let me ask you something. Didn't you think there was something wrong with her talking about me to the other patients?"

"I…" she stuttered, confused. "I didn't know. Some of the other kids were talking about it one night at dinner. I assumed you'd said something."

I sighed. "I never talk but I told them all my business. Yeah, that makes sense."

"You're right," she agreed. "It was stupid of me."

I rolled onto my side and wrapped my arms around my middle. I would not be comforted. Jesse's arms were not there to hold me and would never again. I missed him so much my body ached. And after nearly two weeks of being strong, all I could do was ball up, fetal, and cry.

Brenda wasn't there the next day. She usually came in around lunchtime and stayed until bedtime, which was ten. She did get two days off a week, so at first I didn't think anything of it, but when she still didn't return I started to wonder. There was no way my accusation could have gone unnoticed by the other techs, and with the number of drama queens I was living with, no doubt someone tattled to someone higher up on the ladder. But my aim had not been to get her fired so I hoped that hadn't been the case.

Joel and I were in the elevator again when I asked him about it. "She didn't get fired, did she?"

He looked at me before speaking. "You know I'm not supposed to talk about it."

I snorted back. "Yeah, because confidentiality is so revered here."

"She wasn't fired. Just suspended a few days. It might be good to stay clear of her for a while when she gets back."

"Maybe she should stay clear of me," I muttered as the elevator doors opened and I stomped out.

I started school the following week. This was a joke. The classrooms were housed in an older part of the building, which was part basement because the building was built on slanted land. So even though it's referred to as the basement, it's really not because the loading docks came up to one side. There was also a second floor in this older section that held only three small classrooms. The main part of the school had about six classrooms, a tiny library with little more than a collection of National Geographic magazines and a few tattered classics, and a padded room used as a gym. I was glad I didn't have to participate in some stupid PE class because the walls were covered in red wrestling mats, giving off a hot, closed-in, sickening feeling. Mostly when I walked by I just saw kids shooting basketballs into hoops.

By now my teachers in Deerfield had been requested to start sending in my work. I suspected it'd had taken this long not only because I was a risk, but because my mother wasn't willing to alert my school as to my whereabouts. But so far nothing had come in, which didn't surprise me. They probably forgot who I was and had taken me off the roll altogether. My hospital teachers gave me stupid things to do, like read science books and write paragraphs on them, or algebra problems that were two years behind my level. It was boring but better than staying upstairs all day. My favorite was the vocational class housed in a large room next to the loading docks. There was a large, thick door that stayed locked at all times that led to the outside. Even though this class had the most students in it, there was virtually no interaction with them, which I liked. The room was sectioned off into little booths, each holding a vocation of some sort. You started at one and worked your way around the room. My first project was to remove a tire from a wheel that was mounted on the wall and change the brake pads. At another booth I sat down and recorded DJ scripts as if I was on the radio. This one was great because it had a turntable and I could listen to music.

Everyday we'd line up with our units, wait for someone, usually a tech named Dennis, to collect us and lead us back upstairs for lunch. After lunch we'd line up in the common room at the door leading to the back stairwell, go back down until the end of the school day, line up again, wait to be escorted again. Then we'd do it all again the next day.

One day I got a pass to go to the library for a little while. There was nothing going on in the science class. The teacher's name was Dan and I liked him. He was the most laid-back person in the entire hospital next to Joel, maybe even more so because he didn't have to live with the patients and see all the drama. I sat in the small library doodling some more when a kid came in and sat down across from me at the table. He looked vaguely familiar. I think I'd seen him in the dining room, which meant he was from that other unit.

I could feel him staring at me so I raised my eyebrow at him as if to say, "What?"

He slid a piece of paper across the table to me. I read the words, "I love you." I think I threw up a little in my mouth. This kid was young. And delusional. And probably needed to get out of the hospital and back outside as soon as possible.

When I didn't say anything, he pushed another scrap of paper at me. *You're pretty. I'm John.* We just looked at each other for a minute before I got up and left the room.

I didn't know why John's confession made me sick to my stomach, other than the fact that he was about fourteen and had no idea what he was talking about. He couldn't possibly be in love with me, knowing nothing at all about me, or having ever spoken to me. It wasn't his fault. He was just a stupid kid locked up for some stupid reason. I noticed a lot of the kids were like this. After a while you get a warped sense of reality in this place. There were kids "dating" all over the place, which was crazy when you thought about it because we weren't even allowed to touch members of the opposite sex from our own units. So how these kids managed to forge relationships between other units was beyond me. Even Mark had something going with a girl named Robin from John's unit.

There was one way that some of the other patients had been able to sneak past the no contact rule. I hadn't seen it for myself, but I'd heard rumors. A few doors down from mine was a small laundry room. It was literally a closet with a washer and a dryer. It stayed locked all the time, so either a tech had to let you in, or if someone else was in there they could open the door from the inside. I'm not sure what would happen if a boy and a girl were ever caught in there alone, but from the whispers it sounded as if things had happened in there before.

Carly and I started to get along pretty well, too. I actually liked her once I got past our initial conversation the night I moved in. She was very funny and for the first time in nearly three months I found myself laughing.

We had a game. It was stupid but it amused us. Late in the evening, same as the first night I met Mark holding that bin of jello and juice, someone always came around and went door to door with snacks. Sometimes it was jello, sometimes it was individually wrapped apples, and there were always small, plastic containers of juice. I knew that once I got out of here I'd never drink that kind of juice again. It was the apples that Carly and I made a game of. It started one evening when I was sitting on my bed, literally biting my toenails off because we weren't permitted nail clippers, and Carly was on the other side of the room, leaning against the window sill, looking bored and turning a plastic wrapped apple around in her hands.

"Hey, Jade, heads up," she called. Before I realized it the apple sailed towards me, and I barely caught it before it knocked me on my forehead, while Carly laughed from the other side of the room.

"Oh yeah?" I threw it back. What started out as a leisurely attempt at catch turned into more of a battle of the apples. We threw them as hard as we could, bruising them with every catch, until eventually they'd fall to pieces in our hands. Even the plastic didn't always prevent a mess when it broke and apple bits exploded everywhere. We thought this was extremely amusing, which if you're ever locked up you'd be surprised by what you find to be hysterical.

Another pastime we enjoyed, though for the life of me I don't know how we figured this out, was tampons. Those little suckers can hold a lot of water, and when thrown at a wall with enough force, they stick and dry in place until scraped off. This talent was most rewarding one night when Dennis came into the room to see what all our cackling was about, only to feel water dripping on his head. He looked up and found a large, saturated tampon hanging above the door. He shook his head as Carly and I laughed and turned and left the room without a word.

*   *   *

Our nightly gathering of group therapy session was starting to get harder for me to sit through. Now that it was obvious that Brenda had told people things about me, it was almost as if she expected me to start talking about it. As the techs walked up and down the hallway, knocking on doors and announcing it was time for group, I dragged myself into the common room, dreading the next hour, and sat down.

"Hey," Mark said, sitting down in a big arm chair next to me. "How's John?" I looked at him, a little surprised, and saw the mischievous smile on his face.

"Very funny," I whispered back as we waited for the room to fill.

"Poor kid," Mark mused.

"How's Robin?" I asked him sweetly.

"Hey, now don't go there," he warned me with a chuckle. "Robin's a pretty cool chick."

"Yeah, but it must be hard holding hands with someone who has to stay at least four feet away from you at all times."

The room filled up and Brenda and Joel came in, taking the last two seats. As usual, Brenda started with a period of reflection, asking others who'd shared concerns recently how they were coping and how they felt about everything. Some of them were so eager to share. Maybe that was the difference between me and them. Even though I'd been ignored by my parents, I was able to find release through my friends and my choices. Perhaps some of these kids never had another outlet.

When Brenda looked at me I knew what was coming. There was silence in the room as everyone waited, aware of what was going on between me and her right then.

"What's the point?" I finally asked her. "You've already told them. Now you think I should clarify it? You want some popcorn, too?" I couldn't help it. I disliked her so much. If the hospital knew what was best for my rehabilitation they would have moved her to another unit.

"Jade, I didn't tell everyone everything. What happened was a case of extenuating circumstances. I'm sorry that it became so misconstrued. However, I still feel that it's time you begin sharing and healing. If you keep it all pent up it's going to destroy you."

"When are you going to get it?" I seethed at her. "It already has!"

She sat back, nonplussed. "So that's it? You're just going to give up?" I just shrugged back. "What are you going to do when you leave here?"

"Exist."

"Really? Was it all worth it?"

"Doesn't matter," I shrugged again. "It happened. Can't change it."

"You can learn from it."

I didn't see how. I thought about most of the others in here with me, stories of depression but with no real provocation. Those kids probably just needed a good dose of Paxil and some private psycho-therapy. Well, except for Karen. She definitely needed to be watched. Then there were other stories of angry, bored kids, not so different from where I'd started from, and yet the worst they'd ever done was maybe set off the fire alarm at school. So, okay, yeah, I probably could learn something from everything that's happened, considering most of it was the result of my own actions.

"What do you want me to say, Brenda?" I asked her in a tired voice. "That I did a lot of drugs?

That I ran away and got into trouble? That my friends were nothing but criminals? That I was homeless and alone and desperate? That I sold drugs and my body? That I was beaten and raped? That someone I depended on died, and that I blame myself?"

You could hear a cricket chirping from miles away.

"It's a start," she finally managed to say quietly. "But I think we need to tackle one thing at a time."

I shook my head at her. "No, that's all you get. Chew on that."

I stood up to leave the room. She no longer called after me to stay as she had in the past, in vain. We weren't supposed to just come and go as we pleased without permission. I'd walked out of so many group sessions they were all used to it by now. For some reason I caught Joel's glance before I stepped through the doorway. He looked troubled.

CHAPTER SIXTEEN

Is there reason not to change
Stay the same, become a new thing
Walk backwards, step beyond
Never forget where we come from

Lost Weekend by Pete Yorn

At Phillip's request, my parents finally came. You could see the apprehension on my father's face and the disgust all over my mother's. She looked and acted as if she really were in a zoo. It was not unexpected, and yet completely frustrating to see her react to the other patients, including me, with such open disdain.

It was a Wednesday night and instead of putting us in the family circle group that used a larger room on the second floor, Phillip suggested we meet in the private room on my unit. As one of the few available techs, Joel came in and sat down at Phillip's appeal. I was glad Brenda was in her usual place, presiding over the larger group meeting, because I would have refused her into this one. That didn't stop me from inquiring about her lack of ethics with Phillip.

"I think I have a right to know," I said when he stalled. "She told people things about me. You understand what I'm saying, don't you?"

"Yes, of course," he told me. "It's been dealt with."

"It hasn't," I reminded him. "I can't do it. Even if I wanted to, I can't talk about anything as long as she's here."

"You can't just get a technician fired, or even moved, just because you don't like her."

I just looked back at him in disgust. "If my rehabilitation really isn't that important, then discharge me now."

"Jade, you have to learn to let things go."

There were so many things I wanted to say to him just then. So many cutting remarks. It made me realize how little anyone really cared. It was all a game and I was just a pawn. The only person who was going to care was me, and I barely did.

The night did not get any better. My mother sat like a stone statue, the picture of injury, and refused to discuss Jesse or anything that had happened since the day I left. All she wanted was for the rest of us to focus on her pain, acknowledge how she'd been wronged. My father was quiet and useless as usual. Even Phillip could see how pointless this meeting was. If I had ever wondered how long I was going to remain in lockup, I no longer did. Apparently, I wasn't the only one who was content with where I was.

Now that I was seventeen I knew I had more choices than I did before. While it wasn't exactly the legal age in Illinois, in some cases it did apply. I knew that I was stuck in the hospital at the mercy of the world for as long as they wanted, and that once released I would be sent home, but I was not obligated by law to stay. I did not know where I'd go, but this small glimmer of hope gave me something to work toward.

After that meeting with my parents, there were several things Phillip did. The first of which was he never invited my parents back for another therapy session, the second was he rescinded any previous offer to me for a weekend pass at home, and the third was he joined Team Jade. I didn't revel in that one much, even though my parents didn't really deserve their sterling reputations within their professional and social circles. But now even Phillip could see what kind of people they were. It didn't excuse my behavior, but it certainly clarified theirs. He made this clear to me in as few words as possible once they'd left when he promised to do whatever it took to get me healthy and discharged.

"I'd appreciate it if you kept this between us," I said to him.

"Jade, I'm not going to start gossiping about your parents behind their backs, if that's what you mean. Your father is a respected man throughout the University. And contrary to recent events, I do take patient confidentiality seriously."

I nodded. "I know it was probably condescending of me to say it."

"Actually, it was quite generous of you considering everything."

"Not really," I admitted. "I just want to get my life together and move on from them. Let them have what they've worked so hard for. As long as I can find some peace."

We were standing by the elevator. When it came back up, Phillip walked in and smiled at me.

"Consider your requests approved. But I expect to hear you're trying harder to deal with your grief." The doors closed, leaving me and Joel alone.

"What request?" he asked me.

"I guess Brenda will be moved to another unit," I said, turning to him.

"Wow," he said. "You've got some strong connections."

"What?"

"You know, no other patient in the history of this place has ever called their doctor by their first name, right?"

"He's not my doctor. He's a family friend."

"Case in point."

We looked at each other for a moment. He smiled at me like he usually did, with a little lift on one side, and I realized how attractive he was. Not just because he was good looking, but because he was kind. I felt this warmth spread slowly throughout my stomach, and for the first time in months I didn't feel completely hollow. Then again, since I'd been getting along with Carly and laughing some, talking more to Mark, I may not have felt as empty for some time and just didn't know it. It was weird. I must have looked it, too, because his features became concerned as he looked back at me, uneasily.

"What's wrong?" he finally asked me.

"I…I'm tired," I stammered, and turned away from him.

"Jade, wait," he called after me. I turned at the sound of his voice then.

Joel walked closer to me, stopping a few feet away. "Are you alright?" I nodded quickly, not really sure of what I was feeling. "I don't believe you."

"I really can't talk to you about this," I said. I didn't want to for so many reasons, but mostly because I couldn't reconcile my love for one person with my feelings for another, and I had no suspicion that Joel felt any particular way about me other than as a patient. And a very messed up one at that.

He nodded his head toward the private therapy room. We were still alone on the unit, which was unheard of. "Come on," he said. "This is what I'm here for. Let's talk."

I followed him in to the room and sat down anyway, though I insisted that I had nothing to say. He only looked back at me for a moment, his eyes searching mine.

"Fine, then I'll talk," he said. "I've been working here seven months now, and I've never seen anyone come in who is quite like you. Truth is, my internship was completed a month ago."

"I'm sure I'll make an interesting topic for your thesis," I said, my stomach turning.

He considered what I said before saying, "There are plenty of others who I study for that." I was sure he was thinking of Mark and Karen, just as I was. "It's wrong, I know, to become so invested in a patient. There are so many rules against it. I try to keep my distance, but I..." he paused, and I inched, unaware, closer to the edge of my seat, waiting for the next words to come out of his mouth, completely without any idea of where he was going.

"I can't seem to get you out of my head. I mean, I am genuinely concerned about what happens to you."

Well, that didn't clear up much, but in a way, I was relieved. I knew deep down that any attachment I had to Joel was a result of meeting someone who was nice and real for a change. Not someone who wanted anything from me, not someone who had an angle. The only word I could come up with to explain it was "rebound." I'd been dependent on either Jesse or Kelly for so long that I'd forgotten how to rely on myself. I didn't know where to aim these misplaced feelings I'd had for Jesse so I was directing them at the nicest guy I knew. Typical.

"Thank you," I said slowly, not sure how to respond.

"Can I ask you something?" I nodded. "What you were saying to Phillip about moving on from your parents in peace, what did you mean?"

"Oh, I guess I'm just coming to terms with what my life will be like once I go home."

"Which will be like what?"

"Well, if I stay with my parents it will be just as it was before I got here. But you could probably see that even without knowing them before." He nodded because he could.

"Then what do you mean by coming to terms with it?"

I shrugged. "Knowing I won't stay, that I don't have to." It was like a weight lifted off of me when I realized that I could start my life anyway I wanted, anywhere I wanted.

"Help me out here, Jade," he was shaking his head. "Statistically speaking that would mean you'd go right back to where you were before you came in here. On the run, using drugs, stealing…. getting abused." But I had no intention of going back to that place ever again.

"I don't have it all worked out just yet," I admitted. I knew it wouldn't all be okay overnight. It was going to take time. I had to finish school. But I wasn't going to waste anymore of my life. If I had to live it then I might as well try to be happy.

He smiled. "Okay," he said sincerely. "I know you can do it."

I went to my room then, actually feeling a little lighter than I had in a long time. Carly returned with the rest of the patients a few minutes later.

"Hey," she said, coming in the room. I was sitting up in my bed doing an exercise Phillip suggested I try where I write out all my feelings towards Jesse. I guess it was supposed to be some sort of goodbye. I didn't think it would help, but since I wasn't likely to get closure any other way, and I had so many emotions running around inside me, I figured it couldn't hurt.

"How'd it go with your parents?" she asked, sitting cross-legged on top of her bed and facing me.

"About as awkward and horrible as expected," I said absently.

"Well, from what you've said they do seem a little uptight," Carly agreed.

"Ain't that the truth," I muttered as I flipped the notebook shut. I tapped the light switch by the door and we both slipped under the covers.

"I have to confess something," I whispered in the dark.

"What?" she whispered back.

"I might have feelings for Joel." Silence. "Is that wrong?"

"Why would it be? He's gorgeous."

"Because of Jesse, that's why. It's too soon. It's not real."

She snorted. "There's no such thing as too soon where a heart is concerned." Oh, listen to Dr. Phil over here. "You aren't betraying anyone. Wouldn't Jesse want you to be happy?"

I was silent as I admitted to myself that she was right. Of course, he'd want me to be happy, and safe, and alive. That's why he wanted me to go home in the first place, why he tried to leave me. And why he got shot. Guilt was a terrible thing.

"Besides, anyone can see that he cares about you." Carly continued, meaning Joel.

"What?"

"Sorry," she muttered. "More gossip."

"Do your best to stop any rumors, please, Carly," I begged her. "There's nothing going on between us and I couldn't bear it if he got fired because of me."

"I will," she said. "But I promise it was just me and Mark talking. No one else."

Here's the interesting thing about Mark. He had Brenda wrapped around his little finger. She adored him. Which made me think to tell Carly of my conversation with Phillip. Then I asked her to keep that information private. If the others wanted to suspect I was the reason she'd been moved, that was fine, but it wasn't a topic open for group discussion as far as I was concerned.

"I wonder if Mark will be mad," I mused.

"Eww, she's like forty years old."

"It's not like that!" I giggled. "Well, at least not for Mark. But she would give him extra privileges, you know, so he might not appreciate the fact that she's been moved."

Of course, when word got out that Brenda had been moved it was all the rage in gossip throughout the unit. Several people eyed me, but I couldn't believe most of them cared about her so much as wanting something juicy to grab onto. I ignored all the queries, and Mark didn't really seem to care one way or the other, which was just like him.

*   *   *

After what seemed like several weeks I had a dream about Jesse. It was very similar to the ones before where I floated over a course of perfect green grass, the tips of flowers tickling my feet as I glided past them. Approaching a figure in the distance, I came closer to Jesse who stood still waiting for me. He had his familiar little smile on his face. His hand stretched out toward mine as I took it. He pulled me in closer and I felt the familiarity, the warmth.

"Where have you been?" he asked me, his face buried in my hair.

227

"Somewhere you can't come," I shivered, holding him tighter.

"Stay," he whispered.

"I can't."

"I'm not the same," he said.

"I know."

He began to fade then, my arms circling closer in, holding on to nothing as the feel of his body between them, the feel of his arms around me, disappeared.

"No!" I said desperately. "Wait! Jesse, wait! Don't leave me again!" He smiled and placed a hand on my cheek, though I couldn't feel it anymore. And then he was gone.

I woke up screaming his name.

I tried to write the things I was feeling. I really did. But most of the time I realized that I didn't even know what I was feeling. There weren't accurate words for it. It wasn't so much about saying goodbye. I'd never be able to live my life, satisfied with any kind of literal goodbye, not even if I'd had the opportunity the night we were raided by the police and Jesse was shot. How do you say goodbye like that? Is anyone ever really ready? So instead of an actual letter, or even journal-like writing, I just scribbled words. Whatever I was feeling at the time. The word I wrote the most was *anger*, but it had so many meanings because I was angry about so many different things. Phillip thought this was progress. He explained that anger was the easiest emotion for me to express, but most likely it was covering up deeper feelings such as guilt and regret. I admitted that I had it all, the whole range of emotions warring inside of me. I didn't know what to do with any of it. I couldn't ask for Jesse's understanding or forgiveness. I couldn't even grant it myself.

Phillip had me come to his office on a daily basis. When he said he was willing to do whatever it took to get me healthy again he wasn't kidding. I liked going to his private office because it got me as far away from the unit as possible while still in the building. All the private doctor offices were in a separate wing of the building. Coming in the main doors that led to the lobby and reception area, the five floors of the hospital rose up on the right, while the two floors of private offices were to the left. This was in part because a lot of out-patient therapy sessions were held for people who were not admitted.

We sat together every day, sometimes for an hour, sometimes for two or more. If he had the time and thought I was making progress Phillip would keep me as long as he felt I needed. There were days I just cried. Other days I sat still, numb, dumbfounded, helpless. We started at the beginning and started to work our way through the order of events, but soon found that it wasn't going to work that easily. There were some things that carried a greater burden, things that were harder to move past, than others. Phillip found some of my revelations surprising, such as how almost getting raped didn't scar me nearly as much as what had happened in the alley.

"Do you think if you had been raped in that field, you'd feel differently?" he asked me.

"I'm sure I would," I said. "I think that because Steven actually did something to me that the other guy didn't, had a lot to do with it. But there's more to it," I said thoughtfully. "In the alley…I made the decision to do it, even when I was fighting him, part of me was allowing it."

"And that's harder for you to accept than getting picked up and dragged away by someone who was going to force himself on you? Which, by the way, let's not make light of the fact that Steven did force himself on you."

"I know it doesn't make sense," I admitted. "But I'm not interested in being a victim."

"It makes sense," Phillip nodded. "You have a harder time dealing with the guilt you feel over your actions. But that doesn't mean you aren't a victim."

"Well, then I'm victimizing myself," I concluded. He raised his eyebrows, clearly impressed with my self-revelation.

"You're doing well, Jade," he said. "I think you'll be ready to go home soon."

Since going home wasn't my main goal I could only shrug indifferently. That would happen regardless of how I felt, but here in this place was where I was able to face my fears and insecurities. I knew I couldn't do that outside of these walls just yet.

I didn't dream about Jesse again after that last time. It was weird. Almost like he was really saying goodbye. For so long I clung to those dreams, to any piece of him that I could hold on to. Now I knew that I needed to let him go. There was no going back to where we'd once been. No bringing him back. I still had to come to terms with my anger over this, but where he was concerned, I couldn't allow his memory to keep me prisoner any longer.

The next time I went to AA, Joel wasn't there. Instead Lori took me. I wanted to ask why Joel hadn't been around for a few days but I was afraid the answer might be that he left for good now that his internship was over. He'd said he stayed longer, worked more hours because of me. Not in so many words, but that's what it seemed like. I couldn't help thinking about him, looking for him, and being disappointed when he wasn't there. I chalked it up to feeling lonely. Joel was one of the few I trusted. It was hard to feel alone all the time, but I knew I wasn't going to live in the hospital forever. At some point I was going to have to say goodbye and go home.

I'd also earned the privilege of going down to the main cafeteria to eat on the weekends if I wanted. It wasn't that the food was better or anything, but I liked it because it got me away from my unit and the monotony. There were usually other patients there from different units, and we were allowed to sit with whoever we wanted and talk as long as we were quiet. It was all fun and games until Ray, a guy from the third floor, put a piece of ice down the back of my pants. I jumped up, screeching in surprise as the cold, wet cube worked its way down one of my pant legs. Dennis shook his head, keeping a smile in check.

"I don't get how you kids manage to make friends with patients from other units," he said, walking me back to the elevator.

I shrugged. "It's not that hard if you go to school. But I met him in AA."

"What do you need to go to AA for?"

"Apparently I'm an anonymous narcotic user. So I stand up and say, 'Hi, my name is Jade, and I'm a narcotic,' and then they all say, 'Hi, Jade.' It's so stupid because no one is actually anonymous."

"You're a narcotic, huh?" he teased.

"Yeah," I laughed. "I'm an actual drug. How else do you say it? Narcaholic?"

"You're funny, Jade. I think you'll be out of here soon. You seem to be doing pretty well these days."

"Dennis?"

"Yeah?"

"I don't feel well."

"It's normal, kid. You're going to be fine."

CHAPTER SEVENTEEN

So here we are, the witching hour,
The quickest time to divide and devour.
And I fell apart but got back up again.

Alibi by 30 Seconds to Mars

Four months after I arrived, Phillip decided I was ready to go home with the explicit instructions that I continue therapy with him on an out-patient basis. "I don't want to see you admitted again," he warned me. "You're going to be fine."

I didn't feel ready. There was a part of me that had become accustomed to these walls. In here things made a different kind of sense. Outside I'd have to face everything in a more real way. I'd been clean for four months, so I was fairly sure I'd be okay with not going back to using. It's not like I ever had a real addiction before. I pretty much just used for fun. But I knew I never wanted to experience detoxing again. I walked back to my room in a daze, the fact that I was going home in a matter of days making me anxious. Carly was sitting at our small table and I sat down across from her.

"I'm going home," I said.

She smiled. "Me too. Dr. Jones just told me. Isn't that great?"

"Yeah," I nodded, putting a smile on my face for her. "I'm happy for you."

Her smile faded. "But not for yourself?"

I shook my head and looked down at the table, my throat working. "I don't think I'm going to do very well out there. I didn't before."

"How would you feel about it if Jesse was waiting for you?"

I thought about it and then shrugged. "The same. Too many things happened. I wouldn't want to live that way again."

"Well," she smiled, trying to brighten the mood. "We'll have to stay in touch. We don't live far from each other, right? I'm just in Franklin Park, that's not too far from you."

I did my best to mentally prepare. It was going to happen either way. Lori and the techs wanted me to talk about it in group therapy, to express my feelings about it. I still wasn't saying much though. The only ones who knew how I felt about getting out were Phillip and Carly. Just because I was days away from leaving didn't mean I was going to start sharing now.

I didn't have to go to AA since it was my last night, but Joel had come back and I knew it'd be my last chance to talk with him. We stood in the elevator quietly.

"I hear you're going home soon," he said.

"Tomorrow."

He nodded and then looked down at his feet for a second. "That's good."

There was a pause as I considered what was real and what wasn't; what was real and what was fantasy; what was real and what definitely wasn't going to happen ever. What was it that I really wanted? And did I want it or did I need it? I began to wonder if there was something wrong with me, like I had to have a person in my life to fixate on. First it was Kelly, then it was Jesse. Did I really need another person to give my life purpose, someone to always lean on, depend on? Someone else to define me?

"Where have you been?" I asked him.

"My extension ran out so it took a few days," he replied.

"I thought maybe-"

"What?"

I had no idea what to say and for a moment I even felt stupid. "That.... you were sick or something." I practically whispered the lie. I didn't know what I'd thought, I only knew that I was prying and then couldn't for the life of me figure out why.

He gave me a small smile as if to say "I'm fine, thanks" as the elevator slowed to a stop and a bell dinged above us as the doors started to open. I stepped through, sure my face was flushed, and from behind me I heard him say, "Jade."

I turned and looked at him, watching as the door shut between us.

He didn't pick me up at the end of my meeting. Lori came instead, chattering about how glad she was for me, how she hoped I'd do well on the outside, and not to worry about anything because she just knew I'd be okay. Back on the unit I didn't see Joel anywhere, but I found an envelope addressed to me on my bed. Carly had a mischievous smile on her face as I approached the bed and picked it up slowly.

"What am I doing?" I whispered to her, still looking at my name written on the paper.

"You don't even know what it says," she chastised me.

"It doesn't even matter," I complained. "I have all these feelings inside that I can't make any sense of, and I can't figure out for the life of me what he'd have to say." Then I felt stupid again because for all I knew the paper was some sort of release form he needed me to sign so he could write that thesis someday. But then I recalled how he'd said my name as I was exiting the elevator, as if there was something he wanted to say and then thought better of it.

"Aren't you going to read it?" she asked when I didn't move. I swallowed hard and shook my head. "Maybe it would be better if you went home and waited a while. You know, give yourself a chance to work things out in your head and decide how you really feel."

But I knew it wouldn't matter. A few months from now we'd move on, forget about this weird roller coaster we'd been on. Out of sight, out of mind. That's the way it should be. And that's even if the letter said any of the things I thought it might, which didn't necessarily mean I wanted it to. And if it didn't then what did the contents truly matter anyway?

"You don't have much faith in him, do you?" She was persistent. She reminded me of Corie. I looked up at her then.

"Why should I? I hardly even know him." I looked back down at the envelope and sighed.

"Well, I think you should read it. It's not every day a tech leaves a personal note for a patient the day before she leaves."

"You are too romantic," I chided her. "He's probably warning me not to go all fatal attraction on him."

She just made a *piffling* sound, and said, "Do whatever you want. You're out of here anyway. But just for the record, once you go home there wouldn't be anything wrong about it. He's only five years older than you."

Jesse had only been three years older than me. What a difference a privileged life made.

The next morning after breakfast I said my goodbyes to Carly and Mark before they went off to school. Anne was picking me up and I still had two hours to wait before I was officially discharged. I sat in my room at the table, my belongings neatly packed and waiting on my bed. The unit was virtually bare, with the techs running around doing random things throughout the building. The few patients who were in robes were collected into the common room, watching a movie with Dennis.

I heard a slight rap at my door and I looked up, surprised to see Joel standing there.

"Hey," I said.

"I came to say goodbye," he said.

"You're not going to take me downstairs?" I asked.

"I can if that's what you want."

I did want.

We were silent for a minute, then he asked, "Did you read the letter?"

I shook my head and looked away.

"Oh," he said quietly. "Okay then."

More silence.

I looked up but he was already gone. My stomach felt twisted in knots and I wished more than anything I knew what was going on inside of me. Sometimes I still missed Jesse so much it was impossible to hold back the tears. I closed my door and found the letter I'd pushed to the bottom of my bag. My fingers fumbled as I ripped the envelope and opened it to find a single piece of paper inside. Sitting down, I pressed a hand to my middle and began to read, realizing that it didn't even matter what it said, because either way I was going to have to deal with more feelings I wasn't ready for.

Jade,

This is the strangest place I've ever been in my life. I can't even begin to excuse what a selfish purpose this letter serves. I wasn't going to write it, to say anything to you. I should let you go home and get on with your life. And if that's what you choose to do anyway then I wish you all the best. The thing is, I meant it when I said you were the reason I stayed after my internship ended. They offered me a permanent job but I didn't want to deal with contracts, because I know that once you're gone I won't want to stay.

You don't always think much of yourself, Jade, I can see it. You've been through a lot and I know that you still have things to work out. It might take years for you to heal. Just don't ever lose sight of the fact that you are truly a strong and amazing person. I hope you remember that when you go home and things seem hard. And know that you're not alone in this world. There are things worth living for and people who care for you.

Take care, Joel.

So that was it? A pep talk?

I stormed to my door and thrust it open. The hallway was empty. I could hear the movie coming from the common room, but there was no one else around. I started toward the empty nurses' station, spying Joel's long legs from just inside the private therapy room where I found him sitting in a large chair surrounded by his text books.

"What the hell is this?" I demanded, coming into the room, holding the letter up. He looked up surprised. "Am I missing something?" He stood up and looked out into the hallway, then back at me. "This doesn't say anything!"

"What did you want me to say?" he asked cautiously.

I stopped. What *did* I want him to say? I sighed. I was doing it again. Making assumptions, jumping ahead of myself. I was determined to destroy any ounce of self-respect I had.

"Jade, you're clearly not ready," he said sincerely. "And I should have known better. I'm sorry. I stopped myself from saying anything in the elevator and I should have stopped myself from writing that letter." He was gesturing toward the paper in my hand.

"You're right, I'm not ready. But I can be selfish, too." I pressed my lips against his.

His hands shot out and braced himself against the wall behind me, but his lips did not leave mine for several seconds. Finally, he tore himself away, pushing with his arms off the wall to back away from me.

"Dammit, Jade, you're still impulsive!"

"What the hell do you want from me?"

"I want you to be happy!" He put a hand on my cheek and said in earnest. "I want you to go home and be strong. Make new friends, laugh, have fun. Finish school and find something to do that you're passionate about. Find peace. And if someday you need a friend, then that's what I want, too. Because I know this road won't be easy for you and I really do care about you."

My heart was pounding in my chest. He sighed and dropped his hand to his side. He pointed to the letter in my hand again, and said, "My number's in there. Use it if you want."

I nodded, swallowed, and turned from the room.

Anne was going to be here in less than thirty minutes. Looking into the mirror in my room for the last time, part of me wished I could stay right here where things made sense. In spite of everything that had happened in the last four months, I knew that dealing with Jesse's memory, the dreams, my guilt, and all the horrible things I'd done, was nothing compared to facing it on the outside alone. But I knew I couldn't stay in here forever. Hiding behind the protection of these walls hadn't prepared me.

They couldn't have. I had to do that on my own. And then I realized that maybe that's what Joel had been trying to say all along.

Dennis walked me down to the elevator and stayed beside me as we met Anne and Phillip in the lobby. I smiled at him and said goodbye. He said he was glad I was leaving, which is what they say to everyone because it meant the patients were well. I knew I was better than I had been four months ago, but I also knew that forgiving myself and letting go of Jesse was going to be a daily battle for a long time.

Anne didn't say much as we walked out to her car. I stopped and took in a fresh breath of air. "It's warm out," I commented. She gave me a worried look, realizing the last time I'd been outside was in winter. I'd completely missed spring.

Riding in the car was surreal. In a way it felt like my first time. She apologized for our parents not coming to get me, but neither one of us were really surprised. I was just thankful my mother didn't pick me up, trapping me for the forty-minute drive with her burning a hole in my ear and complaining about every little thing she could think of. I asked her what they'd been saying at home about me, about me coming back, and she replied with, "Very little."

"I have some news," she gave me a small smile. "Tom and I have set a date for the wedding."

Wow. It was like a stab to the heart on so many levels. Their date had been set once before and I missed it. "I'm sorry," I whispered.

"It's okay," she said. "We're not in a huge hurry anyway. We both have to finish school. It's really better this way. And we found an apartment in Gurnee because it's close to where he works, but I'm still packing. It'll be a while before I officially move out of the house."

I nodded, listening. Not that we were ever super close, but I always felt I had an ally at home with her there. Now it would just be me against them.

"So, anyway," she went on. "I just wanted to throw it out there for you, you know. In case you ever need a place to go. You can come stay with us."

"Thanks." I blinked hard a couple of times and then the dam broke.

"Geez, are you okay? I'm sure it's not going to be that bad at home."

"I'm just so scared," I admitted.

"Of what?"

"Of everything!"

"It's going to be okay, Jade. You just need time to adjust."

We pulled into the driveway and I looked at the house. It was familiar and strange at the same time. Once I had thought of it as a prison. Now I didn't know what it was. I grabbed my small bag and willed my feet to move. Making my way up the long staircase, I stopped at the first door on the left and looked into my room. It looked the same as the last time I'd been in it except the bed had been made and everything was piled neatly instead of strewn everywhere. I was sure that had more to do with the cleaning lady than thinking my mother had come in to make it welcoming for me. I dropped my bag on the bed and sat down, realizing that I wasn't coming back with a single thing I'd left with. Where was all my stuff anyway? What had happened to Jesse's car and all of our belongings? I wondered who had taken our tents down, who'd cleaned up after us, and what garbage can in Texas held all of it.

I thought about Kelly then. I didn't know where he could be. It'd been three months since I heard from him. No doubt he was no longer in Elgin, in that half-way house. I still had about a month before school started, but if I didn't hear from him before then, I'm sure word would get around eventually. For all I knew he could be anywhere, doing the same old things. If that was the case it could be months before I got a phone call from him in some distant place.

* * *

My school year started with the explicit instructions from Principal Leighton that I was to make up the missing credits. Usually by senior year a student's class time was reduced by a good two hours compared to an underclassman. Since I'd missed an entire semester I had a full load including two P.E. classes a day. It was the only way I would be able to graduate on time if I didn't want to return the following year as a fifth-year senior. I didn't care much either way but figured I'd be glad come next June with a diploma in my hand.

I went to school every day just like I was supposed to, but I felt tired, overloaded, and helpless. My friends were glad to see me and asked all about my wild trip across the country. Some of them said that they had seen Kelly once or twice over the summer, but no one knew for sure where he was living. I didn't say much about the trip, just a few of the funnier moments.

There was talk about a party coming up at the Base; a back to school bash planned for the following Friday night. I honestly debated over going. I didn't even know if I was allowed to go anywhere. I didn't think I was grounded but I hadn't bothered to ask if I could go anywhere since I'd been home. I hoped that the four months I spent in the hospital would satisfy my parents' need to punish me for the things I had done. Up until then I hadn't cared to go out, but on Friday night I decided against my better judgment to take a quick detour past the Base to see if the party was still going on. When I reached the opening in the woods I could see cars lining the street. I parked behind an unfamiliar car and started through the woods.

As I walked through the dark trail it occurred to me that I had not forgotten the way. It was still as familiar as ever, and before I even reached the runway I found myself feeling relaxed for the first time since I got home. There was just something about being in such a familiar place. Yet my heart was heavy when I remembered the last time I'd been there.

Fifteen minutes later I stepped up onto the first runway and stopped to listen for voices being carried over with the breeze. It sounded as if the majority of the people were coming from the two hills straight ahead, and I headed in that direction. When I was about halfway there I passed a group of drunk guys going in the other direction.

"Who's that?" one of them called out to me. We got closer to each other and the speaker of the group walked right up to my face. "Holy shit, it's Jade. I haven't seen you in like a year, man!" He grabbed me by the shoulders for a quick bone-crushing hug. "I thought you had moved away or something. Didn't you? Wow, it's awesome to see you."

"Well, I'm back," I said, pushing him off me. "Who's out here tonight?"

"Oh, man, everyone is here tonight. It's the best Base party ever! We're going over to the clearing, there's a bonfire over there and everything. Come check it out with us."

"Thanks, but I'm gonna see who's over here first. Anyone in the bunker?"

"Hell yah, there's people everywhere tonight! I haven't seen this place so crowded in my whole life," he cackled and walked away.

I continued the rest of the way toward the hills and found at least fifty people milling about, either sitting on the small hill or standing between the two and talking. Someone had brought a radio and music was playing off in the distance. The first group of people I walked up on was a bunch of hippie friends from school, most of them already graduated. Since they hadn't seen me yet I got a round of hugs.

245

"Hey, everybody!" Gordon yelled into the crowd. "Jade is here! Woo-hoo!"

"Hi, Jade!" the crowd yelled back. It reminded me of an A.A. meeting where the alcohol was allowed.

"Jade!" a voice called from about ten feet away. "Up here!" I looked over and saw Lynn waving at me from the top of the small hill where she sat in a circle with about six other people.

"Hey," I said, sitting down next to her. "What's up?"

"Just chillin'. You need a drink?"

"No, I'm good. Have you heard anything about Kelly?"

"Sure, I saw him."

"When was that?"

"Like an hour ago?" She squinted at me with glassy eyes and asked me, as if I knew the answer.

"You mean he's here?"

"Yeah. Well, he was. I don't know where he is now." Suddenly she leaned backward and yelled down the hill. "Hey! Has anyone seen Kelly?" A plethora of answers were tossed back up.

"Kelly who? Is she a babe?"

"He's in the bunker."

"Kelly left."

"I saw him at the bonfire."

Lynn raised her hands and shrugged at me, a droopy smile on her face. "There you go," she said.

That wasn't very helpful.

I said I was going to look for him at the bonfire and crept my way down the small hill. I made the long trek back down the first runway, then turned right where it ended at the sewage field. Being back at the Base, I could almost feel Jesse's presence. If I imagined hard enough that he was there, waiting for me at the bonfire with Kelly, I could really almost feel it. It was dangerous of me to do that to myself. I knew better, yet I wanted to *feel* so badly. Just…anything really, but especially him. I knew that he was gone, and I'd been dealing what that for four months. It was getting easier to accept even though I wished with all my heart it weren't true. I still believed that I could have more willingly left him if I had known that it would have ended this way. I felt a huge void that would not have been nearly as bad had I known he were still alive, even without me.

I thought about the things Phillip and I had talked about, about me about not making Jesse into something he wasn't. The truth was he wasn't a pillar of society; none of us had been. I didn't fault him for those things because I had been just as much to blame. What I saw, however, was a person who had been caught in a cycle and just didn't know how to get out of it. It didn't vindicate him for the bad choices he made, it was just a fact. There had not been a way out for him. I knew he wasn't a martyr, no matter how badly my broken heart wanted to make him one. I saw the truth for what it was yet could not forget the caring person he was inside. We all have our faults. We all make mistakes. One good quality does not always outweigh a bad one, but all qualities should be considered.

The shorter, weed-covered runway stretched out before me as I followed it to the small clearing. I could see light from the fire before I even reached it, and heard the voices of people singing and talking, while others played guitars.

There was a large crowd of people gathered around the bonfire. I approached them from behind and wondered how I was going to get through this tight mob of fire-hoggers. I circled the group about halfway when I heard the familiar laugh. He had an unmistakable cackle. My heart leapt into my throat and I willed my stomach to stay calm. Pushing through the crowd, I stepped closer to the fire to try and locate Kelly. I finally spotted him about ten feet away, standing with three other people behind one of the guitar players, who was sitting on the ground and staring into the fire, his fingers playing chords as if he were in a trance.

"Kelly!" I called out, trying to get through the thick crowd of people. They were all just standing around like a bunch of cows chewing on their cud. I wanted to push them out of my way but stepped over them instead as best I could. My foot accidentally mashed someone's hand, and he replied lamely with an "Oww."

Kelly looked up, his eyes adjusting to the blazing fire in front of him. "Jade? Holy shit, is that you?" He pushed his way out of the small group of people and rushed over to me. Tears sprang uncontrollably to my eyes as I felt him lift me off my feet and crush me tightly against him.

"Jesus, Jade, I've been so worried about you," he crooned into my ear. When I continued to cry he soothed me, saying, "Shh, it's okay now. Don't cry."

"I can't stop," I said. "It's all I do. I can't help it. I hate it. I didn't know where you were and I was all alone. I'm so tired of being alone."

"You're not alone. I told you I would always be there for you, didn't I?" I nodded into his shoulder, still weeping. He finally set me back on my feet and looked into my face. "Are you glad to be home?"

"Not really," I sniffed.

"Come on, let's get out of here, huh?" He threw an arm over my shoulder and walked me away from the clearing.

I couldn't stop crying. I didn't realize that seeing him would mean so much to me, but it was harder, too, because he reminded me of Jesse, of everything we'd been through, and because the last time we'd been together was the day Jesse died. He let me cry for a bit, not saying anything, just rubbing my shoulder as we walked slowly.

"Where you living at now, Kelly?" I asked.

"I'm staying at Tori's house," he said. At my surprised look he said, "Yeah, it's crazy how things work out. It's not what you think," he paused as I digested it. I didn't know what he thought I was thinking. Tori was a friend of both of ours, and it was no secret that she *really liked* him, but she was another one who was tired of never knowing where he was or if he was safe. I could see her putting her crush aside enough to offer him a safe, reliable place to live. I had no doubts that him moving into her parents' house was not motivated by romance at all.

"I think I'll stay there for a while, you know?" he went on. "Her parents are cool, I've known them a long time, and they really wanted me to come stay. I'm just so tired of being on the road, never knowing what I'm doing."

"Me too," I agreed. I didn't miss that part, either. "At least now I'll know where to find you."

"Hey, what did I tell you, Jade?"

"I know, I know. You'll always be there for me."

We reached the end of the runway and I stopped. "I have to get home."

"What? You just got here and I haven't seen you in four months!"

"I know, but I'm on parole still and keeping peace with my mom has been really hard."

"How's it going?" he asked, meaning my parents.

"Not well. Kelly, I never realized how difficult my mother really is. I used to be so resentful because she ignored me, but now I think I like that better. I don't think she even likes me."

"Listen," he said, putting both hands on my shoulders and facing me. "She has always been difficult. You have never been able to please her. You just have to worry about making yourself happy, okay?"

"Yeah, okay," I mumbled as we started through the sewage fields and the woods as he walked me to my car. But it was easier said than done.

CHAPTER EIGHTEEN

But you always find a way
To keep me right here waiting
You always find the words to say
To keep me right here waiting
If you chose to walk away
I'd still be right here waiting

Right Here by Staind

"Phillip has been leaving messages," my mother told me one afternoon as we crossed paths in the kitchen.

I figured she was wondering why he was calling her line instead of mine. I shrugged.

"Why aren't you continuing with your therapy?"

I didn't answer at first, not sure what to say. I was more interested in knowing why my own mother wasn't more involved in seeing me continue my therapy. I mean, isn't that what a parent does? But then again, maybe I was more surprised to find myself questioning that at all when I've never needed much from her before, nor did I ever want it. She had never seemed much interested in being involved in the healthier more productive aspects of my life anyway, so this current thought left me wondering what I really wanted or expected from her at this point. I was a bit surprised at myself.

"I just want to put all this behind me," I finally said, trying to be honest with both her and myself for once. It wasn't as if I was hoping for some miraculous change of heart from her, because let's face it I wasn't sure I was capable of it either. Having a different kind of relationship with her was ideal, but not very realistic. Especially considering neither of us knew what that actually meant. Keeping the status quo had been working out pretty well so far and we both seemed content.

She sighed and looked me over for a second as if considering what to say. "I'm not sure I agree that avoiding Phillip's help is the best way to do that," she finally said carefully.

In the past I'd cut back a biting remark about how I felt toward her opinion, but I considered the situation more carefully, realizing that she may actually be trying to heal things between us. I mean, I had to assume that a parent would want to have some kind of amiable relationship with their child, even my parent.

I nodded noncommittally.

"I'll take you to see him if you like," she offered. When I didn't reply, she said, "Think about it."

Think about what? Her taking me or me going to see Phillip at all? I guess all of it was worth thinking over, but really, I just still wasn't ready to do anything about it. In my mind I felt as if I'd paid for my crimes. I didn't want to see Phillip anymore and rehash everything. I didn't see what good could come of it. I wasn't lying to myself anymore. I knew exactly what I had done and why, and what the root of my problems were; which were real and which weren't, and I knew how much of the blame rest on my shoulders. I was just trying to breathe now. But I still felt like I was held together with string. Some days I felt like a tightly wound ball of yarn, consistent and unyielding, but other days I felt more fragile, as if I were slowly unraveling.

Shouldn't I have a better grip on myself by now? After all this time I still didn't know what my purpose was. Maybe that was what unnerved me the most, not knowing what was coming next, and even worse, not wanting anything.

When I finally did go back to see Phillip I drove myself. I hated going back to the hospital where his office was. The entire drive there my stomach was in knots and I could feel the stress building up between my shoulders. By the time I got there, was buzzed through the two sets of doors and sitting in Phillip's waiting room, I had a monster of a headache.

Phillip smiled as he opened his door and saw me. He looked around the small room quickly, realizing that I was alone. "Your mother didn't bring you?" He genuinely sounded surprised.

"No." I stood up and followed him into his office and sat down in my usual chair, just to the right of his desk.

He frowned. "I was hoping that the two of you were working things out."

"We're fine."

"That means that things are just okay."

"What's wrong with okay? We're not fighting anymore."

"But you're not growing either." When I didn't say anything he asked, "Do you do things together?"

Silence.

"Do you even talk?"

I was exhausted and I'd only been there 90 seconds.

"You know," he said. "Most of your therapy focuses on your relationship with your mother. I don't see how things are going to get better if you don't let her share in your healing process."

"That's not why I'm here," I told him. My head went to my hands where I mindlessly rubbed my temples.

"What's wrong?"

"I have a headache," I whispered.

He nodded and watched me for several seconds. Finally, he got up and returned with a cup of water, which he placed on the desk near my elbow, and extended a hand with two aspirin.

"Thanks." I swallowed the pills and hoped they'd be enough.

Phillip sat down again and sighed. "Well, at least you're here. I don't blame you for neglecting your treatment once you went home, but from years of experience I could have told you that you weren't entirely ready to put it all behind you. Going home is just another step in the process. It didn't mean that your treatment was complete or that you had fully recovered. It only implied that you didn't need to be-"

"Locked up?" I finished for him.

He didn't respond in any way I expected. He only said, "It was the best thing for you at the time. I understand why you're bitter."

I laughed ruefully, but only for a second. The word bitter didn't seem strong enough a word for the barrage of emotions I felt at any one time. Mostly I was just numb, but if the moment was right then anger would be my prevailing emotion.

"Now that you've been home for several months and back into the mainstream of life how do you think you've been doing?"

"I think I'm doing fine," I said stubbornly. "I don't ditch school, I get good grades, I have a job, I don't fight with my parents, and I'm not doing any drugs."

"Hmph."

"What?"

"Sounds like you're existing but not really living."

"Is that what you're here for, Phillip, to judge the quality of my life? I thought your job was just to make sure I wasn't going to OD or prostitute myself or something."

"Now you're just being difficult."

I thought about it. After all he was a psychiatrist. He was supposed to use psychology on me. The problem with that was I'm too used to it. Psychology doesn't work on me anymore because it's all a bunch of crap.

"Fine," I admit. "You're right. I'm still bitter."

"About what exactly?"

"About everything," I said. "About losing Jesse and what we had. About our world being ripped away from us so unfairly. About not even having accurate memories to comfort me. And about the fact that some stupid rookie cop shot and killed him when he didn't deserve it."

Phillip nodded as I ranted. "I agree with you. It was a horrible thing about Jesse."

"That cop should have to pay for that. It's not right. I don't even know what happened to Jesse. Where he's buried, where his things are, or what was that cop's excuse for gunning down an unarmed kid."

"He wasn't unarmed," Phillip reminded me. "Which I know leaves a lot of gray area, but the fact is he had a gun and he was a threat, and the police did what they felt was right. I never doubted for a minute that the officer who pulled the trigger didn't struggle with the realization that Jesse's gun wasn't loaded, but it doesn't change the fact that there was a warrant for his arrest and all evidence pointed to a very troubled threat to everyone's safety."

"I was safe!" I yelled at him, pointing to my chest. "He died because he was trying to keep me safe."

"Listen to yourself, Jade," Phillip said softly. "Why would he need to keep you safe if you weren't already? The minute you drove across the country with him you were in harm's way. And I think he knew that."

"Don't talk about him like you knew him." But it was true. Jesse knew it and I knew he knew it. That's why he pleaded with me to leave, why he deserted us and then came back. I was the only one who was too blind to admit that the only way it was going to end would be badly.

"Sounds like you're telling me that the only reason you came back here was because you're still angry over losing your good time with your friends"

"First of all," I growled, "he was more than just a good time. There's a hell of a lot more about what happened during those months than you know about. It wasn't all just some big party. I wanted to come home." He looked at me doubtfully, and I had to add the word, "Eventually. But I wanted him to be able to go home, too. I wanted that for all of us. I didn't want to see him running for the rest of his life. It tortured him, you couldn't know that, but it did. But since he didn't feel he could ever go home I was prepared to stay with him forever."

"What reason did you have to abandon your entire life to live like a criminal?"

"I loved him."

He shrugged. "I get that you think you did, but that's not what love really is. It's not an emotion, it's an action."

"It's sacrifice, and I was willing to make those choices for him. I don't expect you to understand. But in the middle of all that chaos, for once in my life, being with him made sense. Everything just made sense."

This is where Phillip would say that the deeply rooted reasons for that are psychological and it was born from my childhood and my relationship with my parents. I'd heard it all before; he'd said it all before. This conversation wasn't entirely new ground. But he didn't have to say it because in that instant I knew the truth for what it was. And over the months in the hospital and even since coming home I'd faced all of that, accepting and admitting several other truths, the first of which was that I suffered no illusions that Jesse was someone he was not. But he filled a hole in me and that was bigger than anything else in my world.

He nodded thoughtfully and was silent for some time.

"In the irrevocable aftermath you still have some other things to work on. You're still alive, regardless, and now you're what? Wondering how to go on? Trying to figure out what you want out of life?"

"Yes," I admitted. "I feel so lost now."

"That's why you're here."

In the coming weeks I spent periodical spans of time with Phillip. It was strange how I came to lean heavily on him, once again, just as I had in the hospital. The feeling wasn't all that different from actually being in the hospital, where at the beginning I fought and bucked the system only to conform and rely on it. Was I so easily swayed? Was I really that weak and pliable that I could be brainwashed into becoming whoever someone else wanted me to become?

I thought about those questions more and more often. I thought about Kelly and our relationship. Years of influence shaping me into the person I thought I was. I certainly can't blame him for all the choices I made, but I could admit to myself that from the start we'd had a very strange co-dependency between us. I'd always known that even if I didn't have the words for it. He needed to be mothered, and I did, too, but it was easier for me to step into a maternal role than vice versa. Besides, if I had expected that from him I would have been sorely disappointed.

Which made me look at other things more closely. Like how Kelly disappointed me all the time because I constantly expected things from him that he couldn't give. I knew he could probably say the same about me, but where his needs and wants were more physical, mine were imbedded in the primal need to just be loved and accepted. Kelly didn't seem to care if he was accepted, but being the con artist that he was, you'd never really know what he was feeling anyway. So, in the end I had to admit that I never really knew Kelly all that well either.

Then I thought about Jesse. Not in the usual ways but looking at him and our relationship from start to finish from a different point of view. I thought I'd understood him so well. I assumed I could read him and give him what he wanted. Even if it was entirely true, is that how two people are supposed to function together? With one person always anticipating the other's needs and moods? Jesse never really revealed himself to me all that much. And in many ways, he was more of an enigma than Kelly was. Maybe I was drawn to people like that, people who were emotionally unavailable. Because in a way I was too, and I can see now that Kelly and I had always made a pretty good pair in that aspect. But I hadn't ever realized it before how I did that. But it made sense now because we'd all been missing something in our lives, something that comes from the nurturing of home.

So, the hardest part of all of this was realizing that the whole thing was a façade, a big co-dependent and unhealthy circle of making the same bad choices over and over. We needed a family and so we formed one. And no amount of therapy was going to change the fact that I had lost the only family I'd ever felt I'd belonged to.

I could see my mother trying in little ways, but it was obvious that she just wasn't capable of change. This was the person I'd always known so I wasn't all that disappointed. Even if I felt like I had changed and didn't see why other people couldn't do a better job of it as well. But we all had our crosses to bear and in true fashion, she just didn't see the bigger picture. It was okay, really, because I'd grown past that childhood need for her, even if she couldn't understand that. I couldn't see what our future relationship would be, but for now it seemed as stagnant as always and somehow I felt comfort in that. Like if she started to hover and ask to paint my toenails or something I'd probably run away screaming, afraid she'd become a pod mom. The fact that she was consistent made living with her easier. Phillip thought that was sad, but even he had to admit that I needed to focus on getting myself together anyway. Someday I'd have to go out on my own and live a productive life, parent or not.

So that was what I'd been trying to do, and that was what I needed him to help me with even if I couldn't put it into those words. All I wanted was to get past the loneliness and the pain and the confusion. I needed to find a new reason for being;

a reason that motivated me, something that didn't involve another person, because I'd always done that with Kelly and Jesse. I'd made them my purpose.

*   *   *

I went to school, passed my tests, and worked my part-time job at a take-out restaurant. But nothing I did seemed to knock me out of my funk. I didn't even want to hang out with my old friends. Most of my relationships had been strained since my return and it didn't seem as if we had anything in common anymore. It wasn't that they were bad people or anything, but I realized that the only thing that united most of them was their desire to get high, and that wasn't a top priority for me anymore.

At school everything was fine because I could focus on work but gone were the days of phone calls and plans for every weekend. Even the girly notes from Lynn, Lisa, and Carrie had stopped along with spontaneous trips to the mall, ditching class to laugh and talk together, or sleepovers. We were still on a friendly basis, but it wasn't the same. We had grown apart.

The days seem to wear on endlessly. It was as if I had nothing to look forward to, and I found that equally depressing. When was I going to find value in life just for the sake of value?

Christmas came and went, the only benefit of it being a break from school. For the first time in my life I was dedicated to improving my scholastic aptitude for no other reason than to prove I could, though it was burning me out a little. The two-week winter break was a welcome respite from all my attempts at over-achievement, if for nothing else than to keep my mother off my back, because I knew that even a straight A report card wasn't going to impress her this late in the game.

* * *

"It's good to see you again," Phillip said to me. I was sitting in my usual spot in his office, picking at my nails and not saying much. Over the past weeks I'd fallen back into that comfortable routine I'd always had with him, and I think he felt relieved, as if it were a sign that I was coming back to life.

I knew what he meant even though I'd been coming to see him twice a week for the past month and a half. I still didn't have anything to say on the subject because the person he recognized I no longer did.

When he saw that I had nothing to say, he asked, "What are we going to talk about today?"

"I want to talk about Joel."

He nodded. "You know, I heard about that kiss. You realize that he could have gotten into a lot of trouble for that. All employees have to sign contracts of conduct, even interns."

"I didn't really think about it," I said honestly. But I was wondering how he knew, and how many other techs, too. Were there cameras up in the ward? The thought had never occurred to me, but it seemed possible.

"Even on your last day you were fighting the rules." He was shaking his head.

"Would you have expected anything else from me?" I smiled and held my hands up momentarily. He chuckled but it did not meet his eyes.

"Why do you want to talk about Joel? Have you spoken to him since you went home?"

"No," I shook my head. "He said he only wanted to hear from me when I was ready. I knew he wouldn't reach out to me first."

"And how do you feel about that?"

"Relieved."

Phillip's eyebrows shot up as he considered what I said. "It's no great sin if you're attracted to him, you know. No one would blame you. After all, life does go on, and you can't expect to hold a torch for Jesse your whole life. It's not very realistic and, quite frankly, it wouldn't be fair to you."

"Well, it sounds great when you say it, but it's harder to actually put it into practice."

"So, you're saying that you feel guilty, like you're betraying Jesse? Does that mean that you really do have feelings for Joel and you're just denying yourself?"

"I don't know," I shrugged. "I mean, yes, I guess I would feel guilty. And I have," I admitted when I saw Phillip raise an eyebrow at me. "But real feelings for Joel? I think it's just concern on his side, and for me...I don't know. I still can't always tell what's real, you know?"

"Jade, if you're waiting for life to align itself, you'll be waiting a long time. You can't always trust your emotions. Sometimes you just have to experience things."

"Easier said than done," I muttered. Then I held up a hand and said, "I'm not sure I understand this. You obviously weren't surprised when I mentioned his name, and you're not giving me the third degree for my impulsive behavior. So, what's up with that?"

He almost chuckled but reigned it in. "Let's not pretend that your situation was ever the norm, shall we?" I nodded glumly. "Reiterating the rules to you would be moot, and I was never officially your doctor. In fact, to make things even weirder, you never had an official doctor like every other patient in the history of this hospital. Not that that makes a difference in any of this, but maybe because I was closer to you in the familiar respect than typical doctor-patient relationships, I really just wanted to see you get better. And frankly, if flirting with an intern helped you heal then I wasn't against it. But just for the record, I am the only one who knows anything. If those circumstances were different, I assure you things would have ended badly for Joel."

"How did you know about it?"

"Joel is the son of a very good friend of mine. I helped him get the internship and as a consequence of having watch him grow up, much as I have watched you," he reminded me. "Joel trusted and confided in me. I knew he was intrigued by you. He asked me before his internship was over if he could stay longer because you were the best subject here to study."

So, he would write his thesis on me.

"Let's talk about something else, like making friends. You said that you've become estranged from your old group of friends. How are you doing on making new relationships?"

"I'm not."

"Why not?"

"Friends disappoint, and I'm tired."

"That's horribly cynical," Phillip told me. "You'll get awfully lonely."

"I just don't have the energy."

"Find some," he said sternly but not unkindly. "Make yourself do it. Start out small with baby steps. You'll never know if you don't try."

I could see he meant it, as if he were giving me homework or something. He was always following up and inquiring about my progress from past sessions. Nothing passed this guy's attention. I knew he wasn't going to let up until I had something to report, so until then I knew the only thing to do was to do as assigned.

I wasn't sure if it was cheating or not but I decided my reentry into the social scene would be through my family. Not my parents, but my extended family. They were the nicest people I'd ever known, which made it really hard to imagine that my father actually came from the same gene pool as my uncle. I also had cousins, two of which were about my age, and I'd always got along well with them. Since my mother was who she was, we'd rarely ever made an appearance at my aunt and uncle's annual Christmas gathering, but this year I decided to go alone. And just as I suspected they opened their arms to me, surprised and happy that I'd come.

The day was nice. I visited with family I hadn't seen in over a year and didn't say anything about the past year, knowing that they had no idea what I'd been through. When they asked me how school was I said it was going well, because for the first time it actually was. When they asked if I'd been seeing anyone, I quickly detoured the topic. Only two people actually noticed I'd been missing and asked me about it, my favorite cousin Lars and his girlfriend, who I'd been friends with at school, and I found that when given the opportunity I truly just wasn't ready to tell anyone.

"Is that bad?" I asked Phillip at our next session. "Because it felt like I'd be giving up a secret if I told anyone, and part of me likes the idea of keeping it to myself."

"Maybe you're using it as an excuse to hang on to your pain," he offered.

"Hmm," I mused. "Maybe."

"This isn't a secret in the sense that you get happiness from knowing something, Jade. This is something that you need to put out there so that you're not carrying it all by yourself anymore. You may even be embarrassed by some of it, but you need to share it, take responsibility for your actions and learn how to live with it. Pretending it's something that holds Jesse close to you isn't healthy. I want you to think about that."

I nodded and said I would, relieved that he didn't give me a new assignment.

CHAPTER NINETEEN

I feel the beating of your heart
I see the shadows of your face
Just know that wherever you are
Yeah, I miss you
And I wish you were here

From Where You Are by Lifehouse

New Year's loomed ahead and with it the anniversary of the day I met Jesse. I felt his absence even more during those snowy wintery nights, standing out the back door. Only this time there were no strange cars coming up my driveway, no beautiful strangers with dark, stormy eyes standing in my kitchen. Knowing that Jesse would never once again cross the threshold of my backdoor left me feeling lonelier than ever. It wasn't smart of me at all to purposely go somewhere, do something, or smell something familiar, all just for the brief revisit of feeling him close. There were times that the intense feeling of familiarity brought me to tears and then I'd be ashamed for sabotaging my healing process.

There were days I spent with Tori, though she had a new boyfriend and stayed busy with him. I didn't see Kelly much but since I knew where he was I found it comforting enough and realized that I didn't need to see him as often. Tori said he'd started dating a new girl whom he met at a party in

Libertyville, and it was at that time that I thought of Corie.

I was still on Christmas break when I came across an old phone number written on a slip of paper in my room. I didn't even remember how I got it, not ever seeing the need, but it was here none-the-less, and on a whim I decided to call on the off chance that she might be there. I was expecting to hear a recorded message saying that the number had been disconnected, when instead a young girl answered.

"Corie?" I gasped.

"Yes, who is this?"

"It's me, Jade."

"Jade? Oh, m'gosh! How are you? Where are you?"

"I'm at home. I have to admit I didn't think you would be there."

"I just got back. If you had called a few weeks ago I would still be in Wisconsin."

"Wisconsin? What were you doing there?"

"I was sent to live with my aunt and uncle. They're very loving people but it still felt like jail in a way. I hated it."

"How's it going with your dad?"

"I don't like living with him either, but he's calmed down a lot. He tried manhandling me at the police station when he first came to pick me up and the cops didn't take that too well. That's why I was sent to Madison. He spent a few months in jail and has had to do a lot of community service. When I decided to come home Social Services said they'd be watching. They've already been here once to evaluate us."

There was a brief silence between us as I digested what she'd said. For some reason I had pictured her in some kind of institutional lock-up as I had been. Hearing that she was shipped off to live with relatives didn't make any sense to me. Why did it seem as if I was the only one who'd been imprisoned? If moving had been the answer, I had an aunt and uncle right here in Deerfield who would have taken me in and loved me the same as my cousins. But then I thought about my mother, knowing that she would never share our family secrets with anyone.

"Jade, what happened to you?"

"They put me in a hospital," I said. "I was in there for four months."

"How are things going?"

"Okay, I guess," I sighed. "Oh, hell, I don't know. I feel like I'm just going through the motions most of the time. I just keep thinking about everything. I can't seem to stop. I mean, I know what we did was wrong, but in a crazy way we did it for the right reasons. Do you know what I mean?"

"Yeah," she murmured, but I noticed she didn't go on about it. "So, you're having a hard time, huh?"

"Don't you think about those days?"

"Oh, man, I think about it every day!" she admitted. "But I'm getting better. Some days are better than others, you know?"

"Yeah," I mused quietly, lost in my own memories. "Corie, do you remember that night very well?"

"Better than I want to."

"What the hell happened? I just don't understand any of it."

"Jade?" she said it carefully. "You do know what happened to Jesse, don't you?" I could hear it in her voice, fear that she'd have to be the one to tell me that he was dead.

"Yes." The tears were building up again, stinging, threatening to spill over. "He was shot in the back. Kelly was screaming. You were crying but I couldn't see you. I couldn't see any of you, but I could hear what was going on."

"Shot in the back? Who told you that?"

"Kelly," I sniffed.

"No, Jade, I saw the whole thing. He was shot in the front. That's when I freaked out and got shoved into a police car."

Hearing that only made it worse.

"What! Why?"

I heard her take in a deep breath and hesitate. It didn't occur to me when I first made the call that this conversation might be hurting her as well, that it might bring up bad memories, knowing she and Jesse had been friends for years, but I had to know.

"He had that gun, Jade. He came barreling out from behind the trees with it, screaming at them to let you go, saying you hadn't done anything, that it was him they wanted, and then some dumb rookie took aim at him. That was it. After that we all went ballistic. Jesse didn't even have any bullets."

"Oh, my God!" It came out a squeak. Emotions were flowing through me so quickly that I almost couldn't breathe. First grief, then anger, then intense despair all battling inside me at once. "So, you're saying he was trying to protect *me*?"

"Oh, Jade, don't go blaming yourself for this. It wasn't your fault."

"How am I supposed to feel? My last memories of Jesse are all messed up. I don't even remember anything from the time we were in Texas to the time I woke up in the hospital. How many states is that? And now you tell me that Jesse was shot because he was trying to get to me? Me! Not you, not Kelly, but me. This whole thing is my fault. I was the one who pushed for us to leave Elgin and drive all over the damn country. Jesse even tried to get me to go home to protect me but I wouldn't have it. It's all about me and my stupid, selfish, thick head!"

"It's not your fault," she said again, more sternly. "It really isn't, Jade. Now you can go on blaming yourself in order to make sense of things, but it won't change the fact that he's gone. What you can do is accept that he loved you, that you gave him more in those few months than he'd ever had in his whole life. He was a better person because of you, and I know that he was happy. Maybe for the first time ever."

"I'll bet he wasn't happy when he got a hole in his chest," I spat out sourly.

"As far as I'm concerned he died nobly. I don't blame you and I'll bet that Kelly doesn't either."

I bit back my comment that Kelly couldn't blame me because he clearly didn't remember it.

Instead I gripped the phone to my ear, silently weeping in mortification as the tears rolled down my face. Corie was making sense; I knew her words weren't just lip service, yet I felt the need to deny myself any abdication of responsibility where Jesse's death was concerned.

"How's Kelly?" she finally asked.

"He's alright, I guess. He went to a half-way house in Elgin at first. Now he's living with a friend in Riverwoods. I don't see him much. He doesn't know where you are, Corie. He thinks he's not allowed to know or to ever see you again. But if you want I can give you his number."

"No," she said. "It's probably better this way. It's taking time but I'm getting over him and everything that happened, and I'm sure he's over me, too."

"I guess it wouldn't be the same, huh?"

"No. But that's not necessarily a bad thing."

We talked a bit longer, updating each other on our new and boring lives, reminiscing over good memories with the guys, laughing over Jesse's beat up, old station wagon. We discussed the possibility of his having a grave somewhere in Elgin, though admitted neither one of us would probably go there even if we knew where it was. I shared some of the funnier moments I'd had in the hospital, making her laugh, and even told her about Joel.

"If you like him, then you should see him. Don't feel guilty about it," she said.

"It's not like that," I struggled with the words. "He's just a genuine person who cares about me. I've never had a friend like that before who didn't have ulterior motives. Sometimes it's hard to know what's real, you know?"

"You'll figure it out."

When we hung up some time later I felt better, yet heavy-hearted at the same time. There was no way anyone could convince me that Jesse's death wasn't in some way my fault. But I did find solace in Corie's words and held fast to the knowledge that Jesse and I both were better people for having known one another.

*   *   *

Second semester started and I was grateful I was getting closer to graduation. Pretty soon I'd be eighteen and have a diploma in my hand. The time for thinking harder about what I'd do after high school had come. I bought a used car with my own money and planned for possibly attending the community college in the fall. I pushed myself out of bed every day.

One thing I knew for sure was that I needed to move out of my parent's house as soon as I graduated. There was something stifling me there. Perhaps it was a combination of too many memories mixed up with the immobility of my parent's affinity for me. Either way I didn't feel as if I could truly move on as long as I was there. I wondered if that meant that I was trying to run away from it all, but even Phillip agreed that I probably needed to make some changes.

"I spoke to Corie," I told Phillip. "Back at Christmas time."

His eyebrows went up in his usual way, but didn't say anything about me staying silent on the subject for so long. "Did you? How did that come about?"

"I was curious," I said.

"About what?"

"About what had happened to her, if she was home or somewhere else. I really didn't expect her to be there when I called. I just thought I'd try anyway," I shrugged. "Somehow I felt closer to Jesse that way."

Phillip nodded, understanding. "And she was home?"

I nodded. "She told me things about our last night together. The night we were all arrested and Jesse died. She told me things I didn't know."

"How did it make you feel?"

I sighed. "Worse. More confused."

"You're going to have to face it all," he informed me. "If you ever expect to move on, you will have to let go of this guilt you feel."

"It's more than guilt," I said.

"I realize that," he said. "But the feelings of loss and resentment aside, under it all you do feel terribly guilty, and yet there really isn't any reason why you should."

"Yes, there is," I argued. "Jesse died because of me."

He was already shaking his head from side to side, as if anticipating my argument. "No," was all he said. "And you need to come to terms with that."

"I don't know how."

"Slowly," he said.

I decided that I would do it Phillip's way. I certainly had nothing to lose and I was so tired of fighting these feelings of guilt. If anything, I needed to put everything into perspective, and Phillip was convinced that I would see things more clearly his way. So, I started from the beginning. I felt stupid at first because Phillip already knew it all, but he encouraged me to go on as if he were hearing everything for the first time. He told me to say it all, explain every detail, how I felt, if I was cold or hot, angry or happy, all of it. He told me to continue to write things down as they came to me, as I had while admitted, and recreate it in a journal. "Writing helps clear the mind," he'd said, and so I did it.

I wrote and talked for hours and days and weeks. It was exhausting, but once I agreed to do it Phillip would not back down and let me fail. I had to reach deep down and be truly honest about every tiny detail; how it made me feel at the time and how I thought I felt about it now. It didn't matter how minute the piece of the puzzle was, Phillip made me inspect each bit of information with new eyes.

There were times I cried. I bawled, actually. There were times I screamed and raged and banged my fists on the table, shook my head and denied that it had been real. There were times I whispered because they were virgin words spoken out loud, words that I wouldn't even admit to myself in the depths of my mind. I promised to give it my all and I did. And whether it was unfortunate or lucky for me, Phillip knew me well enough to know that I was giving it everything I had.

There were times when I thought for sure he'd readmit me to the fourth floor. He watched me and my outbursts carefully, but I realized that as long as I was putting one hundred percent into my own therapy, he wouldn't have me locked up again no matter how unstable I seemed to be. Part of me was relieved, because for months I had truly questioned my own sanity, and once or twice I even considered the safety and familiarity of the hospital walls. He may have suspected, because the one time I mentioned it he said I didn't need it anymore. So patronizing. Just like a psychologist.

It was hard to see what Phillip's plan was, but as I made my way through the story and the memories and the feelings, I started to understand why I'd needed to do that all along. I'm not saying that had I done that from day one in the hospital I would have been cured nine months ago, but it's possible that I didn't need to suffer so much by myself all this time. It was my way to do things differently. I usually needed my head banged a few times anyway. Nothing learned came easy for me. That's probably why I had the year I did.

Weeks passed, and then months. My birthday came and went with little fanfare. I think my parents felt out of their depth, which I found pathetic, but I didn't care in the end because I preferred not having to spend any time with them anyway. Anne and Tom took me to dinner.

I quit my part time job because it didn't offer any training or opportunities for advancement. If I was expected to actually pay rent and utilities, I'd need a better source of income. I thought about all the possibilities that were available to me through the community college, but even during the next two years I'd need a reliable job. I didn't feel very qualified to do anything but took a job as a waitress in a popular restaurant, guaranteeing me a reasonable income.

* * *

On a cold, boring Saturday afternoon in the middle of April, my phone rang. I heard the trill of the ring, two, three, then four times, not really interested in answering it. A few seconds later Anne called from inside her room where she was just finally packing up her room to complete the move into her apartment with Tom. When I didn't answer she popped her head in my doorway to find me lying on my bed, arms flung wide and an ankle crossed over an up-drawn knee.

"Jade, the phone is for you."

"Who is it?" I asked in a bored voice, though I didn't really care.

"I don't know, some guy."

"Who, Kelly?"

"No, a real guy." That made me laugh and I rolled over onto my elbow, reaching for my extension.

"Hello, Jade," came the familiar voice. I knew it even eight months later.

"Yes?"

"It's Joel."

"I know."

"How've you been?"

"Oh, okay," I lied. "You?"

"Good."

"Oh, that's good." I sounded like an idiot. I felt like one, too.

There was a pause and neither one of us knew what to say. All I could think about was the fact that he'd called me first. Part of me was glad, but another part of me was caught surprised and unprepared. All that *thinking* hadn't gotten me anywhere because deep down I didn't believe it'd be an issue.

"I'm sorry," he finally said quietly.

"Why?"

"Because I promised I wouldn't do this. I told you I'd wait for you to make the choice, and now I've taken that choice away from you."

"No, it's okay," I said honestly. "It's good to hear from you."

"I'm not trying to make things harder for you, you know, if my calling is digging up things better left in the past."

I sorted of *pfft'd* because it wasn't likely that any of my past would ever easily be left behind, and smiled, then realized he couldn't see me. I said, "You sure this isn't some follow up call so you can finish the ending of your thesis?"

He let out a breath and sighed. "You're right," he said when I remained quiet. "I was studying you, among a few others. You had an amazing experience. Much more intriguing than anyone else who'd come through those doors during the time I was there. It doesn't change the fact that I got to know you, even when I could see you didn't want anyone to, and that it only made me care about you.

You weren't just some case study. You should know that. I really do want to know that you're okay."

"What if I'm not?" I wanted to know.

"I would be surprised if you'd said you were," he said bluntly. "I'm not calling to creep on you or freak you out."

"Really, Joel, it's okay."

We talked a little longer and I could feel the tension ease from my shoulders. All the confusing moments, thoughts, misunderstood gestures, crazy run-away ideas and theories I'd had since first meeting Joel- they all dissipated like fog in the sun. Maybe it'd been a good thing all of it had happened that way. If I had to be confused and neurotic, then Joel was the best person to be that sort of enlightening inspiration for me. I was finally figuring it out. And when I remembered how I'd tried to explain my relationship with Joel to Corie, I realized for the first time that I had been right. It was relieving and I found that when proposed we get together and get a bite to eat and catch up, I didn't hesitate to say yes.

We hung up and I bounced off my bed and took a spin around my room, trying to figure out what to do first. I headed for Anne's room and found her on her hands and knees in her closet, surrounded by boxes and clothing that had been strewn everywhere.

"I need your help," I said without ceremony. "I have plans tonight and nothing to wear."

She sat up on her heels and looked at me in surprise. "Really?" When I only shrugged, she said,

"Well, don't go over the moon about it or anything. I'm sure he's just as apathetic as you about it."

"It's not like that," I said, sighing and sitting on the bare floor.

"You're going to be okay," she assured me. "You just have to give it time. And going out is a good thing. There are other guys out there." I knew she wanted to say *better* guys, but thankfully she respected my feelings and refrained.

It wasn't that she hadn't like Jesse, she hadn't known him. It was just that from her point of view he was the reason I got into trouble. It wouldn't have made a difference to argue with her, to tell her that I knowingly did those things just to be with him, because either way it didn't put him in a better light. Jesse was who he was and I'd slowly been coming to grips with it. Right or wrong, I loved him anyway.

"Most of my stuff is packed, and I couldn't tell you which box to look in." I had expected a little more effort from her.

"Please, Anne. Please? I lost most of my clothes, and I haven't had a chance to get new ones." Actually, I hadn't wanted to, which was a bit of a wakeup call. I'd just been existing in the same, limited wardrobe for months.

She studied the boxes, flipping a few open to see what was inside, and decided she had something that would do nicely. I made a mental note to go shopping one day soon. It was time I got out of the same few blue jeans and t-shirts I'd been wearing for nearly a year.

"What are you going to do with your hair?" Anne asked me. "You gonna curl it or put it up or anything?" She was definitely more girly than me.

"No," I laughed at her. Jeez, we weren't going to the Ritz! "I told you, this isn't a date."

"Nothing wrong with a girl looking her best," Anne murmured as she held out a cropped cranberry sweater and matching suede boots.

I took care getting ready. This would be the first time Joel would see me without the garish, bright neon lights of the hospital reflecting off my naked skin, or the hard well water to leave my hair dry and frizzy. I never felt as if I looked very girly or pretty in the hospital, and realized I wanted Joel to see me in the real world, looking well, when I remembered all the times he watched me flip out, cry, scream; the time he had carried me to my room; the time he'd unbuckled me from the restraints…. The more I thought about it the more I realized that regardless of what my neurosis believed Joel had every right to make a case study out of me.

My hair was done, makeup finished, and I had just pulled on the last boot when I glanced at the clock. Fifteen minutes and counting. I'd had four hours of prep time and I was ready just in time. I'd never make it as a femme fatale.

Opening the door I felt one last rush of exhilaration, but it was gone as soon as Joel appeared on the other side and I saw the familiar face of the friend I had grown to trust. He stood relaxed, leaning on one hip as his hands hung loosely out of his front pockets, and a small smile on his lips. He was dressed in jeans, his white button up oxford shirt untucked and casual, and a jean jacket. Both sleeves were rolled up to just below his elbows, and on his feet were Timberland boots, making him look wholly attractive in a completely different way.

"Hey," he said lazily. He hadn't moved a muscle. He looked like he was made to just stand still calmly like a model, like he didn't have a care in the world.

His blue eyes sparkled as he smiled at me. "You look good."

"Thanks. So do you."

He glanced down at himself and chuckled, his eyes coming back up to meet mine. "So, you wanna get out of here?" He turned toward his car, which waited in the driveway.

"Yeah. Let me get my jacket."

I closed the front door behind us as I followed him to the car. He opened the door for me and waited until I was seated inside before shutting it and making his way around to the driver's side. Once inside, he settled himself behind the wheel and cranked the keys in the ignition. As the engine turned over, a soft purring sound came forth.

"Mmm, I like this car," I said as he flung an arm over the back of the seat and began to back down the driveway. "What kind is it?"

"It's an '86 Monte Carlo Super Sport."

"It's my new favorite car," I said matter-of-factly.

CHAPTER TWENTY

Guess I'm contagious, it'd be safest if you ran
That's what they all just end up doing in the end
Take my car and paint it black
Take my arm, break it in half
Say something, do it soon
It's too quiet in this room

Blood in the Cut by K. Flay

Sometime later we found ourselves sitting across from each other in a booth in a restaurant in Riverwoods. He filled up the space by telling me what he'd been doing since he left his internship and what the experience had meant to him, what his plans were now that he'd graduated college.

"So, you did write that thesis after all," I teased.

"I did," he smiled back. "And yes, you were in it, as well as a few others."

"I can well imagine who," I laughed.

"So, really," he said. "How do you feel these days?"

"Not as confused as I've been."

"Is that good or bad?"

"I'm not sure yet," I said honestly. "I keep thinking I need more time. But it never seems to change anything."

He nodded slowly, digesting what I was saying. "Maybe you if you started living instead of just existing you'd find how much easier things can get."

"Have you and Phillip been talking about me?" Strange how the thought didn't upset me as it would have a year ago.

He only responded with a boyish smile that was unexpectedly adorable, causing me to giggle. Then I looked up and saw Kelly standing about five feet away and glaring at me.

"What?" I asked him, as if months hadn't gone by since we'd seen or spoken to each other.

His face was red and I could see his fists were clenched. I raised an eyebrow at him, wondering what he was getting so fired about, and then noticed the small dark-haired girl standing next to him, looking ill at ease and very unsure of what to do.

"Excuse me," I said to Joel as I slid out of the booth.

"Jade," Kelly said as I approached him. It sounded like a question.

"Kelly," I parroted.

"What are you doing?" His eyes flashed to Joel and then back to me.

"What are *you* doing?" I looked pointedly at his newest girlfriend and then back at him.

"Is this funny to you?"

I blinked. What the hell was going on here? "Kelly, are you high?" I looked at his little friend and repeated the question to her, to which she shook her head, clearly confused by his behavior.

When Kelly didn't answer, I yelled loudly, "What!"

A few people sitting nearby turned to stare. Kelly's girlfriend turned red. "Oh, honey, you can't be that easily embarrassed if you're going to be hanging out with him," I told her in a patronizing way.

"Shut up!" Kelly said. Jesus, now I knew he'd lost his mind.

I could see out of the corner of my eye Joel stand up. I turned and held up a hand.

"Shall we go outside?" I asked Kelly.

"Fine," he turned on his heel and stalked out in front of me.

"Kelly?" the young girl asked uncertainly as Joel threw some bills on the table and followed us outside.

"Just go inside and have a seat!" he barked at her.

I looked at her, seeing the flush on her face, that familiar pre-bawling look that so many girls before her had had. "Still the same, I see," I said, looking back at him. But I cared more about how he spoke to me than I did about her, so all I really wanted to know was what his problem was.

But he didn't say anything. He just continued to look at me accusingly. I shook my head, beginning to feel myself unravel. It was so unfair of him to do this to me. If looks could kill I'd be dead. What a hypocrite.

I took a deep breath and said, "I think we're done, don't you?" It took everything in me to say that without breaking down. He had no idea how it was killing me inside to realize that I had to let him go; to actually say goodbye when I never thought I would.

"After everything we've been through?" he accused me. "After all the times I came for you and saved you?"

"When was that?" I screeched. "What the hell do you want from me?"

He looked ready to throw a punch and I could feel Joel moving closer, though I knew in my heart that Kelly would never lose control and hit me. That was one thing I was sure of. He wasn't afraid to push me back, but he'd never hit. He still hadn't said anything, which made me madder because it only meant that I was right.

I threw up my arms. "I hate you for doing this to me. Nothing about this has been easy, and to think of all the people in the world to do this to me that you would make me feel guilty for living my life. Look at her," I pointed to the crying little girl who I knew after tonight he would never want to see again. "You're living your life, so I guess that means that I'm supposed to be sitting at home like some basket case. Is that what you wanted?"

"No!" he growled, but I could see it was a lie.

"Because someone has to pay for our sins, right? It's obviously not going to be you, because you don't even have a conscience, so it must be me!" I shoved him them, hard, screaming in his face. "Jesse's gone and this is all I've got! Well, thanks a lot, Kelly, thanks for nothing!"

* * *

If there was any one person who could reduce me to a blubbering idiot it was Kelly. There wasn't anything Joel could do, nothing I'd allow him, except to take me home. In front of my house he looked at me, unsure of what to say, and I was sure that he was sorry he'd ever turned in his thesis before getting a glimpse at this chapter of my story. I mumbled a "thanks" and stepped out slowly, walking blindly toward the door. After I let myself in and stood shaking and crying in the dark, I realized that Joel's car stayed in the driveway for a long time.

I had no idea what prompted Kelly to say what he did. Even though he didn't actually say a whole lot, all the implications were clear and it hurt me even more had he come right out and accused me of any number of things. Maybe not knowing exactly what he was mad about bothered me the most. Did he feel I was betraying Jesse? That just wasn't like him. But did he feel betrayed because I no longer needed him? That seemed more likely.

The bottom line was Kelly was selfish. I had always known that. I knew he wouldn't be showing up or calling me to apologize, even if he did remember it. He was a coward and if confronted he'd have ten different excuses, none of them making up for what he did. But knowing these truths didn't make the pain any easier, because in the end I'd lost him, too. Actually, if I was being honest I'd know that I'd lost Kelly the same night as Jesse. We just didn't know it until now. I didn't know who I was anymore. Every facet of my personality had abandoned me in some form or another.

For the next several weeks I focused only on final exams and packing up my room. My parents didn't understand why I was in such a hurry to move out when I could stay there for free, but I didn't expect them to. It wasn't something I could explain and I found that I didn't even care to try when I saw their confused expressions. They still thought this was all about them and me being defiant. I didn't know how to tell them that I had to start over, that the pain was too strong and that the emptiness was consuming me, yet again. I didn't know how to explain that I couldn't breathe anymore.

If looking back a year I thought I'd been an unlikeable person then I had no idea what to think of myself now.

The part of me that just wanted to give up thought that finishing these last few weeks of school was stupid. As I settled into my one-bedroom apartment in Grayslake so that I could be closer to the community college when I started in the fall, I knew that I'd be glad I made myself do things this way. I could easily make a living off of waiting tables and pay my bills, but someday I might want more. I couldn't imagine when or what that would be, but just in case.

I commuted to school every day, finishing up my exams. The day of graduation I didn't even bother attending. It was all behind me as far as I cared, and knowing I'd passed was enough for me. On my last day of class I gave the school secretary my new address so my diploma could be mailed to me.

I worked. Life wasn't very interesting but I didn't really care much. After all those months spending time with Phillip and thinking I was healing and moving forward, I realized that it was all a bunch of crap. Deep down I didn't feel that moving forward was truly possible. Either that or I didn't really care. I still didn't know the difference.

I didn't speak to anyone I knew in what I called my former life. I didn't want Kelly finding me so I avoided Tori. Only Anne and my parents had my number, with strict instructions not to give it out to anyone, though there really weren't that many people I could even think of who'd be looking for me with the exception of Phillip and possibly Joel.

I took double shifts as often as I could. There wasn't anything else to do. I didn't make any new friends, though the people I worked with were nice enough. It didn't matter. There wasn't a single person alive that I could spend any time with. Most people irritated me, and my tolerance was running at zero. I bought what little furniture I couldn't live without and hoarded the rest of my income. With classes starting in just two months I was sure I'd need the nest egg sooner than I'd like, though my first plan was to apply for a Pell grant at the college.

I found I enjoyed community college more than I ever could have believed. Perhaps it was the breaking up of the monotony of my days for the past few months with nothing but work to show for my time. I liked being able to choose which classes I could take and finding how easy the work was when completely engaged in a subject I liked. Two-year degrees were more plentiful than I thought, and after wasting a semester on easy classes like creative writing and computer skills, I decided that a degree in the medical field would most likely yield me employment for the rest of my life. I debated becoming certified as a dental hygienist, perhaps liking that job the best because small talk would be at a minimum with patients' mouths propped open with cotton, being that chit chat was not my thing. But in the end, it didn't appeal to me as much as working as an x-ray technician where I'd be in a dark room mostly just with machines to keep me company.

To some it might have sounded lonely. To me it sounded like refuge.

Months passed and the second anniversary of when I met Jesse came and went. I found that being in a new place helped stifle the choking memories, though nothing could ever stop the smell of the air during a snow, or the wet, white flakes themselves from affecting me the way they did. Winter was always the hardest for me and I found I resented every minute of it.

Other things triggered the memories, too, things that I wasn't seeking out on purpose as I used to, such as a scent familiar to Jesse's or the trickle of water that sounded too much like a small, babbling stream on the cusp of spring. It was times like these that I found myself caught in a trance, tilting my head to the side, trying to hear it or smell it better. And then I'd shake my head, disappointed that I could still be so easily entranced; that I was still looking for traces of him just so that I could feel warm and whole again. So that breathing would be easier for just a minute.

Functioning this way wasn't really that hard. I know people at school or at work often wondered about me, but after four months in the hospital stares and whispers just didn't penetrate. I wasn't mean. I didn't avoid speaking to people. I just didn't socialize outside of the restaurant or school. And since we weren't all living within the same walls, the people I came into contact with every day didn't see the need to focus on what I was or wasn't doing. I liked that.

Spring was hardly better when I remembered the warm night Jesse and I were ripped apart, and it began my four-month imprisonment. It was odd how I mourned the day of our meeting more than the day of his death. Perhaps because I had a clearer memory of the first. Because that was when the hole filled up and I was truly able to breathe, for a short time.

It was weird how I still instinctively avoided dark haired and dark-eyed men. So many of them could spark a memory of Jesse in an instant. I hated the way my mind did this on its own and I couldn't wait for the day when it slowly subsided. It seemed that even as I was trying my hardest to move on, my subconscious continued to make comparisons. But then I embraced it, hoping that as long as I stayed honest with myself where Jesse was concerned I might be able to gain a better perspective of myself. For the most part it worked. I'd see a tall, broad-shouldered man from the back and instantly think of Jesse, and then remember how his strong arms carried me, running away from a field and a threat. And then I realized that I was safe because of that. I was better off now. And I could visit memories in a different way. In a way that allowed me to be thankful for where I was now.

I saw other things too that surprised me. Blond-haired men with blue eyes brought Joel to mind, and I found myself comparing them without even meaning to. At first, I was shocked, but even more so when I realized that I was grateful for his friendship, for showing me that I could trust in someone else and rely on them in a healthy way. Even if circumstances had made it so that we never spoke again, it was okay. He accomplished what he'd set out to do.

And then the unthinkable happened. I was at work, just at the start of a shift so luckily there were not too many people in the restaurant yet, when I noticed a young man being led to a table with several others. At first, I didn't think about it too much, the way the back of his head looked so similar to Jesse's both in color and style. It was one of those small things that nag at your conscience, though you can't quite place it. He wasn't even sitting in my section so I had no reason to look twice. But as I walked by I heard a familiar voice call out.

"Excuse me, Miss?" I stopped in my tracks, not even knowing if the voice was directed at me. Looking into a pair of strangely familiar eyes, I gasped. Whatever question he was going to ask me was lost on his lips when he saw me standing there literally petrified. His eyebrows knitted together momentarily, as if trying to make sure I wasn't about to throw up on him. His friends looked on curiously and their waitress finally appeared, taken aback by my shaking.

"Jade? What is it? You alright?" Bailey asked me, alarmed. I gripped her arm for purchase without even thinking about it. It alarmed her even more and she asked me again if I was okay.

I never took my eyes off him. Instead I managed to whisper, "What is your name?"

He looked at me sadly for a moment, and then said, "You know what my name is, Jade." And then I fainted.

When I woke up I was in my manager's office. He looked down on me with a layer of sweat on his upper lip as he paced the small area. My heart was thumping so wildly that for a moment I forgot how I'd gotten there. Surely this was all just some horrible nightmare. I knew that I'd imagined it all and now Phillip was sure to admit me back into the hospital. I'd completely lost touch with all of reality.

"Lord, you know how to give a person a fright!" Mack was saying as I struggled to sit up. "Don't rush it now. Luckily that young man caught you before you could go breaking your skull on the floor, but you look a little peaked just the same."

"What young man?" The tears came on quick and forcefully, causing Mack to look even more distressed. Through my weeping he insisted I go to the hospital but I ignored him. "I just want to go home," I said. But even that didn't sound right to my ears, because I didn't know where home was.

"You can't drive right now," he answered. "Is there someone I can call?" I shook my head. He clearly wasn't surprised by this.

The door to the manager's office opened and Bailey poked her head in. Seeing that I was conscious, she smiled with relief then said, "Jade, are you okay?" She came and knelt on the floor next to me.

"What?" My head snapped in her direction but all I got were the spins.

"What was that all about?" she asked. "That guy was really shook up. I mean, after he carried you in here he just took off, left his friends and everything."

The sobbing came then. Uncontrollable heaving that moved my whole body. Mack looked ill at ease and Bailey asked for some privacy when he cleared his throat a few too many times. When the room was empty except the two of us, she said softly, "What is it?"

I shook my head, unable to open my mouth and say anything that might not make me appear completely insane; unwilling to even consider what I might have just seen. I had made it up, I knew it know. I knew that I was destined for a life of loneliness, with nothing but faded memories. Now every guy I see with dark hair and eyes was going to put me in a near catatonic state.

She left without another word and I tried to pull myself together quickly so that I could get out of there and drive myself home as soon as possible. My legs were a little wobbly as I stood up, but I could see that Mack was relieved I was able to walk on my own. Bile threatened to creep up my throat but I swallowed it down and did my best to appear as if I were completely fine.

"I'm sorry," I said. "I'll be fine tomorrow," indicating my shift. But he didn't seem too concerned.

"Call if you need more time," he said. I nodded and pushed my way out the door, though I didn't feel as though sitting alone in my apartment with only my thoughts would be a very productive use of my time.

I went straight to the locker room and grabbed my stuff, then darted through the restaurant as obscurely as possible. I still felt shaky as I made my way through the parking lot toward my car, but at least the tears of hysteria had subsided for the time being.

"Wait!" he called out just as I had inserted my key into the lock, and I look up to see him running toward me. An image of Jesse running out of the woods flashed across my eyes and I screamed. He stopped suddenly about ten yards away.

"Jade, it's me," Jesse said, walking towards me slower now. "Please don't look so scared."

"I don't…I don't understand," I whispered. And then I started gagging, bent over the curb and throwing up on the small patch of grass between the parking lot and the highway. Hot tears mixed with my tangled hair as I struggled with reality. And then I felt him touching my back, softly saying my name, and all I could do was sit there and bawl.

"I'm sorry," he was saying. "I'm so sorry."

"I thou…I thought you were dead," I accused him when I could finally catch a breath. I still had my head down, close to my updrawn knees. I could hear him and speak to him but I still didn't believe it.

"I know," he said sadly.

"How could you just let me think that!" I wailed.

"I didn't mean to, Jade, honestly. I…" he stopped short and circled my wrist gently with his hand. "Will you please look at me?" I shook my head and pulled my hand away.

"It's not real," I whispered to myself.

"Jade, I am real!"

"No!" I screamed and looked up at him. "You left me all alone when you said you would be there. And you weren't! You died and left me alone!"

"I'm sorry," he said again. "Please let me explain."

"Explain what? How suddenly you're not dead? How you didn't come looking for me…ever? How Corie and Kelly think you're dead, too, or is this some cruel joke and everyone knew the truth but me? Why did you do it, Jesse? Why?"

"I thought it was best," he said lamely. "It seemed like the right thing to do by you."

"Kind of like when you abandoned us at the campsite?" I reminded him. And suddenly I was angry. I stood up and jerked my car door open.

"Where are you going?"

"I'm going home," I said it, happy that I could.

"Where's that?"

I slid behind the wheel and turned the ignition. "I'll let you wonder," I said.

CHAPTER TWENTY-ONE

I want to be a good man, I want to do right
I don't wanna be a criminal for the rest of my life
I want to be a good man, I wanna be saved
I want to be a free man but I feel like a slave

Good Man by Devour the Day

I didn't go to work for a couple of days. Mack called to make sure I was alright and assured me that covering my shifts wouldn't be a problem. He called again two days later under the pretenses of checking on me but I could tell he was more interested in knowing whether or not I planned on returning to work at all. I had to admit that quitting occurred to me about a thousand times over the past few days, but I assured him I'd be back in another day or two. I went to see Phillip. What angered me the most was the lack of surprise on his face when I revealed that Jesse was alive. I was piqued to say the least.

"Explain to me this look on your face." I said it much calmer than I felt.

"I can't imagine what a shock it was for you to see him," Phillip said instead. "I completely understand your anger, but it does not belong directed at me."

Maybe not but he was the only person in front of me at the moment. And one who apparently knew the truth, no less.

"So, you knew?"

He shook his head. "No. No one here knew."

"That makes no sense." I said it slowly, enunciating each word carefully. "You don't look like you thought he was dead."

He sighed. "I only know what the police told me when you came in. I knew much more about the fate of your friends then I ever said, but those were confidentialities that I didn't feel were conducive to your treatment."

"Skip the mumbo-jumbo, please. I was your patient. Not them. You didn't owe anyone else confidentiality. You could have told me *something*! Why did you lie to me?"

"First of all, I didn't *lie* to you," he told me. "I only knew what I was told when you first came in, and that was that Jesse had been shot. The fact that he'd been taken to a hospital in Texas didn't assure anyone that he would survive the gunshot. I was also informed that should he survive he would serve time for skipping probation. As far as I know no other charges were brought against him."

The room exploded in silence. I sat thinking of everything Phillip had said. Clearly his idea of truth was not the same as mine. I still felt completely manipulated and lied to. So that was it – the hospital was just some last attempt at punishment for an unruly daughter. Just one more attempt at control. It was so pathetic, and like a puppet I'd played into it.

*   *   *

Every shift I worked I wondered if he'd come back to the restaurant to look for me. I was edgy to say the least. It had been over a week since I found

299

out Jesse was alive and I hadn't seen or heard from him. What did it mean? Did he care so little for my feelings that he would really stay away forever? He had no idea the torment I'd been through these past two years, and it was obvious that he'd changed and didn't want anything to disrupt that. I didn't know what to do with the hate that was boiling up inside of me. I'd spent two years mourning him. Two years of not being able to identify myself, and just functioning on auto pilot. Two years wasted on memories.

I had so many questions and no answers. I didn't go back to Phillip. Regardless of what he said I still felt lied to and it didn't matter if he was my last link to my former life. I was born again, relieved of my misery and guilt the moment I realized that Jesse, while quite still alive, was indeed lost to me. But then I thought of Kelly and Corie. They must not have known, still didn't, in fact. Jesse survived and decided it was best to leave everything and everyone from his past behind. The more I thought about it the more I realized that I couldn't blame him. What were any of us really, if not reminders of his mistakes?

But he did come back. Just when I'd reconcile myself to forgive him and let the past go, he showed up at my apartment door.

"How did you find me?" My voice came out flat, but I couldn't allow myself to feel anything anymore. I stood in the doorway, blocking him from entering, and watching as he casually leaned against the door frame as if this was just another social call. My heart was hammering wildly in my chest and it felt ready to explode. I could feel the red creep up my neck and hoped he couldn't see what he was doing to me.

"I followed you," he said in a no-nonsense tone, as if I should have been prepared for this inevitable visit. "I didn't want to try and talk to you at your work."

My right eyebrow shot up but I didn't say the plethora of things on my mind. The first of which was why did he wait twelve days to come back? He had no idea at all how those twelve days were harder for me than any day in the past two years. He had no idea how suffocated I've been.

"Can I come in?"

Part of me wanted to say no and close the door for good. But I didn't know how I was going to be able to breath for the rest of my life without at least getting some answers. There was something comforting in believing he was dead and knowing I'd have to find meaning in my life again. But knowing he was alive and without any need for me, left a hole too deep. So, I stepped aside and allowed him to enter.

He didn't say anything at first. He just looked around the sparse room and finally landed his eyes on me, still standing near the door.

"You planning your escape?"

I think he meant it to be funny but I didn't respond. He sighed and sat down on the arm of the couch. He studied his hands. "I've wanted to see you so many times," he said slowly. "I thought about you every day. I just thought that maybe it was for the best, letting you go. By the time I recovered you were all long gone and had been told I was dead. I had prison in front of me and I knew I'd never be anything but trouble for you."

I didn't say anything. I was trying to absorb his words but they didn't make sense. Nothing about this person sitting in front of me made sense. This was not the Jesse I knew. This person was actually using words. He just looked at me for a moment, waiting to see if I'd say anything; waiting for the old Jade to fight back or throw a temper tantrum and demand some answers. If that's who he came for he'd be waiting a long time for her.

"I was stunned to see you the other day, working in that restaurant," he continued. "I couldn't believe it was really you. I actually forgot just for a minute that you thought I was dead. But then you fainted and everything went crazy." I listened. "That didn't go well at all, out there in the parking lot that night. I'm so sorry you found out that way. That was never my intention."

"Your intention was for me to never find out," I concluded. My voice was hard and cold, but it was everything I could do to keep from bawling or gagging, or both.

"No." He was still calm, shaking his head and trying to explain himself. "I didn't want you to find out that way, but I guess there really couldn't have been a good way." Well, he had that much right. But I still didn't know where either of us would be right now had he never come in for dinner. I'd most likely still be thinking he was dead and trying to get on with my life. So, regardless of what he was saying, it was still pretty clear to me what his intentions really were.

"It's just that I'm trying really hard, you know, to turn myself around. I can't go back to that place I was in before."

I watched him struggle with the words as I stood in front of him, arms crossed, defiant and angry. And he was humble. It infuriated me. At that moment I couldn't decide who was truly more selfish; him or me. Based on all our actions over the past two years, I really couldn't sum it up. And here he was saying that *I* was the bad influence now.

"Well, now I know, so you can go back to your life." It was harsh but I didn't know what else to say. His expression indicated that was not what he expected from me at all. In fact, he looked a little pissed.

"What?" I demanded when all he did was stare at me. "You certainly haven't bothered to ask how I've faired these two years. You're not really *looking* at me so you must not care. It's obvious you're only concerned with yourself, and I can't really say that I blame you. You're right, you know that? It was a freaking hot mess, that place we were in before. We all nearly destroyed ourselves. Why wouldn't you want to forget about us and move on?"

"I'm not trying to forget about you," he growled. I shrugged at him as if to say, "Oh well!"

"But you did," I said it more calmly than I felt. The time for yelling and ranting was over. It wouldn't change anything and he had every right to want a good life. "And I wish you had just stayed away."

The tears came now and I let them because it didn't matter anymore. After today it would truly be over and he could live with all the guilt and regret just like I did. I couldn't absolve him of any of it; I wouldn't. Because if I had to live with it then so did he.

"Things were hard enough. I was finally getting over it all and making sense of things. And now you're here. And I don't know what to do with that. You're saying that you just want to go back to your new clean life. That's fine. But go now so I can learn to put myself back together *again*!"

He didn't say anything. He looked back at me clearly surprised at my words. But I don't know why he should have been, or did he really not realize how much I had loved him? Or maybe it was because I was so obviously weak. Either way he didn't appear to know what to do or say to me.

"That's not what I meant," he finally said. "I didn't forget about you. I did want to look for you. But I didn't even know where to start. I couldn't just walk up to your parents' house, you know that. Your number was disconnected and it was clear that you didn't even live there anymore. I didn't know what to do," he shrugged helplessly.

"So, you decided it was best," I finished for him.

There was a long pause before he said quietly, "Yeah, I did."

I sighed and sat down at the table, still a considerable distance between us. I understood how he could be alive, of course. Considering Corie's and Kelly's distorted memories, and my lack of them as well of that night, it all did little to assure me that anyone was really coherent enough to remember what really happened. He was shot, yes, that much we did know, but obviously it hadn't been fatal. He didn't need to explain that once he recovered he was sent back to Illinois to face the charges that had been against him prior to our fleeing the state. This new, clean-cut look he was sporting, the different friends, all normal law-abiding looking people that he'd been with the other night. He even smelled different. But how did he sleep at night knowing everyone thought he was dead?

"Well, just so you know, I wasn't better off," I said icily. "I heard you get shot. I saw you on the ground, bleeding. I had nightmares for months, reliving it over and over again. Maybe you thought you were better off without me. I won't even try to argue that. But I loved you. And there was a time when I was sorry I never told you that, but I'm not sorry anymore. So, you can go back to your life and not worry about me."

"Why do you keep saying goodbye?"

"Because that's what you want."

"You don't know the first thing about what I want you're so busy trying to kick me out the damn door!"

I fumed. "You're right. I have no clue what you want. I can't tell what you're thinking or why you're even here. All I can assume is that some form of guilt motivated you to come and explain yourself."

"Well, then you'd be wrong," he said it roughly. "I came here to tell you how glad I was to see you again!"

"Was that *after* you saw me faint at the sight of you and you realized that you didn't want to let me go on thinking you were dead?"

"First of all, let's get a few things straight," he pointed a finger at me. "I've only been out for a couple of months. They gave me a place to live and a job. I didn't get a choice, but I made some friends and tried to move on with my life. Do you think it's easy being an ex-con? I knew I'd never get a decent job and I'll always have to fight for my rights. What kind of life could I possibly offer you? I'd already practically ruined it once. And Corie's and Kelly's, too. I wasn't about to do it again."

"I don't talk to Kelly,'" was my reply. "But I can assure you that you are not to blame for his decisions. I'm surprised you even let that sit on your conscience."

"I'm surprised you don't talk to him anymore."

"A lot of things have changed," I said. "Besides the last time I saw him he didn't seem to care very much about my feelings. It made me realize a lot of things about him that I refused to see before."

"And Corie?"

I shrugged. "I don't talk to her either. What makes you think I'd need either of them?"

"Nothing," he said. "I'm relieved, actually."

"Really?" I said dryly. "Does that make walking out of here harder for some reason? Knowing that I'm not relying on someone else?"

"Maybe," he admitted. "But I haven't walked out yet."

"I don't know what you're waiting for."

"Maybe I'm waiting for you to tell me to stay the hell away from you."

"You really need me to say that after two years?"

"No. But I want to hear you say it anyway."

"I won't ease your conscience," I told him.

"Is that because you don't really want me to leave, or because you want me to suffer?"

I eyeballed him. What did he want from me? Is he saying that he's suffering by staying? By not being released by me? In frustration I threw up my hands. "I may be angry but this is not about some weird form of revenge. I really did love you, Jesse. My heart broke into a million pieces when I thought you were dead, and it broke again every day after that. They put me into some mental hospital and I didn't even remember how I got there or where Corie and Kelly were. I kept thinking they should have been with me, and they weren't. And no one would tell me anything. I didn't even remember that you'd been shot. I thought you were coming for me. And then you didn't. And they made me remember. I had no answers. No closure. Nothing made any sense. And now you're here telling me that you just want to leave the past behind, and I can't blame you because I do, too. But I can't just say that I don't love you and that I want you to leave me again, because it will never be true."

I wasn't telling him to stay; I wasn't telling him to go. He was just gonna have to decide for himself. He wiped at his face and I could see redness around his eyes. Whatever he wasn't saying looked like it was killing him inside. He was struggling, but I couldn't do anything less than be completely honest with him at this point. I had nothing left to lose.

"So, whatever you really came here to say, just say it."

He wiped at his eyes. "I guess I came to hear you say that you forgive me."

"Fine, I forgive you." It sounded stupid even as I said it. Forgive him for what? For dying? For living? For wanting a better life? Isn't that what everyone wants?

"And I came to tell you that I really do love you," he said slowly. "I just didn't know if it would make things better or harder." I shrugged. Odd how it didn't seem to do either. "Damnit, Jade, just tell me now what you want from me, because I can't stand this anymore."

"I want you to stay! And I want you to love me," I cried desperately. "What the hell do you think I want?"

"I don't know," he said heavily. "I was just afraid that we couldn't ever get past everything and start over."

"Jesse, do you want to stay?"

He looked back at me for a minute before replying quietly, "I never would have left in the first place."

I nodded. "Then stay."

THE END

Additional songs that helped inspired the telling of this story:

Way Down We Go by Kaleo; *Oh Lord* by In This Moment; *Slipped Away* by Avril Lavigne; *Fire* by Barns Courtney; *Around Me* by Flyleaf; *Hurricane* by 30 Seconds to Mars; *6 Underground* by Sneaker Pimps; *Trembling Hands* by The Temper Trap; *We Could Run Away* by Needtobreathe; *I Never Told You* by Colbie Caillat; *White Flag* by Dido; *Hands Open* by Snow Patrol; *My Last Breath* by Evanescence; *Landing in London* by 3 Doors Down and Bob Seger; *Beggin' For Thread* by Banks; *Nitesky* by Robot Koch; *The Weight of Lies* by The Avett Brothers; *Waiting for Spring to Come* by John Butler Trio; *Painted Desert* and *Outlaw Blues* by Pat Benetar.